...ymond Andrews:

...EE **RED**
...ILDCAT **TENNESSEE**
...WEET'S
...ADIO **BABY**

...Gems—EMI Music Inc.
...pyright Secured. Used by permission.

...*rshed*

...of America

...g-In-Publication Data

..., Cousin Claire : two novellas / Raymond
...nny Andrews.

...(hardcover) : 15.95
...men--Georgia--Fiction.   I. Andrews, Benny,
...hond. Cousin Claire. 1991.   III. Title :
...Cousin Claire.

                    91-16676
                    CIP

Other books by Ray

APPALACH
ROSIEBELLE LEE W
BABY S
THE LAST R

Published by
PEACHTREE PUBLISHERS, LTD.
494 Armour Circle, NE
Atlanta, Georgia 30324

Design by Candace J. Magee
Composition by Kathryn D. Mothe

Manufactured in the United States

10 9 8 7 6 5 4 3 2 1

Library of Congress Catalogin

Andrews, Raymond.
[Jessie and Jesus]
Jessie and Jesus ; and
Andrews ; illustrated by Be
p. cm.
ISBN 1-56145-032-4
1. Afro-American wo
1930- . II. Andrews, Rayr
Jessie and Jesus. IV. Title
PS3551.N452J4 1991
813'.54--dc20

Some who made my move back South worth the packing:

Bob & Barbara Russo,

Bryant & Marilyn,

Sweet Baby Sue . . .

And, most of all,

The Elegant One.

Jessie and Jesus
AND
COUSIN CLAIRE

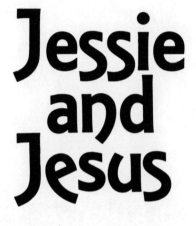

Jessie
and
Jesus

JESSIE REMEMBERED HER SIXTH BIRTHDAY WELL. Too damn well. It began with a breakfast of hot oatmeal with plump raisins washing down her gullet, followed by even hotter cocoa, brazenly interrupted by:

"Jessie, after eating you and me are going out back of the garage to pick blackberries."

With this announcement to her daughter, Mildred Mitchell, a tall, big-boned, fair-skinned black woman, stood up and began taking the dishes from the dining table.

"But I wanna go with Daddy!"

"You go with your momma, Sugar Dumpling. You can come with me later on," Sid Mitchell rumbled to his daughter softly from the head of the table, where sat his shorter, broader, and much-darker-than-his-wife's body behind a steaming mug of coffee, teeth clenching a smoke-spiraling pipe.

"But Daddy, how come I can't come with you *this* morning?"

"Because Momma wants you to go with her to pick the blackberries so she can make our little Sugar Dumpling a birthday pie today."

"Then will you come with us to pick the blackberries?" Jessie left her unfinished breakfast and in two swift steps leaped from her chair to her favorite seat, atop her daddy's knee, whence she threw both arms tightly around Sid's thick neck. "Will you, Daddy? *Pretty* please!"

"But Sugar Dumpling, I can't this morning," he said, taking his pipe from his mouth, now being brushed by the hair of Jessie's head. "Next time."

"That's what you *always* say—'next time'—every time I have to go with *her!*"

"Now Sugar Dumpling, I've told you about saying 'her.' Always say 'Momma'"—who had just departed the kitchen via the screen door and could now be heard out on the back porch feeding the dog. "And this morning you've gotta go with her, er...*Momma,* because she got...got something to tell you."

"What she...."

"*Momma.*"

"...Got to tell me?"

"Momma will tell you that when you two get together by your-selves."

"How come *you* can't tell me?" Jessie tightened her grip around her daddy's neck while putting her face right next to his to dig deep into his eyes with her own pleading, oversized, soft browns.

"I can't. It's something Momma has to tell our little Sugar Dumpling. It's woman's talk."

"Oh."

To the sunshiny warm patch of wild blackberries growing directly in back of the garage, Jessie wore for the first time the brand new field straw-hat, blue denim overalls, and baby black brogans her daddy had bought her for her sixth birthday. Unafraid of the bushes' briars and chiggers, this denim-wrapped dynamo began quietly plucking from their stems the dark, ripe berries. All the while, waiting. Waiting for her momma, picking the berries at an even faster pace and plopping them into the gallon waterbucket sitting on the ground at their feet, to tell her the "woman talk" her daddy had promised her she would be told.

"Jessie," Mildred said, after nearly five minutes of berry-picking silence, "you are six years old today and getting to be a big girl...."

"Daddy say I'm *already* a big girl."

"...And Daddy and I think it's about time you had somebody around the house to play with."

"I got Daddy to play with."

"He's grown. I mean somebody like a little sister or brother."

"You mean a little baby?"

"Er...yes! Would you like to have one to play with?"

"Where is it coming from?"

"God is going to give it to us."

"Why?"

"Because...because Daddy and I asked Him to give us one so you will have someone to play with."

"Will it be a baby sister or a baby brother?"

"We won't know until the day God gives it to us."

"Doesn't God know?"

"God loves to surprise. Which one would you like to have?" Here the older woman stopped picking berries to look down at her daughter...who stood looking straight back up at her momma from out of a pair of *hard* browns and answered,

"I'd rather play with *Daddy*."

"When God gives us the new little baby are you going to stop playing with me?" Jessie, still dressed in her birthday present outfit, wanted to know from her daddy (wearing a field straw-hat, blue denim overalls, and black brogans) later that same afternoon while following him on his daily tour of chores around the barnyard of the family's dairy farm.

"Nooo, Sugar Dumpling." Sid stopped what he was doing at that exact instant to squat down before her. "What makes you think that?"

Throwing her arms around his neck while staring softly into his eyes with her sweet baby browns, Jessie told him, *"She said you would."*

Then came that day when Jessie was hard at work as usual following her daddy around providing him with his daily quota of unanswerable questions, only to be abruptly interrupted by the sudden appearance through the big red barn door of her momma, wearing her nice clothes and carrying a small suitcase. "I'm ready," she said. That's when Sid took Jessie in his arms and told her that he and her momma were going to the hospital in town to "get the baby" and bring it back home and she would have to stay with the next door neighbors until their return.

"Why can't God bring the baby to our house?"

"God's gotta heap of babies to bring today, Sugar Dumpling." Moments later he and her momma were driving, baby-bound, off in the car.

She lost no time in telling her neighbor girlfriend, Reenie, "My daddy and mother went to town to the hospital to get the little bitty baby God's leaving there for me to play with and are going to bring it back home to me in the suitcase."

"The stork always brings ours right to our house and it don't have to use a suitcase."

"Y'all got too many to fit in a suitcase."

Early that evening on his way home from the hospital Sid stopped at the neighbors' to get her.

"Where's the little baby?" she asked the instant she saw her daddy.

"In the hospital with Momma. Tomorrow I'll fetch them home." Sid grabbed her up into his arms at the front door. Before even greeting the neighbors he proudly announced, "Sugar Dumpling, you got an eight-pound baby brother!"

She never forgot the light in her daddy's eyes when he said that. Sitting in his arms she wondered, did he look that happy when she was born?

"I named your baby brother 'Sidney Junior.'" The happiness in her daddy's voice hadn't subsided one bit even as they were riding the half-mile home in the car.

"How come when I was a baby you didn't name *me* 'Sidney Junior'?" she blurted back.

"But, Sugar Dumpling, you are a *girl*."

In bed, later, she cried because she was a "girl" until she fell asleep. Awakening in the middle of the night from a bad dream, she left her room to go and snuggle in bed beside her snoring daddy.

Taking one look at the wrinkled, gnarled critter God left at the hospital for her to play with, Jessie became in complete awe of it. Whereas her folks had feared she might be jealous of the new baby, from the moment it reached home (outside the suitcase) she began smothering it with such attention that before long Mildred found herself fighting back jealously over her daughter's total devotion to the child. Jessie acted as if she was the mother rather than Mildred, who already knew that her daughter had always loved Sid much more than she did Mildred, one reason being that the father, against the strong wishes of the mother, had spoiled the child rotten. From the day they knew they were going to get married Sid had made it clear to her he wanted a child, right away.

And it was an accepted belief in Plain View that Sid had always gotten what, or who, he wanted. Take for example getting a wife...and property. Mildred Allen inherited seventy-five acres of dairy farm land from her widowed mother, who died when her only child was eighteen. Sid got the job milking Mildred's dozen cows shortly before his twenty-first birthday. Before he was twenty-two he had married his twenty-eight-year-old, old maid bosslady. In short order, Sid, with his good head for business and even better one for politics, was running his wife's, and his, dairy farm. County politics kept him out of World War II when his dairy was ruled essential to the war effort. Five years of marriage created Jessie, whose birth was so difficult for the mother that she lay abed hoping to die. Mildred was so sick following Jessie's earthly arrival that she didn't even remember writing her name on the many papers Sid kept bringing to her bed of affliction to sign. When she finally recuperated and got home she was greeted by eighteen new heads of cattle, twenty-five additional acres of pasture, and a brand new pickup truck. But the *real* "welcome home Momma Mildred" for her was to learn that the dairy was no longer hers. It was now Sid's. Said so right there on the paper just above where her name had been signed...by her.

Yes, all agreed, Sid had a knack for getting what he wanted. But almost five years of marriage passed before they finally had a baby, and it was a girl. Deeply disappointed, Sid named it "Jessie" because, he said, it sounded more "boy." Yet from the very beginning he took to calling her his "Sugar Dumpling" and never referred to her by any other name, even in public. He was hooked on his daughter. As soon as she learned to walk he took her by her little hand and wouldn't let go. The child didn't hang around the kitchen, or any other part of the house, with her mother and could only be found in these "female" places solely out of necessity. She was *always* with her daddy. "Daddy's girl" insisted upon wearing overalls at all times and could be found in the barnyard, garage, tool shed, pasture, forest, or anywhere else out of the house, and always with Sid—and just like Sid, folks said. Sometimes Mildred had to fight to keep out of her mind the silly thought of her losing her husband to a daughter she'd never owned. Meanwhile, the couple never gave up on having

another child, and finally, after more than six years, they had a second one. A son. This one *her* child. But now here was the daughter, who wanted no part of the mother, trying her best to take from Mildred this male too! And Mildred also knew that just as soon as Sidney Junior started walking he, as well, would be taken by his little hand by Sid and led out the door away from her. What was she, she sometimes found herself wondering, just something to have and take care of children for her husband's use? No, she had to keep telling herself, just as soon as Jessie got a little older she would begin getting interested in girl things and, as Sidney Junior would someday be to his daddy, become a great help, and companion, to her mother. Mildred prayed.

Jessie's love of her baby brother kept her in the house more now but *only* to attend Sidney Junior's needs. No maid work. Even the rest of the community wasn't long in learning about Jessie's attachment to her baby brother, since from the time she first learned to talk the little girl wasn't one to hide her thoughts, whether in words or deeds, from the public. Jessie's tongue sported no scars. But now her publicly demonstrating such affection for her little baby brother made everyone breathe somewhat easier, figuring the spoiled-rotten-by-her-daddy Jessie would become a more kind-hearted and considerate child, especially toward the community's other youngsters. Everyone waited.

Jessie wanted the baby for herself. But right from the start she discovered a major obstacle to ownership. Her momma. While the daughter was readily available to help the mother with Sidney Junior's diapering, bathing, dressing, rocking, cuddling, burping, kissing, and playing, Jessie realized early on that for that *most* essential of all the baby's needs, food, no way was she ever going to supply the teeny-weeniest bit of competition for those eminent feeding ritual providers: breasts. Came nursing time, Jessie, watching the little baby God sent here especially for her to play with suddenly forsake her and *everything* else around him to turn into all mouth to noisily suckle on Mildred's big, purple-nippled teat, would be overwhelmed by a strong sense of inadequacy. Feeling the outsider, unneeded, she would quickly leave the scene in search of her daddy.

One time when she had been alone with the baby she had tried to nurse it herself but neither of the two tiny spots on her chest would stretch far enough out when she pulled on them. Then she leaned over the baby with her naked chest up against his lips hoping he, as with her momma, would latch onto the tiny spots with his mouth and begin suckling. Instead he just turned his head away and smiled...or suffered gas. That's when Jessie started to hate her momma's breasts.

Came the night she started to hate the rest of her momma.

Awaking from a bad dream, she got up and headed for her parents' room. Walking through the partly opened door she stopped and blinked her eyes several times, not so sure she wasn't still dreaming. With its high headboard resting up against the room's rear wall, her parents' large bed faced the door. The light was on. Her daddy and momma were lying on the bed with no covers on them. They were buck naked! It was totally confusing to her what they were doing but she could see her daddy lying on top and in between her momma's legs, stretched wide open. Wider than Jessie had thought was possible for anybody's legs to stretch. Her momma was sounding like she was crying, or hurting. Her daddy was moving up and down on her momma, not saying anything. The big bed was shaking like it was about to break down. She stood right in her tracks until this discombobulating sight told her she shouldn't be where she, again the outsider, was, and sent her running back to her room to lie abed trying to decipher what her eyes had just witnessed. She fell asleep hating her momma, who earlier had taken away her little baby brother, whom God had sent here especially for *her* to play with, by having breasts to nurse him with. Now tonight she was in there somehow stealing from Jessie *her* daddy by letting him lie on top of her between her real-wide-open legs. She slept the rest of that night self-consciously pressing her legs tightly together.

The very next chance she got alone for any length of time with the baby she managed to get him from his crib in her parents' room over to their bed. Taking off all her clothes and then his, she lay on the bed on her back and put him atop, facing her, his bottom half lying between her as-wide-open-as-she-could-get-them-until-it-hurt legs. Then pushing him up and down on her, she began making crying and hurting sounds. But for all of her moving him up and down she couldn't get the big bed to shake like it wanted to break down. After a few minutes of this strenuous, senseless exercise, she got bored, figuring her parents strange. Sidney Junior smiled...or had gas.

Jessie remembered the day well. Too damn well!

She, now nine and old enough to be of help, was working with her daddy doing some carpentry out in the tool shed when her momma walked in with Sidney Junior.

"Sid, watch the baby here and let Jessie come and help me in the kitchen with the canning. If I don't get it done today everything's going to spoil."

"But I wanna help Daddy!"

"Now, Sugar Dumpling, you go on and help Momma with the canning."

"Why can't I help you? I don't know how to *can!*"

"Listen, Jessie!" She had *never* heard him call her that before, nor did she recognize his sudden, harsh tone of voice. "Momma needs you to help her out in the kitchen...where the womenfolk *belong!* We menfolk will work out here in the tool shed where *we* belong. Right, little man?"His voice, and face, reverted quickly back to smiling as he stood proudly beaming down at his son.

Stunned! Jessie stood staring, mouth open, speechless, not believing what she had just heard coming from *her* daddy, now taking Sidney Junior by the hand and walking away from her to show the boy around the tool shed. Spinning around, Jessie tore past her momma, who stood looking somewhat surprised by her husband's handling of this, abrupt, changing of the guard, and ran from the building crying.

Jessie's place was now in the kitchen helping her momma. Maid work! She hated every single minute of it! From as far back as she could remember she'd helped her daddy do *everything*. He had taught her to saw, nail, chop wood, milk, drive, swim, play baseball, bale hay, and numerous other important, *boy*things. And now he didn't want her! Her momma needed her in the *kitchen,* the *womenfolk* place! Sidney Junior, a *boy,* was now taking *her* place with *her* daddy outdoors. Why wasn't she born a boy? Why did God make her a girl? Girls did *nothing* interesting! She wanted to be a boy!

But for Jessie the worst was yet to happen. That came a couple of years later when one day she suddenly became aware of something being wrong with her body...but she wasn't quite sure what. She wasn't hurting. Yet she was bleeding. There was blood all over her panties and running down her leg. At first she wasn't sure where it was coming from. She wasn't cut. Then, Lord, she saw!

Her first instinct was to run screaming to her momma. But she didn't. And, Lord knows, she couldn't tell her daddy. She began to cry. Now that she was dying she had no one to tell! Was she being punished? For what? She'd already lost her daddy and been exiled to the kitchen, where for the past couple of years she'd daily danced with boredom. And now here she was bleeding to death. God, hadn't she suffered enough? She knew she had to somehow stop this bleeding herself before she bled to death. That's when she thought of:

"Reenie, Reenie!" Hollering, Jessie ran all the way to the house of her, she felt at that moment, only friend in the world, who was out in the backyard feeding corn to the chickens.

"What's the matter, Jessie?!" A concerned Reenie stopped her throwing of the grains of corn to focus fully on her frightened-looking friend.

"I'm bleeding to death!"

"Bleeding where? Down *there?*"

"Yes...how did you know?"

"I started last month." Reenie went back to throwing corn.

"Started *what?*"

"I thought you knew."

"Knew *what?*"

"Missis Mildred never told you? Mama told me...."

When Jessie came away from the home of her best friend she was mad. Mad because her mother hadn't told her about this bleeding business beforehand. Mad, *and* embarrassed, because she had to find out about this bloody mess from, of all people, little Reenie, whom she knew more than. But, most of all, mad because now she felt she knew why her daddy liked Sidney better than he did her. It was because Sidney was a boy who didn't bleed like she, a girl, was now doing. Her daddy, she just knew, had known all along that one day she was going to bleed and then he wouldn't want her any more. God, she began crying again, it was so unfair.

She was crying too because of what her body was suddenly causing her to do. Reenie, besides proudly telling her that they were now both women, had given her something to absorb the blood. Now, walking home, she felt extremely self-conscious, feeling the whole world was watching her walk, knowing from the way she moved that something was *up* her. Personally, at that moment she would much rather have stayed a little girl instead of suffering this uncomfortable, icky feeling of being a bowlegged, stuffed-turkey, bleeding *woman*. Gross!

But bleeding or no, Jessie still loved her daddy and wanted him back from Sidney Junior. And she swore to God, who had made her a girl in the first place, that someday she was *going* to get her daddy back. No matter how.

~ Chapter 2 ~

When he came home to Appalachee, Georgia, from World War II on Thanksgiving Day Eve, 1945, he swore he wasn't going back to his old job at Nickerson's sawmill where he had worked before being drafted. With a war under his belt he felt he deserved better. He wanted an "inside" job like the one he had had in the war as an orderly room file clerk filing Army regulations and other important papers and where just before getting discharged he had been learning to type on the typewriter. But he was quickly brought back down to earth by everyone telling him that the war hadn't changed anything at home and the only place in Appalachee where a colored man could be sure of spending any amount of time inside, besides his own house and grave, was inside the jailhouse.

But this just made him even more determined to find an orderly room type job somewhere in Appalachee where he would be in charge of filing important papers while continuing his practicing on the type-writer. Before entering the Army he hadn't seen but one typewriter in his life—the one in the principal's office at the colored high school in Appalachee. And even then the few times he was ever in the principal's office (no student liked being in there as it usually meant trouble) he hadn't paid much attention to the machine, and had absolutely no idea how it worked. He only noticed that it sat on the same desk as did the telephone, which he hadn't known how to use either until he got to the orderly room. But when he donned his Private First Class uniform of polished and shined brass that the Army was good enough to let him keep and marched spiffily over to the high school, he met a new principal. One who told him he was very sorry, "Private" (thus knighting him with his new name), but the school had no need for a former war filer of Army regulations and other important papers and a practicing typist. Despite this disappointment the orderly room veteran now had a greater appreciation of the principal's office than he'd had as a student. On the desk now was a new telephone, no longer a mystery to him. On a new desk nearby sat a new typewriter...with a new, pretty young woman behind it.

Still in uniform, the Private marched straight to Appalachee's two other colored typewriters, the offices of Blackshear's Undertakers and Doctor James Allen. Here, standing at parade rest, he was politely told that neither office needed the services of an ex-orderly roomer.

Later, while talking to others, it was suggested he go up to Atlanta, or some other big city, where there might be more of a demand for former orderly room personnel—or go to school on the G.I. Bill, or even reenlist in the Army. But the Private was such a homebody that after having just spent over three years away from Appalachee, he couldn't tolerate the thought of ever leaving it again— even in search of another orderly room with piles of ready-to-be-filed Army regulations and other important papers, a telephone with a dial, and a virgin typewriter. Thus the Private stayed home.

And, true to his word, he didn't hit a lick of work on the sawmill. Nor at any other job. Always known for his tightness with money (able to squeeze the balls off the buffalo without waking the Indian on the other side of the nickel, it was said), the Private had saved practically every penny he earned in the Army. On payday when most of the soldiers went out and spent their money on drinks and women or stayed behind in the barracks and gambled it away, the Private just hung out at the orderly room sucking on a Coca-Cola and munching from a bag of salty peanuts while swapping orderly room stories with the C.Q. Now out of the Army, he began living on these savings while, always in full military dress from staunch cap to shiny toe, he daily sat on the front steps of the jailhouse over back of the courthouse. Here on the jailhouse steps, while consuming his daily diet of soda crackers and sardines, or pork and beans, with a dessert of Coca-Cola and salty peanuts, the Private had at his back a captive audience. To these behind-bars inmates he sat talking by the hours...days...weeks...months...years about his varied war experiences in the orderly room back during the Big One.

~ Chapter 3 ~

All of her life, first by her daddy and then by her husband, she had been called nothing but "GAL!". Even on the day her husband of twenty-three years brought home a new, teenaged wife and kicked her out of their house in the cotton mill section of Yankee Town for not having birthed him any babies, his last word to her had been "...GAL!". Possessing nothing but the faded cotton dress she wore and her stack of romance magazines, she struck out walking along the Oconee River until arriving four miles downstream at Muskhogean County's seat, Appalachee, where she stopped to cool her bare feet and rest her butt atop the front steps of the courthouse. When first asked her name down there on that very first day she automatically shot back with "GAL!". And in Appalachee that's who she instantly became. And, to Appalachians, Lord, GAL! was "something." Forty-one years old but still wearing a younger woman's shape when she came to roost atop the courthouse steps in the summer of 1946, GAL! had long blonde hair scragglying in every direction off her head down her back, big blue trusting eyes, a pointed nose, and a quick, snaggletoothed cackle for a laugh. And, Lord, on just her second day in town she had all of Appalachee talking...and looking. From high atop the courthouse steps this long-blonde-haired, snaggle-toothed cotton mill refugee, while sitting popping her chewing gum and intently reading one of her romance mags, immediately began attracting a crowd below. All males. Staring up. Lord, GAL! wore no drawers!

The discoverer of this bare fact on that locally historic day was a young colored boy who dutifully reported what he'd seen to the nearest white man. In those days it was immoral for a southern black male to look under the dress of a white lady...and unlawful to get caught looking. Ordering the boy to forget what he had seen, the white man immediately went about his God-assigned duty in such a dire emergency of protecting this sacredly sinful sight from the eyes of blacks by quickly shooing them from around the courthouse and making the area off limits to all male members of the darker race. Black females were permitted in the area. Meanwhile, like flies to honey, white males hurriedly flocked around the bottom step of the courthouse to stare up the widely stretched hem of GAL!'s dress. It wasn't too long before the law came to look. Word went, and by nightfall every Godfearing little old lady of

Appalachee had either gone out and bought or selected from her own personal stock a pair of unmentionables for GAL!. Many of the males (the Godfearing shoving for a better viewing position along with the Godless) stood at the bottom step long past sundown hoping to see her try them all on. Which she did, over in the police station under the protective eyes of the law.

The following day GAL!, back on the courthouse steps sitting between two piled-high stacks of assorted colors, sizes, and styles of underpants, drew an even bigger crowd than previously. Perched up there popping gum and reading her romance mag, she was wearing a brand new pair of pink panties of silk (her first ever)...and nothing else. Back came the Man. This time she was *ordered* by the law to keep off the front steps of the courthouse or she would be punished to the utmost: sent back to her husband. This was more than enough to make GAL! put on her dress, grab her romance mags and piles of panties, and go scurrying around the corner of the courthouse to the *back* steps. Fewer steps and less traffic than around front, yes, but the backside of the courthouse was destined to become GAL!'s throne, where less than one hundred feet away stood the jailhouse—atop whose steps sat a short colored man in a spiffy soldier's suit with one stripe on each arm endlessly talking up through the bars to the inmates beyond.

For the next three years GAL! sat atop the back steps of the courthouse popping gum, talking to passersby and herself, reading her romance mags, and wearing drawers across from the Private, who rather than go back to work at the sawmill sat and told World War II orderly room tales to the men behind bars. During all of those years no one ever saw GAL! or the Private, whether by sound or sight, acknowledging the existence of one another. This was back when white ladies and black boys didn't rap publicly 'twixt t'other, no matter how crazy they were.

Everybody knew the Private slept in the one-room house he was born in over behind the fertilizer plant. But where GAL! slept was a mystery. From dawn to dusk, come rain or shine, sleet or slime, she was atop her back-courthouse-steps throne seven days a week. But just as soon as dark dipped, GAL! was gone. True, it might not've been known where she slept, but everybody passing her throne saw what she daily ate. Soda crackers and sardines, or pork and beans and Coca-Cola and salty peanuts for dessert.

In fact this diet appeared to've been agreeing with GAL! too much there in the summer of 1949, when her weight suddenly shot up, eventually even worrying her, the nonworrier, enough to send her to the free clinic. Here a doctor told the in-the-midst-of-menopause GAL! that she had a cyst growing inside her belly that should be cut out sooner than immediately. No slicing up the GAL!, vowed GAL! before waddling back to her throne to pop her gum, talk her talk, and read her romance mags.

Word went, bringing the wingless buzzards to hover around the back of the courthouse awaiting the bloated queen to burst atop her throne.

These human buzzards were hovering back of the courthouse the day GAL! suddenly stopped popping gum in midpop, dropped her romance mag, and fell back with a scream. The cyst had burst! It excreted from beneath her silk unmentionables in the form of a six-pound female. Black. Lord!

~ Chapter 4 ~

Claiming that the baby, born of her until-now-barren body, was "God's Miracle," GAL! named the little girl Jesus. "Besides," she said, "ain' nobody 'bout to call Jesus 'GAL!'."

The old and the newly curious came from the far reaches of Muskhogean County to crowd around the back steps of the courthouse to behold with their own God-given eyes this proclaimed-by-GAL! Miracle, watching the long-scraggly-blonde-haired, soft-eyed white woman sitting on the top step nursing, burping, and napping her black baby while popping gum and in between reading her romance mags. Everybody looked for it...but nobody saw it. The halo.

Nor did anyone ever again see sitting across the way atop the jailhouse steps, the Private.

In those days of racial segregation in the South, Appalachee's authorities, heretofore of the belief that it was biologically impossible for a white woman to birth a black baby, hanky-panky even God Himself wouldn't touch, felt it was the white man's burden to do something about this unlawful freak of nature. But what? Arrest somebody? *Crucify* somebody? Who? The baby? The mother, a *white* woman? The police finally brought GAL! in for questioning and when asked who was her baby's father, she simply replied, "GOD!" But, if anybody did, the police knew God was a white Christian man who hadn't messed around since Mary. Yet not knowing God's blood type, nor knowing what chapter of the Old Testament to find it in, the police had to let GAL! go—but with the stipulation that she keep away from the courthouse. The house of justice, the law felt, was no place for a black baby to be seen by decent Christian folks sucking on a white lady's tits. This sent GAL! to sit on the bench nursing her Miracle black baby in the small park located in the town's center, the favorite spot for black nannies to bring Appalachee's elite white youngsters to crawl, crow, romp, roll, and roar. Before GAL! could burp Jesus from her first nursing in the park, a policeman, with strict orders to come back to Appalachee alone or himself be gone, had mother and daughter in the back seat of the squad car speeding up the Oconee to Yankee Town.

Word beat wheel. The car was met up there by a mob, led by GAL!'s husband, who guaranteed the lawman that if the white woman and

God's b
daughte
GAL! w
while h
the-law

Bu
Yankee
still-sha
brakes
County
ordered
several
outta A
gone. J

~ **Chapter 5**

It was the summer of
September she would
County Colored High
of her family's dair
to transport all
very first day
of the buil
he woul
at sch
the

Jessie's fourteenth birthday. That upcoming
be entering the ninth grade at Muskhogean
School located in Appalachee, six miles northeast
y farm. She didn't ride the bus provided by the county
its schoolchildren from their homes to class. From her
of school her daddy had driven her right up to the front door
ding every morning and when classes ended in the afternoon
d be waiting at the same spot to drive her back home. Arriving
ool ten minutes before classes began and leaving five minutes after
y ended each day didn't give Jessie very much time to associate with
er schoolmates. Yet this had been plenty enough time over the years
to've clearly conveyed the understanding to one and all of them that
Jessie was strictly a "doer" and had no time whatsoever to waste on those
who weren't "doing." Altogether not the bosom buddy type, Jessie
exuded an aura that demanded, and got, the respect of all those coming
in contact with her, including adults. Quick to learn, she was always at
the top of her class—up where she was better able to learn the ways and
means of the classroom power structure, the teacher, and how to
manipulate it to her advantage.

Despite having time only for those who "did," Jessie made an
exception to this strict rule of hers in the case of Irene, or "Reenie."

Reenie, three months younger than Jessie, was the daughter of
Mattie and Will Ingram, the Mitchells' nearest neighbors. Will and Sid,
born less than a mile and a year apart, had grown up together. Came
adulthood, they both landed jobs milking cows at a local dairy. After Sid
married the dairy's bosslady, Mildred, the milking job belonged solely to
Will and he'd had it ever since.

Meanwhile, Will married Mattie and they moved onto what was
now Mitchell land to become Sid's and Mildred's closest neighbors.
Moving into a spacious five-room house, they immediately began filling
it up with children. Mattie dropped nine. The sixth of these, born in 1950,
was Reenie, whom no one thought was going to live past sundown of her
first day out of the oven. But she fooled them all and was very much alive,
and well, that summer of her and Jessie's fourteenth birthdays. The direct
opposite of Jessie in nearly every respect, Reenie was quiet, unassuming,

introverted, slow at learning, passive, frail, but, Lord, *sweet*. Just the type of child Plain View's parents wanted to keep out of the path of Jessie, who consistently, and exultantly, chewed up and spat back in their folks' faces much more resilient souls. But for reasons unbeknownst to all, Jessie took Reenie—who rode to school and back with her in Sid's car—under her wing and double dared *anyone* in *any* way to mess with her best...and only...friend. Yet of all Reenie's many other brothers and sisters living in the house on their parents' land, Jessie bothered with none of them. Only Reenie.

Mildred was more than pleased over her daddy-spoilt, headstrong daughter finding a young female friend to daily share her growing girlhood with, as for awhile she had been afraid Jessie just might've been destined to grow up a lone, dangerous, wolf type. Reenie, the mother also felt, was unknowingly playing the role of the sister Jessie never had. Such a feeling Mildred dared not express aloud to her daughter, whom, she felt, once hearing such coming from the mother, would out of spite break up her friendship with Reenie. Thus Mildred kept quiet, hoping that being in the constant company of sweet little Reenie would eventually bring about a softness to her daughter's too-often-harsh attitude toward others. But she couldn't help but feel that Jessie was, somehow, using Reenie in the same manner she did everyone else coming near her web. Mildred prayed she was wrong.

When Jessie was so abruptly and rudely sent crying from her daddy's outdoor world to the indoor world of her momma, she felt she didn't have a friend anywhere in the world. Her daddy, she was firmly convinced, no longer had any use for her now that he had Sidney Junior. Her momma she hadn't trusted at all ever since the long-ago night of the wide open legs. And Sidney Junior? She had loved him like she believed God had meant her to. But now she hated him...because he was a boy. *Chosen*. All she had now was frail, shy, *sweet* Reenie.

Reenie was an enigma to Jessie. Unlike Mildred and, particularly, Sid, who supplied their daughter with more than enough material goods, Reenie's parents, with a houseful of children, weren't able to give her much of anything outside of love—plus a doll every Christmas. And to the bafflement of Jessie, a possession person, Reenie was ever so happy with so little. Whenever she would come visiting the Mitchells and enter Jessie's room, filled floor to ceiling with dolls of all sorts and sizes, they made look sick the little rag doll she would be hugging tightly in her skinny arms. But every time Jessie, a lover of boy toys, offered to exchange with her one of these larger and more expensive dolls for her skimpy rag one, Reenie would just hug her cheap little doll even tighter to her chest, smile sweetly, and shake her nead no. This confused Jessie, who early grew accustomed to other children always wanting from her, whether it be something material or intangible, with her often giving but always with a stipulation. Except in the case of Reenie, who asked nothing of Jessie but to be her friend. A soul without guile. This Jessie didn't, *couldn't,* understand.

Despite their night-and-day differences, from the age of nine onward the two became inseparable. Then, Lord, came the summer of their fourteenth birthdays.

Early one hot July afternoon, Reenie appeared at the Mitchells' on her daily visit. (Jessie rarely visited the Ingrams' house.)

"Hey, Jessie!" said Reenie, entering her friend's room.

"Hey, Reenie. God, it's hot! Let's go down to the pond where it's cool."

"The *pond?* You know we can't go down there!"

"Why not?"

"Because Mister Sid told us to *never* go down there unless a grown person went with us and you *know* that!"

"We don't have to go in the water, silly. We'll just sit on the bank and cool off some."

"But what if Mister Sid sees us?"

"He's not here. He and Mother just went to town and won't be back until late. They won't even know we went down there."

"What about Sidney outside, won't he tell?"

"If he does I'll whip his ass."

"Jessie!"

Jessie led Reenie and Sidney Junior out back of the barn and onto the narrow path leading into the forest for about a quarter of a mile to the pond. One of the first projects Sid had undertaken after marrying was to have this fish and swimming pond dug. Square shaped, it was fifty yards by fifty yards, with the shallowest end being three feet deep and the deepest fifteen feet. The pond being one of his proudest possessions, Sid kept the water clean and properly drained for both fish and bather, with only his and Mildred's friends permitted to use it. Neatly mowed, the encircling grassy bank was where the three children sat, Jessie with long legs dangling over the edge and bare feet touching the cool water below.

"Let's go in!"

"Jessie, you know we can't! We shouldn't even be down here," admonished a very serious Reenie.

"Daddy said for us to *never* come here unless...."

"I've heard it too, Sidney. *I* can swim. Reenie, you can sit up here on the bank and burn up but I'm going in and cool off." Jessie rose to her feet.

"What about me?"

"You can't swim, Sidney. Daddy's going to teach you just as soon as he gets the time. So you stay *right here* on the bank, you hear me?"

"I'm going to tell Daddy."

"You do and I'll whip your little ass."

"Jessie!"

"Shut up, Reenie!"

"I'm going to tell Daddy you said a bad word."

"If you do I'll drag you back down here and drown your little ass."

"Jessie!"

"Shut up Reenie or I'll drown *your* skinny ass now!"

"I mean...you can't go in the water with your clothes on."

"I'm not, silly." In a flash Jessie dropped her dungarees and pulled her t-shirt off over her head, leaving her standing in nothing but silk panties and brassiere.

"Jessie!" A startled Reenie darted a quick glance at Sidney Junior, who sat staring open-mouthed at his sister's near-naked body, and then looked back at Jessie.

"He can't see anything. Take your dress off and go in with me."

"But, but...." Before Reenie could protest any further, Jessie in one flicker of an eyelash spun the shy little creature around with one hand and with the other one unzipped her sleeveless dress down the back, then with both hands pulled it off over her bony shoulders to fall to the ground around her bare feet. Reenie stood stark naked. "JESSIE!"

"God! You got *whoppers!* Wearing that ol' droopy dress nobody can tell you got such *big* ones! How come you don't have on underwear?"

"Momma said," mumbled an embarrassingly confused, barely audible Reenie, "so close to home I don't need to wear any panties. I don't have a brassiere"—all the while stooping to pull her dress up to cover her front from the bulging eyeballs of Sidney Junior.

"God! You need one. Oh, don't mind *him.* He's too young to know what he's looking at anyway."

"Then why does he keep looking at me?" Reenie whispered while watching from the corner of her eye her friend's ogling younger brother.

"Seeing your big tits he thinks you are his mother."

"Jessie!"

"Shut up and let's go in!"

"I can't go in the water like this!"

"Okay, I'll take off my bra and pants." Jessie did so. "Now we both can go in naked."

"Jessie! But, but...." Reenie looked quickly at Sidney, whose eyes had left her body to become glued back to his sister's now-stark nakedness.

"Will you stop worrying about Sidney! He's not even eight yet. Sidney? Do you know what a pussy is?" She patted the fresh patch of hair newly grown down south of her navel and up north of her knees.

"Jessie!"

"I *know* you know what titties are," she taunted, yanking Reenie's dress away from her chest.

"JESSIE!"

Sidney Junior giggled at the screaming Reenie.

"See, he's still a baby, only knows titties. I'll bet you don't even know you are a boy, do you Sidney?"

"I'm a boy."

"How do you know?"

"Because."

"Because what?"

"Jessie! Leave him alone and give me back my dress!"

"Shut up, Reenie! Can you prove you are a boy, Sidney?"

"Boys got short hair and girls got long hair."

"Boys got something *else* too."

"Jessie!"

"Shut up, Reenie! Show it to us, Sidney."

"Show y'all what?"

"Show us what boys got."

"What they got?"

"I'll show you!" Before the puzzled-by-his-sister's-strange-persistency Sidney Junior knew what was happening, Jessie had jumped him, grabbing both his wrists. "Here, Reenie, hold his hands!"

"JESSIE!"

"Shut up, Reenie, and help me here because if you don't I'm gonna tell my mother and daddy you took off all your clothes and showed Sidney your tits! Here, grab his hands while I get his feet!" Releasing her grip on her brother's wrists to that of the frightened-yet-obediently-following-orders Reenie, pulling the boy's hands back over his head, Jessie with her knees pinned both of Sidney's legs to the ground.

Struggling to free himself of the older girls' grasps, a now-frightened, flat-on-his-back Sidney began hollering and crying out, "I'm gonna tell my daddy on y'all!!!!"

"He was *my* daddy before he was yours! Now shut up because nobody's going to hurt you but if you don't stop that hollering we are gonna throw you in the water and let you drown! Ain't that right, Reenie?"

"Let's turn him loose, Jessie, please!" Reenie, on the verge of tears herself, struggled to hold a squirming Sidney's hands on the ground back of his head.

"Reenie, if you don't shut your damn mouth I'll turn Sidney loose and we'll both do the same to you! Won't we, Sidney? *Sidney,* won't we?"

"Yes!" Sidney Junior stopped hollering out his threats to tell his daddy on them long enough to answer through sobs his older sister, who, before he could decide whose side she was now on, from her position atop his legs quickly unzipped the fly of his trousers.

"Look, Reenie! See what *boys* got!"

"JESSIE!" Reenie turned her head away but still held tightly to the wrists of the crying Sidney.

"It's a 'dick'! But it looks more like a little worm! This is what all boys got. A *worm!* Let's see you make it stand up by itself, Sidney. I know boys can do that. Make it stand up! If you don't then I will." Placing the tip of her forefinger beneath her brother's penis, Jessie began flipping it up and down. "Stand up little worm, stand up! Glow, little glow-worm, glow! See, I told you I could do it! Look at it now, Reenie, it's getting stiff! A stiff little worm! Reenie, look!" Reenie brought her head and eyes around to look before squeezing the lids tightly together. "That's what men put inside women. I would never let *anybody* put *that* in me would you, Reenie? Ugh!" Jessie took her finger away and rubbed it back and forth on the grass. "Would you, Reenie?" Eyes still squeezed closed, tears escaping from beneath the lids, Reenie shook her head from side to side. "What are you crying for? You must've seen a lot of worms before with all of those brothers you got! You must've seen some *big* ones too! Well, *have* you?" A nod by Reenie, eyes still closed. "I sure wouldn't want all those brothers with all those worms always in *my* house. But that's why Daddy, and I know Mother too, love you better than they do me, Sidney, because you got a worm between your legs and I don't!" In one quick, agile leap, Jessie hopped up off her brother, now sobbing softer, and went to stand over at the edge of the pond. "Reenie, Sidney has seen everything you got so you may as well leave your dress off and come on in the water with me. How come somebody as skinny as you got much larger breasts than me, who's bigger, older...and better-looking than you? You even started your period before me. Is that why that...that playboy Samuel James got hot nuts for you? It's just not fair!" Then, in a dropped, soft, almost wishful tone, Jessie said to her head-hung, naked friend now standing alongside her, "You are going to make a good mother." Jessie jumped over into the water, pulling in with her a Reenie screaming,

"JESSIE!!!"

Sitting up on the bank staring through a slowly unblurring vision down at the water of the pond, Sidney's first inclination upon being freed by the two older girls had been to run straight home and wait for his parents to tell them what Jessie and Reenie had done to him. But the longer he sat the less he felt like running all the way home crying to tell his parents what had happened to him. He felt, somehow, ashamed. He also felt something else. Something about his sister's bad words, Reenie's titties, and the hair growing where the girls had no pee-pees had made his almost-eight-year-old body feel dizzy right in the pit of his belly. Then when Jessie had played with his worm she hadn't hurt it like he had been scared almost to death she was going to. He had liked seeing all of that big-girl nakedness, especially Reenie's titties, and wanted desperately to prove to them that even if he did have a little worm he was a *big* boy. His daddy had told him so. Feeling like a big boy, he pulled off his short pants and jumped over into the shallow end of the pond.

The girls were way over on the deep end of the pond swimming in between laughing, screeching, and water fighting. In order to get a better view of all that big-girl nakedness, he wanted to get as close to his sister and, especially, Reenie as possible while yet able to keep his head above water. But it took only a few steps before the water was up to his nose. Arching his head backwards and staring upward at the cloudless sky, he kept on moving toward the sound of the girls. Suddenly, as if a rug had been jerked from beneath him, his feet were no longer touching bottom. He couldn't move forward, nor backwards, just bobble straight up and down. Water was pouring into his mouth, nose, eyes, and ears. Every time he popped up he could see the girls, now looking so far away, but through all of the water roaring in his ears he could no longer hear them—though he could feel himself screaming with an unfamiliar voice. He remembered his daddy once saying that if you are drowning you go down three times and then you are drowned for good. So far he had counted going down seventy-five times and he was still bobbing, with his feet trying frantically to touch down. Finally, on one of his pops to the top he saw Reenie swimming toward him. But he wished she would hurry up because that unearthly voice was screaming louder and louder for someone to come and help it.

Jessie, her back to the shallow end of the pond, was having a great time water fighting and felt she was now getting the best of Reenie, who had been the one who started the battle. Diving deep in order to come up behind her water foe for a surprise attack, she surfaced right next to the bank at the deepest point of the pond only to find no Reenie. Reading the enemy's thoughts, Reenie had swum away from the deepest end and was now out of water-fighting reach over at the side of the pond about sixty feet to Jessie's right...then, suddenly, swimming madly toward the shallow end. About to holler out to her quickly departing foe, Jessie heard it. The screaming. Sidney! Godammit, I told him to stay on the bank, was Jessie's first thought. An able swimmer, she shot out straight ahead toward the screams, more miffed than frightened. But about halfway there, where she could now see her brother bobbing up and down, from the corner of her eye to her right she quickly noticed Reenie—who had just recently learned to swim and still had problems trying to stay afloat very long at a time—splashing madly while her open mouth was busily filling itself with water, causing her to sputter and cough. Realizing that Reenie was fast losing control, Jessie, faced with split-second deciding, had to choose between swimming to her baby brother or her best friend. Jessie swam to Reenie.

Sidney Junior felt himself being pressed deep down beneath a wall of gray, crushing water where he couldn't breathe, and now replacing the screaming in his ears was a loud roaring sound that, like the last moments of wakefulness before falling to sleep at night, he never remembered ending.

Mildred went into total shock, and so that following Sunday she wasn't able to attend Sidney Junior's funeral, where Reenie cried and cried and Jessie tried and tried...but couldn't.

~ **Chapter 6** ~

More than a year had passed since the drowning, but like a dark tornado cloud the tragedy yet hung over the community, especially over Mitchell's Dairy Farm. Sid was hard hit by this untimely, shocking death of his only son, whom it had taken him eleven years of marriage to sire— a son whom he was just beginning to slowly, and lovingly, groom to someday take over the family's farm. He blamed himself for not taking the time to teach the boy how to swim. He had been waiting until that very summer for Sidney to turn eight, the age his daddy had taught him to swim and the age he had taught Jessie. But before he got around to passing on the legacy that busy summer God popped His fingers and overnight Sid found himself without a son. Or a wife.

The instant Mildred heard of her son's drowning she had gone into shock, triggering off a crippling stroke. Now confined to bed, unable to walk or talk, she had to be waited on hand and foot. The moment Mildred first opened her eyes from the initial shock, Jessie, standing over her bed awaiting her lids to roll back, told her:

"I heard some hollering and looked and saw him popping up and down in the water on the shallow end. Reenie was closer to him than me and I had already started swimming to get him. I was all the way over on the deep end but I would've gotten to him in time because I'm a fast swimmer, just ask Daddy, if it hadn't been for Reenie. She just learned how to swim not too long ago and when I got close to her I saw she was trying to swim too fast and was swallowing a lot of water, making her cough. I was so close to her that I thought I would help her out of the deep water and still get to Sidney, who was just in shallow water, in time. I was so close to her that I couldn't just swim off and leave her, my *best* friend, to drown. But after I got her to the shallow water and looked around I didn't see Sidney anymore.... Before we went in the water I *told* Sidney to stay *right there* on the bank because he didn't know how to swim and that's *exactly* where we left him when we went in the water. On the bank. Reenie will tell you the same thing. But he didn't listen, just too hardheaded. It's all *his* fault." Jessie for a moment thought she saw, *felt,* a glare in her momma's eyes.

Jessie told the identical story to her daddy of having swum to Reenie's aid first because she was the closest at the time. And, of course, sweet little Reenie, full of guilt while taking upon her skinny shoulders total blame for the tragedy, felt Jessie should've bypassed her, on the verge of strangulation at the time, and swum straight for Sidney Junior. Sid, Jessie couldn't help but believe, thought so too. Mildred just lay staring blankly off into space until, Jessie chillingly felt, the daughter came near and the mother's eyes would emit a cold glare. When Sid had asked Jessie why she had disobeyed him by going down to the pond in the first place, especially taking along Sidney Junior, who didn't know how to swim, she answered him, "The weather was hot and sticky, and I needed to cool off in the water. I didn't want to leave Sidney here at the house by himself and down at the pond I *told* him to stay on the bank until we got out of the water. Reenie will back me up on that. Sidney was just too hardheaded to listen."

Jessie's figuring was that the whole thing was a tragic accident that no one felt any worse about than she did, yet was more Sidney Junior's fault than anyone's for not minding her. At the time of the drowning she'd done all she could possibly do and now there was nothing anyone could do to change what had already happened. With this feeling firmly in mind she became determined that, unlike her mother, she wasn't going to let something she couldn't change destroy her, ever. And, Lord, Jessie didn't lie.

At home she now did the cooking, the only household chore she didn't detest. Mainly she wanted to cook for her daddy, grieving over his dead son and with a wife who was now an invalid. Jessie wanted to take care of him. She now had him all to herself and wanted again to be her daddy's "Sugar Dumpling."

Chapter 7

Beginning in the spring of 1950, practically every night, whether moonlit or starlit or stormy, somewhere in either rural Morgan, Putnam, or Greene County surrounding Muskhogean, someone would report hearing his or her dogs barking wildly as if in fear. In going outside to investigate, the person of the house would see standing just beyond the edge of light the ghostly images of a long-white-haired woman holding in her arms a dark baby (in later years the woman would be seen holding the hand of the child standing beside her) before fading back into the darkness. Nighttime possum and coon hunters told stories of catching fleeting glimpses of a long-white-haired figure floating through the trees. Or the hunters looked up to see female and child silhouetted briefly against the skyline before both quietly disappeared over the horizon. Automobiles passed these creatures of the Georgia nights walking along the highway in the dark, and whenever those few drivers bold, or drunk, enough to offer a ride would stop their cars and wait ahead...and wait...nobody ever appeared. Only the sound of the night would be out there. This would be enough to send the now-frightened driver speeding off down the highway...only to pass the two ghostly figures again...but this time, rather than stopping, the driver would pick up speed. Nobody ever got close enough to touch, or even talk to, this long-haired white haint and its dark child, both of whom were seen only at night.

Then, in the fall of 1965, one dark, rainy, and cold night, the Candy Man was driving back to Appalachee in the pickup truck of the company he worked for, J.W. Edwards Garage, along a Muskhogean back road over near Morgan County, when suddenly he jammed on the brakes. Standing bare of head and feet and coatless in the middle of the muddy dirt road was a young, ragged-dressed girl.

"If you wanna ride, come hop in!" hollered the Candy Man out the window and over the engine at the long, lean, big-eyed, rain-soaked girl not moving one inch out of his headlights.

"Naw!"

"Yo' car broke down?!"

"Naw!"

"Well, wha'cha want?!"

"My maw's dead!"

But, Lord, it wasn't to be that easy. No matter what or how much Jessie did for her daddy he just didn't treat her like, nor even call her, his little Sugar Dumpling of yore. He didn't mistreat her but his mind and thoughts now seemed more and more on things outside the house, the farm, than within. Jessie took care of her father's food and the cleaning of his clothes and his room (he now slept in the spare room), not letting the hired woman do anything for her daddy. She also cooked for her mother but let the newly hired woman do the feeding and care for the sick woman, as whenever she entered Mildred's room Jessie just couldn't shake the eerie feeling that the invalid's blank stare would automatically revert into a cold glare directed upon the daughter. Jessie stayed out of her mother's bedroom.

She knew her daddy missed Sidney (at times when Jessie had a moment to think about him she too found herself missing "the little rascal"), whose name was never brought up around the house. It was right after the drowning that Sid put a high barbwire fence around the pond and posted it with a big KEEP OUT sign. Now only the fish swam in the neglected water with its overgrown banks. Sid began spending more and more time away from home and usually didn't return until late at night after Jessie was asleep. But one time he got home before she went to bed and brought with him not the sweet aroma of pipe tobacco—the masculine scent she'd always associated with her daddy—but the strong smell of liquor. She went to sleep crying.

Then, the very next day, immediately after washing his clothes and before going to her room for the night she, extremely bewildered, went straight to her mother's room. Here, without turning on the light since she didn't want to see Mildred's eyes, she sat in a chair beside the sick woman's bed for several hours without muttering one word before finally getting up and, yet silent, leaving for her own room. She lay awake way past midnight because of her mind refusing to let go the memory of her fingers earlier that evening running through her daddy's ready-for-the-washer overalls and pulling out what she remembered having seen at school one day in the girls' lavatory when Ivory MacDonald had shown several of the curious, giggling females a "rubber." In *her* daddy's pocket! No wonder he no longer had time for her, his *only* child, despite *all* the things she did for him every day to try and make him a happy home—only to find out there was a woman, besides her poor sick mommy, in his life. Lord, Jessie was pissed!

Needing badly to talk to someone, Jessie, one who put off nothing for tomorrow that could've been done yesterday, early that next morning paid a rare visit to Reenie's to confide in her best friend about her daddy now having a woman besides her poor sick mommy. But Reenie was still in mourning over the more-than-a-year-old Sidney Junior drowning, and hearing what Jessie had discovered in Sid's overalls pocket brought instantly from her best friend's eyes a bucket of tears flooding in apparent sympathy for the bedridden Mildred. Jessie knew of no way to find out who the mystery woman was who was making her father go around buying rubbers and cheating on her mommy. She couldn't ask her daddy's best friend, Will, whom she just *knew* knew, because, she also knew, a grown man wouldn't tell a child, especially a girl, such a thing, no matter what. And she wasn't about to ask her daddy because she just couldn't stand the pain of hearing him lie to her. Lord, Jessie was both confused *and* pissed!

It was while in the ninth grade that Jessie's body suddenly put the brakes on its rapid climb to the clouds to begin concentrating on filling in all the hereunto hollow spaces below. By age sixteen everything about her physique was filling in, and out, so beautifully that she was attracting the attention not only of all the schoolboys but of many adult males as well. One afternoon while driving his daughter home from school, Sid stopped at J.W. Edwards Auto Garage, whence he bought his vehicles, to conduct some business. Parking at the garage's gas pump for a fillup, Sid stepped into the nearby office, leaving his daughter alone in the car, since Reenie, sick with a cold, hadn't attended school that day. Having been sitting in class for hours, a restless Jessie got out of the front seat to stretch her long legs while thinking heavily on what she was going to cook her daddy for that night's supper. Halfway around the car she stopped dead in her tracks.

Gassing up the car was a man about her daddy's age wearing a pair of greasy mechanic overalls. But what hit her where she lived, cried, died, and couldn't hide was his face—leathery-bronzed, soft-green-eyed, with a thin salt-and-pepper mustache decorating a set of lips tottering on the edge of a soul-devastating smile. The man's temples were graying but the rest of his headful of thick hair was jet black. This was the most handsome male Jessie had ever seen. As if being pulled, willingly, her gaze dropped down his body where her eyes caressed the long fingers of his hands gripping tightly the nozzle of the long, thick gas hose sticking in the open mouth of her car's gas tank. Drawn back up to his face, her eyes latched onto his green set, and without uttering a single syllable the older man and the sixteen-year-old high school girl stood staring straight on at one another while the sound of the nozzle of the long, thick hose loudly spurted gas into her tank. Then, abruptly, the nozzle bolted, indicating her tank was full, and the man, not moving his eyes from hers, slowly pulled from the hole the hose, dripping. With a rag he wiped the wet spot surrounding the tank before, with those long fingers, slowly screwing the cap back on. All Jessie could hear above the screwing cap was her heavy breathing...while a warm feeling was billowing back of her navel...sensations interrupted by the sound of Sid slamming shut the office door on his way to their car.

All the way home Sid did the talking, mostly about the new pickup truck he was thinking about buying. Jessie did all the thinking—thinking about how that good-looking *grown* man had kept looking at her, a young, teenaged schoolgirl. The way he had looked at her made her feel special. And for the first time in her life she was finding herself glad she was a girl instead of a boy. Boys had nothing girls wanted, except to be one of them. But girls definitely had something *all* boys wanted. *Grown* men wanted. And, Lord, she knew what it was. She then decided that beginning the very next day, rather than wearing her usual dungarees to school, she would start wearing a dress—to show off her, she'd often been told, nice bod, especially her legs. Sitting there on the front seat of her daddy's car, she could feel the power between her legs...vigilant. God! For the first time ever she was glad she was a girl!

Jessie was never to remember what she cooked for her daddy's supper that night, nor even to remember cooking. She just remembered after eating asking him, "Who was that man who put gas in our car at J.W. Edwards today?"

"What did he say to you?"

"Nothing! He didn't say one word. I just stood watching him spurt gas in the tank. He's good at it. Who is he?"

"That's the Candy Man."

"Is that his *real* name?"

"I don't know. All I know is what I hear and all I ever heard anyone call him was 'the Candy Man'."

"It doesn't sound like a real name. I wonder why he's called that? You ever hear why?"

"Because he's no good." This bit almost blurted out following a brief pause.

"Why? What does he do?"

"He's been on the chain gang."

"For doing what?"

"For selling bootleg liquor."

"Is *that* all?"

"That's enough. But he's no good for other reasons too."

"Like what?"

"You are too young to be knowing."

"If I really wanted to know, all I have to do is ask at school. Ivory MacDonald knows everything about everybody in town."

"He's a woman chaser."

"*All* men are women chasers." Jessie stared straight into her daddy's eyes, which quickly lowered to watch his fingers pack his pipe.

"Not like him. He chases married women...and young girls. When he found that old white woman they called Gal dead last year he upped and took in her young daughter for himself like she belonged to him just for bringing in her dead momma in his pickup."

"Oooh, so he's the one. How old is the daughter?"

"About your age. Too young. I hear she's black but talks like a poor white."

"She must like it if she's still staying with him. He's certainly good-looking. Must've broken a heap of hearts."

"Just make sure *you* stay outta his way."

"I might."

She did. For almost a week. Until that recess hour when she stood talking to Reenie right at the edge of the crowded schoolyard next to the street, where came cruising a car. The whole schoolyard hushed, all eyeballs on the white T-Bird convertible. Behind the wheel, bareheaded, white-sport-shirted, dark-sunglassed, sat the Candy Man. The school-yard stood open-mouthed, silent, eyeballing the car now stopped in the middle of the street, waiting, its driver sitting behind the wheel, watching. Looking straight on at the car was Jessie, who in midword stopped talking to a bulging-eyed Reenie and, to the gasp of the crowd, stepped out of the yard into the street (a school rule no-no). Strutting on up to the car in her hip-hugging new mini, Jessie stood talking to the older man just out of the crowd's earshot for several minutes. A conversation ending in shared loud laughs brought Jessie swinging back onto the schoolyard and sent the T-Bird cruising on down the street. A stunned, staring Reenie stood speechless until Jessie told her to "shut up!"

The next day, Thanksgiving Eve, just before her last class of the day, Jessie went straight to her teacher and said, "Mister Massey, my father's birthday is coming up soon and I would like to go into town and buy him a present without his knowing. May I please be excused from your class and go buy it now before he comes to pick me up after school? If there's any work you want me to make up for today I'll make it up next week."

"Jessie, dear, don't worry about making up any work. You know it all anyway. Just go right into town and buy your father a birthday present. He's very fortunate to have a thoughtful daughter like you," said Mister Massey, who then stood watching the back of her mini move maniacally down the hall.

Crossing the street from the schoolyard and entering the small grocery store on the other side, Jessie walked on through the building out the back door and onto the next street over, where she pulled open

the door and climbed into the cab of a parked-against-the-curb pickup whose doors were lettered

J.W. EDWARDS
GARAGE

before it sped off down the street.

She had pleaded with him to go slowly with her because she was afraid. She hadn't let him take off her clothes, except her blouse. He had only his trousers on. His gentle kissing of her mouth and neck while talking ever so sweetly to her, lying on her back atop the bed beneath him, was giving her a powerful sense of being ever so special— especially when she felt pressed against her body the straining bulge of his crotch, whose worm was stiff because of, and for, *her*. Now he was kissing her beneath her bra, sucking the nipple of one breast...then the other one...sending a tingling straight down her body to the center of her source. God! His hand was now under her dress, down *there,* a long finger finding its way beneath a corner of her pants to where she was wet like she had never been before. Lord, she hoped she wasn't bleeding! At the feel of his roving finger exploring her, gently pulling in and out, going around and around, she opened her legs wide...wider...just like.... From where she lay she thought just for an instant she saw standing in the bedroom door a sleepy-eyed little girl in pajamas. But lying there with her legs opening wider...wider...what she heard, then saw, was the door exploding open and her daddy springing into the room screaming "SUGAR DUMPLING!!!" and wielding in his hand a pistol. (For a while there she was beginning to think her daddy was never going to come to preserve his Sugar Dumpling's virginity. But she just knew when he got to school and began demanding her whereabouts, sweet little Reenie couldn't tell a lie.) Hollering "Daddy!!!" Jessie quickly pulled on her bra and leapt off the bed in search of her blouse. As she groped around for it alongside the bed in the dimly lit room, a pistol came flying through the air to land on the floor right in front of her. Looking up she saw the half-naked body of a cursing Candy Man with both hands gripped tightly around her daddy's throat. That's when she picked up the pistol and hollered, "TAKE YOUR GODDAMN HANDS OFF MY DADDY!!!" and pulled the trigger.

Word lost nary a second in getting out about the grown man the Candy Man having offered a ride to the young, underaged Jessie, on her way into town to buy her daddy a surprise birthday present (more than a month ahead of time), and then forcefully taking the high school teenager to his house where he tried to rape her, only to be foiled in his attempt by the father, Sid, who arrived just in the nick of time to preserve his daughter's honor by shooting and killing the would-be rapist.

Lord, Lord, "Sugar Dumpling" was back!

~ Chapter 9 ~

That night beneath the giant pecan tree rising eerily out in the middle of the Mitchells' spacious front yard stood a lone figure watching the house where a solitary light painted an upstairs window. With hours of tears burning her eyes, Jesus had walked all the way from Appalachee to find out firsthand from the one who, for her looks and dress, she called "the Pretty Girl," why the Candy Man had to be killed. Besides her mother, the Candy Man had been the only person who had ever treated Jesus humanely. Everyone else just laughed at her. But after coming way out here to be greeted by such a house, whose size and solid structure instantly intimidated the young nomad, who for her first fifteen years had lived in and out of abandoned shacks, sheds, and barns, in caves, on the beds of forests and open fields, beneath bridges, and anywhere else refuge could be found for the day or night, Jesus, suddenly and frighten- ingly realizing she could never possibly deal with anyone living in such a house, stood frozen in her tracks beneath the giant pecan tree. Lord, she, slowly and sadly coming to grips with the horrid thought, knew it was time again for her to hit that lone, lonesome road, having nobody in the world now but herself...and the one in her belly...Le Bonbon.

Chapter 10

Following graduation from high school in 1968, Jessie entered college that next fall. Most of her classmates enrolled in black-owned colleges about the state and the South, but Jessie, who had always wanted to work with her daddy and, being his only heir, knew that someday she would inherit the family's dairy farm, decided as early as her junior year in high school that she would major in business once in college. Thus, after *telling* her daddy, she decided to attend the best available college to get the best available education: Emory University in Atlanta. Also, though this time she *asked,* Jessie wanted her daddy to pay for her dearest friend Reenie, whose folks couldn't afford to send her to college and whose grades hadn't been good enough to merit a scholarship, to attend Emory with her. To this a startled Sid, well known around the county for his nickel niggardliness, erupted with a flat-down-to-the-ground-and-under-the-dirt NO!

Jessie was serious about wanting her friend to go up to Atlanta with her because ever since the Candy Man killing ("justifiable homicide," the law had ruled in Sid's favor) Reenie had been the only person daring to get too near Sugar Dumpling in public. Jessie hadn't appeared too upset over the matter as others' awe...or fear...of her seemed to pump her blood, but everyone's avoidance of her had made her even more dependent on "little Reenie" for company. And something had happened to Jessie that even she couldn't shake from her mind, no matter how hard she tried to, even though to outsiders it would seem small compared to the Sidney and Candy Man incidents. But not to Jessie. It happened about a year after the Candy Man killing when one night she was suddenly awakened by something sounding like a baby cry. For several nights afterwards she heard the same cry. The cries, which appeared to be coming from the direction of the barn, sometimes continued while she lay awake...and afraid. Too afraid to get up and go outdoors to investigate. Some mornings after hearing the cries the night before, she had gone out to the barn where she found nothing...which scared her even more. But wherever the first cry came from, suddenly they all went back there. Gone. Jessie never again heard them, nor did she mention them to anyone. But she never forgot them, and only when she was with her friend Reenie did the eerie feeling they gave her become stilled.

But sweet little Reenie solved the college problem.

"Who did it to you?! Is he going to marry you?!" raved a shocked, furious Jessie. "He'd *better!*"

"It's all right, Jessie." Tears bubbled up in Reenie's eyes.

"Tell me who it is and I'll tell Daddy and we will *make* him marry you, or pay for an abortion."

"Jessie! I don't want an abortion! I don't want to marry...him. But I *want* my baby. I've *always* wanted a baby." Tears now crept down Reenie's cheeks.

"But the baby *gotta* have a daddy, somebody to take care of it. Who's the daddy?"

"I can't tell you because you'll kill me...."

"It *better* not be ol' hot nuts Samuel James! It just *better* not be!" This broke the dam behind Reenie's eyes, drowning a face distorted by uncontrollable sobs. "I *knew* it! I just *knew* it! You mean to stand here and tell me you *fucked* Samuel James and I, your *best* friend, didn't even know about it? When?! Where?! How come?! How could you do it without telling *me?* Now, now, don't cry." Jessie grabbed and hugged tight the shaking body of her loudly sobbing friend. "Daddy and I will get that sonofabitch!"

"Daddy," Jessie began after supper that night, when just she and Sid sat in the living room.

"Yes, Sugar Dumpling?" Sid puffed on his pipe while rocking gently in his rocker in the glare from the giant color television screen.

"Reenie is pregnant."

"Oh?"

"Yes, she told me this afternoon."

"She's sure."

"She's three-missed-periods sure."

"Does her folks know?"

"Not yet. I'm the first one she told. She hasn't even told that Samuel James yet."

"Who is Samuel James?"

"The boy at school who made her pregnant. He thinks he's a real playboy. He uses girls, and he's had his eye on Reenie ever since...ever since.... Anyway, Reenie wants to have the baby but she doesn't want to marry Samuel. I can't blame her for not wanting to marry that shit...."

"Baby Dumpling!"

"...But *every* child needs a daddy."

"Is she going to tell the boy?"

"She says she's not. I offered to talk to him but Reenie cried and begged me not to. Can you imagine? Somebody gotta talk to that sonofabitch...!

"Sugar Dumpling!"

"...Will you talk to him?"

"Me? That's not my place, Sugar Dumpling. It's got nothing to do with me...nor *you*."

"But she's my *best* friend...."

"Sugar Dumpling! That is *none* of your business. What Reenie and that boy want to do about that baby is between them and their folks and *nobody* else. You hear?"

"But...."

"You *hear* me?"

"Yessir." Here followed a long pause when nothing could be heard in the room but whatever it was that wasn't being paid attention to on the television. Then:

"But since she's my Sugar Dumpling's best friend and if the boy don't want to marry her, then maybe I'll help out a little where and when I can. You hear?"

"Yessir!" Jessie bounced over to give her daddy a daughterly hug.

Thus Jessie went off to college without her best friend Reenie, who stayed home to have her baby...unmarried.

Going off to Atlanta without Reenie was enough to make Jessie just want to *kill* that Samuel James! It was *almost* enough to make Jessie want to tell Reenie about the time she lost her virginity—something, like the scary baby-crying sound, that she'd told nobody about. It had happened long after the Candy Man misfortune, as Jessie thought of it, which had convinced Jessie that the female possessed a special power, spelled "S-E-X," over the male, who would willingly crawl on all fours to any spot in the world, or the house, to "get it." Jessie loved that.

Jessie had been in her senior year when Mister Randolph Blackshear came to teach at Muskhogean County High School. A former marine veteran of Vietnam, Mister Blackshear was tall, dark, and rock-solidly built. In his class Jessie had always sat on the front row where she could be nearer to him, a wearer of skin-tight trousers, in order to hear him better...and see close up his mighty bulge. One day he caught her looking. She raised her eyes to his, daring him, before letting them fall back upon the bulge...suddenly bulging to break out. She was going to let him figure out when and how—and he did, immediately.

"Class, I have on my desk here some test papers that must be corrected by me before the next hour, which gives me about twenty-five minutes. Class dismissed!" Thrilled at being let go early, the students shot out the door like bullets from a rifle. Except Jessie...who got to the door just in time to get it locked in her face, whereupon she dropped her books...and grabbed the bulge....

At his home that night, Mister Blackshear finished correcting the test papers that had been lying atop his desk, after unsuccessfully trying to remove from the batch on top several bloodstains.

Chapter 11

Came that first weekend in November of Jessie's freshman year at Emory. She had called home earlier in the week to tell her daddy that she was bringing home a friend, and Sid had been pleased—and surprised—that in such short order his Sugar Dumpling had met and become friends with a girl she liked well enough to bring home to meet her parents. Jessie had even asked him to make sure her old friend Reenie be there when she and her new friend arrived. The night before her arrival while sitting at his wife's bedside, Sid told the mute Mildred about their daughter's coming and he knew the mother understood because in strong anticipation of Baby Dumpling's first trip home from college he felt, at the mention of the child's name, the sick woman's hand stiffen in his. No love, Lord, like mother love!

Sid and a very pregnant Reenie were seated in the living room when the front door flew open and in popped Jessie—popping out Sid's and Reenie's eyeballs...all four of which were aimed dead on Jessie's friend. A boy! A *white* one, baby.

"Daddy!" Jessie sealed her cub hug with a kiss. "It's soooooo good to see you! This is David. Don't get up." (He couldn't.) "David, Daddy."

"How do you do, Mister Mitchell." The boy had a sweet smile. Was this boy laughing at him, his family, his race? pondered a bedazed, dishrag-hand-shaking, seat-glued Sid.

"Reenie!" Jessie cried amid hugs, kisses, and tears—Reenie's. "My! You sure you aren't going to have that baby tonight, *this* minute? What are you having, triplets? David, this is Reenie, my dearest and oldest friend who rather than go away to college to expand her mind stayed home instead and expanded her knees."

"JESSIE!"

"Shut up, Reenie! Daddy, how is Mother?"

"She's...uh...all right," Sid muttered, his eyes still sticking to that sweet smile.

"Good! I'll run up to see her. David, sit down, anywhere. Except on Daddy's knee. Would you like something to drink? Daddy, is there beer in the refridge?"

"I'll get it!" Reenie belly-bounced to the kitchen.

"Oooh, it feels sooo good to be back home! While I'm up saying hello to Mother, Daddy, you and David get to know one another. Talk about whatever men talk about to one another. Politics? Sports? *Women?* Be back!" Gone.

"Mister Mitchell," the white boy smiled sweetly, "did you ever hear the one about...?"

Following supper, cooked and served by Reenie, now downstairs hosting David, Jessie and Sid sat as bookends to, while talking across the top half of, Mildred, lying staring at the backs of her eyelids.

"Sugar Dumpling, why did you do it?"

"Do what?"

"Bring that white boy here."

"David's not white. He's Jewish."

"That's still *white.*"

"The Gentile whites don't think so."

"He ain't *black.*"

It would've been all right with you had I brought home a black man?"

"When you called and told me you were gonna bring home a friend I thought you meant a friend *girl.*"

"A friend of mine is a friend of mine whether it's male or female, black, white, Jew, or politician."

"Sugar Dumpling, no decent lady brings home to her folks a man she's not married to...or doesn't intend to marry. You...you want to marry this white...uh...Jew?"

"No. I told you we are just *friends.*"

"Y'all must be mighty *good* friends for you, of all folks, to bring him all the way from Atlanta down here just to eat supper. What time are you going back tonight?"

"We are not. We leave tomorrow."

"Tomorrow? What are you going to do with him...tonight?"

"What do you mean?"

"I mean where is he going to sleep?"

"In the spare room. I'll fix you a pallet in here with Mother. I'm sure she will love that. Won't you Mother, dear?" Jessie couldn't see Mildred's eyes, now aimed at the ceiling, but she could feel their iciness bouncing off directly back down upon her.

"I'm not going to sleep on any pallet in my own house!"

"Then David can sleep in my room and I'll sleep downstairs on the living room couch."

"NO! He...he can have the spare room. You stay in your room. I'll sleep in here. That way...."

That way, his pallet pulled by him all the way up to the door, he could lie, fully dressed, awake in his and Mildred's bedroom, separating Jessie's and the spare room, listening for any after-hours hallway traffic. Like lodestones, his ears kept leaping to the door. But all they picked up were his own heavy breathing and pounding heartbeats, along with the sound of Mildred moving restlessly in her sleep, an unusual, excitable condition for her that he attributed to their only child being back home. No love, Lord, like mother love! But he was determined not to go to sleep...going to make Goddamn *sure* there be *no* hallway-hopping in *his* house on this night. No, he wasn't going to go to sleep...*couldn't* sleep...being he was the only thing separating his Sugar Dumpling from that sweet-smiling white, or Jew, boy.

As he lay his lonely guard post between the two rooms on across the midnight hour while protecting his only child's honor, Sid's mind, against all his wishes, started to flicker, picking up pieces of the past. Like those times when Sugar Dumpling used to follow him around even tighter than his fair-weather-friend shadow. God! Why hadn't she been born a boy? Then he wouldn't be lying here on a pallet awake in the middle of the night like a fool. That would be some other father's problem. He knew that sweet-smiling white, or Jew, boy's father wasn't lying awake that night worried about his son's honor. Yes, why hadn't Jessie been born a boy? Here his mind was bluntly butted into by a flashing across the brain of a picture of Sugar Dumpling as a baby lying naked on her back in her crib with him leaning over the railing tickling her with his thick mustache...mouth...nose...face, BURRUBBURRUB-BURRUB!—right atop her little belly button, sending her into spasms of high-pitched giggles, her little legs kicking wildly in the air, up and down...up and down...up and down....

An outside sound shot him up from the pallet to stand with an ear suctioned to the door. But all he could pick up were the loud sounds of heavy breathing and drumming heart, his own. What had made the noise? An opening door? Sugar Dumpling's or the spare room's? The harder his ears strained to pick up the sound of shoe two dropping, the more insistent became his open-mouthed breathing and heavy heart-beats, drowning everything else out. Stooping to peek through the keyhole, he saw nothing moving outside. He was frustrated. Pissed! What should he do? What *could* he do? Goddammit! he thought. This was *his* house and she *his* daughter and he, a *man,* couldn't just stand there peeking through the keyhole like a woman and let Sugar Dumpling take control. The man of the house thus stood up straight, pulled open the door of his bedroom, and stepped out into the hall. Empty. Now what? Sleep in the hall? Goddammit! Sometimes Sugar Dumpling just up and got the devil in her. Got that from her momma. Was she in the spare room? Or *he* in her room?

Moving to grasp the knob of Jessie's door, a shock streamed up his arm to his brain. Locked! It had *never* been locked before. How could she do this to her daddy in his *own* house? Lock him out of her room! Leaning against the door to listen, he heard nothing coming from inside. Should he knock? Knock down the door? What if the boy wasn't in there?

Quickly he moved down to the spare room, thinking that if he didn't find the boy there, he then would know what he had to do. Locked! Lord! Then came screeching across his brain the picture of a half-naked, teenaged Baby Dumpling clutching his pistol with both hands while screaming at the top of her tonsils, "GET YOUR GODDAMN HANDS OFF MY DADDY!!!" a split second before the roar he could still hear these many miles and years away of the gun exploding...filling the room with a tidal wave of red, the Candy Man's blood and brains.... Yes, Lord, that's when the man of the house, spooked, tiptoed away from the spare room. The daddy's "devil daughter" had come home.

That next morning at breakfast, prepared by Reenie, while being gabbed to by a bright-eyed Jessie, every time Sid's red eyes peered up from his plate they looked right smack dab into those of that sweet-smiling white, or Jew, boy's.

Emory barely had black students, none of whom Jessie found to her interest, as the powerless had no place in her plans. A civil rights activist only when and if it suited her personal cause, Jessie's chief interest here, as elsewhere, rested around those who ran things, but she was soon to learn that at this big Atlanta university it was going to prove an impossibility for a rural-area black female like herself to get in tight with these chosen children of the region's elite, Gentile or Jew. Quickly accepting the fact, civil rights or no, that she wasn't in any manner going to put a dent in the school's class-race barrier, Jessie, a born leader and *nobody's* follower, chose not to march.

After remaining in Atlanta that Thanksgiving, at Christmas she came home. Alone.

"Jessie!"

"Reenie?" The women greeted each other at the front door with hugs, kisses, and tears—Reenie's. "Where's Daddy?" Jessie asked, releasing Reenie and stepping out of her hug to wade through her friend's tears on into the Mitchells' house.

"In the living room," Reenie choked between sniffles.

"Daddy!" Jessie's outstretched arms suddenly froze as she stopped stone-cold dead in her tracks to stare at what Sid, sitting in his rocker, held on his knee. "Is that...is that...?"

"That's Sonny, my son," announced a proud, flooding-faced, grinning Reenie at Jessie's elbow.

"God! He's *beautiful!* Hello, Sonny! Meet your Auntie Jessie, who's going to hold and kiss you just as soon as she runs upstairs to say hello to her mommy."

"Where is Mrs. Allen?" Jessie, standing in the doorway of her mother's room, interrupted the strange woman sitting by the bedside reading to Mildred.

"She gone."

"Gone where?"

"Don quit wuk'n, retir'd."

"Who are you?"

"My frien's call me 'Pig.' You Jessie?"

"Yes."

"Then you kin call me Pig too. If I'da knowed you was com'n t'day I would've wo' my wig. 'Scuse my naps." Pig's big, warm, snaggletoothed smile was punctuated by a wink.

Following supper, with Sonny abed asleep and Reenie banging pots and pans back in the kitchen, Jessie sat on the living room sofa talking to the pipe-smoking, rocking-chaired Sid.

"I wish I was as domesticated, as *tame,* as Reenie. In the kitchen she's the Eighth Wonder. You should've hired her to do your cooking."

"I did."

"You *did?*"

"Hired her to cook and clean. Once she had the baby she needed a job. Will got enough mouths over at his house to feed without having to worry about two more. So I thought I would hire her. This way she can bring the baby here and watch him while she works."

"I know she's great at cooking, but cleaning too? Reenie looks so fragile, except for those buck teeth and that big bosom."

"Don't let that skinny frame of hers fool you. Reenie's as strong as a mule."

"Daddy, you are such a *sweet* man! Thinking of little Reenie like that."

"Well, she's always been my Sugar Dumpling's best friend so the least I could do when she was in need was the Christian thing and help the best way I knew how. Anyway, that's all taken care of. How long do you have with us?"

"For as long as you want your lil' Sugar Dumpling."

"I mean, when do you go back to college?"

"I'm not going back."

"What?!"

"I said, I'm not going back."

"Why not? Is something wrong? Are you in trouble...by that...that...? I'll *kill* him!"

"No! I'm not pregnant."

"Then how come? I thought you liked it up there?"

"I did, for a while."

"I *told* you to go to an all-Negro college where...."

"No, that's not the reason. Race means *nothing. Power* is everything!"

"Just what are you talking about?"

"I don't like being a fish swimming in someone else's pond. The thing I want most of all to do I can do right here without you spending the money and me wasting the time for a college trying to teach me how to do it."

"What do you want to do here?"

"Run the dairy with you."

"We'll see."

"But, first things first."

"Like what?"

"Like firing that 'Pig' person. Poor Mother deserves better."

"Sugar Dumpling, what are you talking about? Pig is said to be the best wet nurse in the county. She's good for Momma. Momma's eating and looking much better now. Pig even reads to her."

"Yes, I saw. The comic strips, comic books, the *National Enquirer,* romance novels, and every other piece of printed trash sold in the supermarket. Besides, Mother doesn't understand a single word of what's being read, thank God. Pig, I'm sure, is doing all of that reading solely for her own pleasure."

"No, not the way she takes time to tend to Momma's every need. Momma might not know what Pig is reading to her but that don't matter one bit because whatever it is it's making her feel better. That much I can tell."

"Mother might be eating good now but so is Pig. That plate she took upstairs for her supper tonight was piled so high with food it resembled the Empire State Building. Why doesn't she eat downstairs like Mrs. Allen did?"

"She likes to eat with Momma."

"She probably eats Mother's food too...living up to her name. Just where did you find her?"

"When old Mrs. Allen told me she was ready to retire, I happened to think of Pig."

"Oh, you knew her before?"

"Yes, Pig and I went to school together."

"An old girlfriend?"

"Puppy love, it was called then."

"What is it called now, 'Pig love'?"

"Sugar Dumpling, if I fired Pig who would take care of Momma? You?"

"I can't. From now on I will be helping you run the dairy. But I guarantee you I can find somebody better for Mother than that Pig."

"I am *not* going to bring *anybody* else in here! Pig is doing a *good* job taking care of Momma!"

"*And* you?"

"I'm gonna be out at the barn." Sid got up from his rocker and looked down into the eyes of his seated daughter. "Sugar Dumpling, you are a real pretty girl, a woman now, and since you say you ain't going back up to college ain't it about time you started thinking about other, more important things in life? Like by you being so concerned about Momma's care, and all...don't you think it might do her a world of good if she had a grandchild? What just might help get her well could be a little *grandson.*" Gone. For the first time since being spanked across her baby ass by the delivering doctor Jessie didn't get in the last word. It was just at this time that Pig—a char-black, all-bosom-and-butt, ageless woman—on her way to the kitchen passed through the living room and gave that big, warm, snaggletoothed smile of hers, followed up by a wink. Jessie got sick in the seat.

After Reenie finished in the kitchen and while waiting for her and Sonny to be driven home by Sid, still out at the barn, she sat in the living room with Jessie, now talking.

"Do you like working here better than at your own house?"

"Yes. Here I get paid." Giggles.

"If I could cook and clean like you I would either patent myself or protest loudly for the return of slavery to ease my workload. Oh, Reenie, you are the best friend I've ever had or could ever want. Besides Daddy, my *only* friend. It feels so good to be back home and I'm so glad you are now here cooking and cleaning for Daddy." Jessie reached out to touch her starting-to-sprinkle-tears friend's hand. "Also, now that I'm not going back to Emory, it's good to know my dearest friend will be here to take care of the housework while I help Daddy run the dairy."

"You aren't going back to college?"

"No way, baby."

"Why not?"

"Like I told Daddy, up there in the big, dirty, public swimming hole of Atlanta I quickly learned that I was just another one of the countless, insignificant minnows. But here in the small pond of Appalachee I can, and *will*, be a BIG FISH!" (A shark, Lord?) "How is Daddy doing these days?"

"He's doing just fine. Doesn't he look it?"

"I don't mean his health. Is he still running around?"

"Running around?"

"Come on, Reenie, you know where babies come from by now, I hope. Remember the rubber in the pocket? Have you caught them yet?"

"Caught who?"

"Daddy and Pig, who else? I *know* he's fucking her!"

"How do you know that?"

"My female intuition told me while I was talking to him about her tonight. Sad to say he has such poor taste."

"Jessie, why don't you let Mister Sid live his own life? He's a grown man."

"He's still *my* daddy and I don't like him cheating on Mother, especially with the woman who's supposed to be taking care of her. If, and when, I find out Pig while nursing Mother is fucking Father on the sly, I'll *kill* the hypocritical bitch!" Then, quickly flashing her winningest and warmest smile to her dearest friend: "God, Reenie, you got the most beautiful baby! He sure doesn't look anything like his daddy, except maybe for the asshole part."

"Jessie!"

"What has Samuel James said for himself, or done for the baby?"

"Samuel James left town right after we all finished school last spring and hasn't been back since."

"You mean to say he hasn't even *seen* his *own* child?"

"No, he hasn't seen Sonny."

"Why that Goddamn sonofabitch!"

"Jessie!"

"Shut up, Reenie! That's the very reason you are in the predicament you are in right now—because of your being soooo understanding. It got you pregnant. But I guess it's good he's gone because if he was here he would probably keep you full of baby year round."

"No! I only wanted *one!*"

"You *wanted* one?"

"Yes. And he means *everything* to me. My *whole* life. I don't care if he *never* knows his daddy. Sonny's *mine!*" A long minute of silence interrupted before Jessie, in a dropped, soft voice, spoke.

"It must be wonderful...a real warm feeling...being a mother. Sometimes I wish I was one. If only you didn't have to submit to all of that degrading mating, male domination shit. The last laugh is always on the woman."

"Jessie, it's nothing like as bad as you always make it sound."

"If it's so Goddamn good then why in the hell aren't you married?" Jessie was back.

"I don't *want* to get married!"

"To Samuel James, I don't blame you. Too bad God didn't know how to make the pussy that only certain, special dicks could fit, like Cinderella's slipper, rather than *any* cock on *any* male that can get hard. But I guess then women would be walking around all the time with sore assholes."

"JESSIE!"

"Daddy better come on soon so you can go home and get some sleep. You spend your whole day here. When do you have a day off for yourself?"

"I don't take any days off but any time I want to do anything or go anywhere, Mister Sid always lets me, even drives me to where I want to go. He's been very good to me."

"You know what he wants from me?"

"What?"

"A grandson! He *still* wants a boy! And wants *me* to go out looking for a stud, *any* stud, to sire *him* a *grandson!* Can you believe that, Reenie? My *own* daddy telling me to go out and get fucked!"

"Jessie! Why do you always make everything about babies sound so nasty? There's nothing wrong with Mister Sid wanting a grandson.

You just said sometimes you wished you were a mother."

"Why didn't he say a granddaughter? Or just a grandchild? But a *grandson!* He sees Sonny and now wants another Sidney. He *still* hasn't forgiven me for something that wasn't my fault."

"No, Jessie, that's not why Mister Sid wants a grandchild. He would want one even if Sidney Junior was still alive. *All* fathers want grandsons."

"Sure! He doesn't have to have it. Men have the fun part. Poke in, puke up, and pull out. The rest is up to the woman for the rest of her life. Look at you!"

"But I like that. We always got something, somebody. Men don't feel that way about another human being like women do. A life just doesn't mean as much to them as it does to us. We women are sort of like farmers who love growing gardens and the men are always the ones stepping on and killing our plants."

"You are talking this way because you already have yourself a beautiful baby and don't have to go through all the shit again. Why doesn't God just present women with babies in the manner we were told as children He did? Where in the hell are you, stork, now that I need you?"

"Jessie...you...you don't like men?"

"Of course I do, sillyass! I just don't like them *always* having the upper hand. The advantage, the edge, from birth. Why?"

"Like I keep telling you, you just make things sound even worse by always talking about them so much."

"Perhaps I do. I hope that's the case. Maybe it's best to have a baby when you are too young to think. Just close your eyes and open your legs."

That's when Pig swished through the living room from the kitchen, her nightly snack piled high atop the plate in her hand, leaving Jessie with a big, warm, snaggletoothed smile, a wink...and sick in the seat.

~ Chapter 13 ~

Having always wanted his daughter to grow up to become a "lady," Sid was deeply disappointed in Jessie for dropping out of college after only three months. Plus, he was at a total loss as to what work she could possibly help out with on the farm that was worth leaving college for. But Jessie quickly solved her daddy's dilemma. A natural at numbers, she took over the books, a job Mildred had done up until her stroke and one that had suffered as much as had the woman herself since Sid, a detester of paperwork, took over. Jessie lost no time in bringing her daddy's books up to date and keeping them there and as time went on began surprising Sid by making astute suggestions about the operation of the dairy farm itself, including expansion and new equipment, plus outside monetary investments.

Males, young and old, had always desired Jessie. But, especially since the Candy Man, *all* feared her. It was said that one glare from Jessie's cat-quick eyes could freeze a bolt of white-hot lightning in midair. Then, just as quickly, the white-hot flash from her ivory smile could turn right around and melt the North Pole. And Jessie *felt* male-wanted. She was decidedly pleased with all 120 pounds of her five-and-a-half-foot-tall body of flat stomach, round butt, and long, comely legs. All except for her tits. From the time she'd watched her mother nursing Sidney Junior she'd wanted large breasts. She'd thought she was growing big ones until that fatal day down at the pond when she yanked off Reenie's dress and saw her skinny friend's whoppers, more than twice the size of her own. Sick at the sight of, Jessie felt, such misplaced abundance, she thenceforth became determined to grow bigger boobs than her skinny friend Reenie.

Jessie began her "boobies ballooning" period by, like Reenie, not wearing a brassiere—a practice, she believed, preventing the holding back, up, or in of her breasts' daily growth. She also stopped lying or sleeping on her stomach, thus not squashing and hindering their nightly growth. Daily she stood with knees locked while touching her toes with both hands one hundred times without stopping in order to extend the growth of her swinging-free breasts. Twice a day, morning and night, she stood before the mirror pulling the nipple straight out from each breast as far as it could be extended without bringing tears, or unplugging, and holding for ten minutes before releasing. She drank a quart of milk per meal, swallowing slowly, letting the liquid trickle down into each breast to puff them up. Nightly she massaged each breast gently, then slowly rougher, rougherandROUGHER! before, finally, falling asleep. (If during these nightly massagings her thighs wanted to rub one another, then, Jessie reasoned, it was no business of her boobies.) When none of this seemed to work, Jessie prayed.

Males, like moths fluttering crazily around a deadly flame, had always hung near Jessie. But Jessie wasn't the marrying, or even getting engaged, kind as that to her meant ownership. And, Lord, Jessie wasn't about to be owned by anyone.

Though she wouldn't admit it even to herself, Jessie yet had the hots for her first man, her former schoolteacher, Mister Randolph Blackshear. She saw him in town on occasion and could have him again, she knew, but getting to him was too complicated for her, as he was married with children. And, Lord, no sucking hind teat for Jessie.... Jessie had to be the "main mamma." Thus, wanting to be nobody's concubine, Jessie kept her hots for Mister Randolph Blackshear to herself.

Starting that early morning following New Year's Day, 1969, she went to work for her daddy and for the next six years was to devote herself almost entirely to the operation of the farm. During this period, thanks greatly to her shrewd business sense and Sid's gradual trust in her judgments, the dairy expanded from thirty to one hundred milk cows, acquired a second bull—greatly increasing the yearly number of calf sales—and went from one hundred to two hundred acres of grazing and timber land, thus making the Mitchell Dairy Farm, behind the farms of the families Nicholson and Crawford, the third largest farm in Plain View. Jessie, surprising few, particularly herself, was an authentic chip off Sid's block, as feared as her father when it got right down to hard-core business.

"Reenie!" Jessie made a beeline from the left-open door of her new Mustang to the kitchen following her race-track return home from town.

"Yes?" Reenie stood at the sink drinking a glass of water.

"Guess who's back in town?"

"Who?"

"*Guess,* sillyass!"

"I don't know."

"I know you don't know. That's why I'm asking you to guess."

"Christ?"

"Almost. Samuel James." A dropped water glass.

"How do you know?" Reenie went down on her hands and knees, picking up the pieces.

"I saw him."

"I hope you didn't say...."

"No, sillyass, I didn't. I wanted to but didn't. *You* are the one who's going to say something to him, and *soon.*"

"Why?"

"Why? Sonny is *his* child, that's why. *And* he brought back with him a wife. A *pregnant* one! That's *double* why!"

"How do you know she's pregnant?" Reenie stopped her sliver search to look up at Jessie.

"I saw her belly. But guess what the kick in the ass is?"

"What?"

"Samuel James is now a *preacher!*"

"A preacher?"

"That's right, honey. Somewhere up the line there ol' hot nuts Samuel suddenly saw the Light. Probably while poking around under some married woman's dress when a flashlight was beamed up his butt by the husband. But, listen to this, here's the *real* kick in the cunt. Guess *where* he's going to be preaching?"

"In town with his daddy at Bethel?"

"Nooo, honey. Plain View!"

"Plain View?"

"That's right, baby! Samuel James is the new pastor we've been promised by next meeting Sunday. He just finished theologian school up in Atlanta and, no doubt through his daddy, got the Plain View position. Hell, he's just a year older than us. Imagine someone that young, someone we know, went to school with, a one-time playboy, being our pastor? Telling us how to get to heaven? Someone with nerve enough to bring a pregnant wife back home where he already has an illegitimate child whom he, supposedly a man of God, has never seen nor provided a single penny for the support of? Yes, Reenie, you are going to say something, a heap, to that hypocritical sonofabitch! And if you don't I surely will, even if I have to go up and say it to him while he's preaching in the pulpit!"

"Jessie!" Reenie leaped up off the floor to face her friend while grabbing both her hands and squeezing them tight in hers. "You've *got* to promise me one thing and I promise I'll never again ask you for a favor the rest of my life. Never! Promise me, *please,* that you won't say *anything* about Sonny to Samuel. I don't want him, or his wife, having *anything* to do with my baby because Sonny is mine!"

"But, Reenie, Sonny needs a daddy. *Every* baby needs a daddy."

"*My* baby doesn't. I can take care of him by myself. I'm doing it! If you say *anything* to Samuel about my Sonny I'll take him and leave Plain View!" The dam walled up back of her eyes was on the verge of bursting. The inevitable flood wasn't what was scaring Jessie right that moment, as she had swum too many of Reenie's cries to try and count. But never before had she seen such desperation—fear?—on her friend's, or anyone else's, face as Reenie stood pleading while gripping both of Jessie's hands tightly in hers. "Promise, *please?"*

"All right, if you insist, I promise." This broke the dam and Jessie hugged her sobbing friend. "Only for you. But somewhere, somehow, on down the road that Goddamn preacher sonofabitch is going to pay for his sin against my dearest friend. You just wait and see."

The very next meeting Sunday, the young Reverend Samuel James, Junior, son of the Reverend Samuel James, Senior, pastor of Bethel Baptist of Appalachee, Muskhogean County's largest black church, made his debut at Plain View Baptist Church. Reenie, a frequent churchgoer, did not want to go for this particular occasion. Jessie, a churchgoer only on particular occasions, insisted upon Reenie and Sonny going with her and sitting up front to better see, and be seen by, their new pastor. Reenie relented but only under the condition that Jessie promise again that from her absolutely nothing would be mentioned, or hinted at, to Samuel, or his wife, or anyone else in attendance, about a possible connection between the new pastor and Sonny. And that Sonny wouldn't go. Jessie, that lover of action, hated such restrictions but finally agreed. She also tried talking Sid into attending.

"But, Daddy, the church is christening a new minister today."

"I know."

"Do you know *who,* though?"

"Reverend James son."

"Sonny's daddy."

"Is that why you are going to church today? To cause trouble?"

"No, I promised Reenie I wouldn't...today. But isn't there some-thing you, a man, could do or say to him, now a man of God, about supporting his illegitimate child? He can well afford to."

"What does Reenie say about it?"

"You can't listen to Reenie."

"*I* can. And *you* listen too. Sugar Dumpling, I'll tell you again, stay outta places where you ain't got no business. Reenie been doing all right working here while taking care of Sonny, who's a real fine boy. He follows me around the place like...like...like you useta."

"Yes, I notice—but he's spending this morning with his grand-mother because Reenie and I are going to church together today, and I want you to go too. You haven't been since Mother took sick. Don't you want to go and put in a prayer for her?"

"I can do that here, anywhere. It's just not the same anymore, going to church without her. Besides, Will's waiting on me now so we can do some things out at the barn that got to get done today." He got up and left the house by the front door, just ahead of:

"Whenever I want you to go someplace with me you *always* get out of going by saying there's *something* to be done around here. Please tell me just what is it here that's got to be done so badly that it cannot wait on God?" While saying this last part, Jessie's eyes latched onto Pig's gyrating butt sashaying through the living room on the way to the kitchen...its owner, returning crumb-free breakfast dishes, leaving for the daughter of the house a trailing snaggletoothed smile and a wink. Jessie departed for church that Sunday morning seat sick.

~ **Chapter 15** ~

Once the cotton-picking machine rid Muskhogean of the vast majority of its farming blacks and sent them off to America's concrete communities during the 1950s, the local country churches suffered severely due to the lack of attendance and new membership. But Plain View survived. A new building with electricity, indoor plumbing, central heat in winter, and air conditioning in summer made it much easier to believe in God. Yet since most members now lived in Appalachee proper, many hardly bothered to attend services except on special occasions. This Sunday being one of those special occasions, the church was packed. Not so much to get the Message as to find out if the new, young pastor could get it across to them well enough to keep them coming back again and again to hear more of the Word. But to Jessie, sitting right down front with Reenie, the Message, and how it was presented, carried no significance whatsoever on this day. All through the sermon she sat not heeding a word said, or how, by Samuel—just kept her eyes directly on the young Reverend's, wanting, *daring* him to look back into hers. But not once could Jessie catch his eye. Not even following the sermon when outside the front door the new pastor, with wife alongside, stood shaking the hand of each member of the congregation as they filed singly out of the church.

"Hello, Samuel."

"How are you today, Sister Jessie? Your folks?" His eyes didn't move a hair above her lips.

"Fine, thanks. I'm sure you remember Reenie here. Don't you?" Jessie said, all the while watching his eyes while putting an extra little squeeze on the Reverend's hand before passing it back to Reenie.

"Sister Irene, how are you? And the boy?"

"We are fine, thanks." Jessie still stood double, *dirty,* daring him to meet her eyes with his. But before another word could be spoken between the three of them an older sister of the congregation suddenly reached in and snatched away the Reverend's hand and began pumping it up and down while exclaiming,

"Congratulations, Reverend James! A job well done...." Reenie pushed a pissed Jessie toward the car.

"Did you dig all of that holy shit right there at the end?" Jessie asked

Reenie while driving them home.

"What do you mean?"

"That Goddamn hypocrite propping his pregnant wife up beside him like some prize heifer while shaking the hands of all y'all other folks he's fucked."

"Jessie, you would find a dark cloud in heaven. His wife looked like a real nice lady to me. Also, I thought Samuel, er...Reverend James, preached very well."

"You would. But no matter what you might think something oughta be done about him and his kind. And, believe me, someday something will."

The next meeting Sunday Reenie refused to attend church with Jessie, or let Sonny go, because she couldn't help but believe her best friend was attending not for religious reasons at all...but to hang the preacher. Jessie went alone and sat down front, during the entire sermon staring dead on up at the pulpit with eyes persistently trying to catch and lock into those of the black-robed young sermonizing pastor. Again, no eyeball contact from the pulpit. Later, she stood at the very end of the line exiting the church to shake the hand of the Reverend standing at the front door, his wife alongside.

"How are you today, Sister Jessie?" For a long moment Jessie just squeezed the outstretched hand while staring directly at its owner's face until his eyes, finally, met hers, briefly, before hurriedly dropping back to watch her lips moving.

"I'm doing fine, thank you, Reverend. How are you Mrs. James?" Jessie shifted her cat eyes to the pretty, petite, and pregnant lady, the top of whose head didn't quite measure up to her husband's shoulder and whose smiling face looked like it hadn't long left its teens.

"I'm doing right fine, thank you, Sister Jessie."

"That's good. What is the doctor predicting for the expectant, happy couple here, a son or a daughter?"

"A daughter."

"Good! Ladies first! Perhaps next time it will be a son for you, Reverend James." Her eyes swung back to Samuel's, his diving quickly back down to her smiling (smirking?) lips. "Would you like a son, Reverend James?"

"Whatever God gives us will be satisfactory with me, Sister Jessie," he said, eyes still on her lips.

"Men usually want boys and women girls. But my best friend, Reenie, you know her, Reverend, ended up with a boy. But, my, he's such a beautiful boy! Going on seven years old and just like a baby brother to me. Sticks to my father like daddy was his own daddy. Imagine." Another little squeeze on the hand still in hers. But before another word could be spoken between the three, the Reverend suddenly found himself surrounded by several older sisters of the congregation in need of his immediate attention. Jessie's thought regarding the abrupt intrusion was, silently, "Bitches!" Reluctantly releasing his hand, she stepped aside to turn her full attention upon the pastor's wife. "This must be a long day for you?"

"Yes. But not so much for me as for the Reverend. He's been here each meeting Sunday working back there in his office long before the beginning of service. I'm here ahead of the congregation too, yet always a good hour behind the Reverend."

"Is that so?"

The white Mustang pulled right alongside the black Chevrolet Caprice, the only other car parked in the yard of Plain View Baptist Church early that next Sunday meeting morning.

"How come so early, dear? Are you feeling all right?" spoke the Reverend James before looking up from behind his desk. Then, raising his eyes to see who was standing in the door of his office: "Oh, Lord...I...please excuse me. I thought you were my wife coming in. She always...."

"Not yet. Don't get up." Walking on into the small office, Jessie sat down on the corner of the large desk taking up nearly half of the room. Lighting up a cigarette, she crossed her long, bare legs, a move forcing her short, tight, white leather skirt to slide up her brown thighs to within a hair of where grew hair. Inhaling, she faced the Reverend, tall, ebony, athletically built, but on the verge of developing a preacher's pot in his immaculate dark suit.

"What...what can I do for you so early on this Sunday morning, Sister Jessie?" He was fighting to keep control of his voice...and hold his gaze south of her eyes and north of her thighs.

"Shouldn't it be 'what can I do for you, Samuel?' That's how it used to work with all the girls, didn't it?"

"That's all in the past, Sister Jessie. I've suffered a lot for my transgressions during my youth but have since found the right way through prayer and God. I would very much like to help you too if that's why you are here so early this Sabbath morning." His eyes daring not to drop, nor rise, hung on to her lips by their lashes.

"You forgot your wife. Getting her pregnant must've help shoot you on down the road of righteousness," Jessie said, blowing smoke at him.

"Yes, Sister Jessie," the Reverend replied, not raising a hand to fan the smoke out of his face, "she has been a great help to me and my work. Truly God-sent. I am hoping she and the people of the community get to know and love one another. Perhaps, Sister Jessie, you could be of some help in her case. She's a truly wonderful woman." He gave a nervous smile, with eyes still praying desperately to their God to not let

them fall rolling and tumbling to crash down body and die in sin on her thigh.

"Yes, it's a marvelous idea. I think she should get to know, first-hand, *all* of your old conquests...*and* their children." Another puff of smoke in the face.

"Sister Jessie, like I just told you, that's all in the past and, as *you* should so well know, *all* of us have sinned at one time or another...."

"Samuel, please, don't keep handing me all of this Holy Ghost shit...."

"Sister Jessie, even if you don't respect me, please show some for the house of God."

"...I don't believe a leopard ever loses its spots. Just camouflages them to confuse its prey. But no matter how heavily the makeup is applied, those spots are *still* under there. You can't fool another leopard. Right, Samuel?" A puff of smoke in the face was followed by that Jessie, tundra-thawing smile.

"Sister Jessie," his voice taking on a whine, "why are you coming to me this morning with all of this talk about my past sins? Don't you think I know about them and have suffered enough? You never had to suffer from anything I did to you because I remember specifically you would not have anything to do with me at all. You never so much as once spoke a courteous word to me all those years. So why all of this now?"

"I was afraid you would seduce me." Swiveling atop the desk, she now faced him, her bare thighs at his finger tips. "But now I'm not afraid." She stuffed her cigarette out in the desk's ashtray.

"What...what...what do you mean, Sister Jessie?" Lord, that's when the Reverend's eyes came tumbling from on high down upon those sinful smooth brown thighs.

"You know damn well what I mean. You've still got your leopard spot beneath that preacher suit. Let's see it!" She reached down and grabbed onto his crotch.

"Sister Jessie! Wait...wait! My wife will be coming...." Grabbing her hand clutched firmly to his, standing, crotch, the Reverend was caught between pulling her fingers away...or pressing them down harder.

"Are you still a man or has that little woman pussy whipped you?" She squeezed harder. He didn't pull her hand away. "Let's see if you are man enough for *me*. Now!" She slid off the desk to swiftly unzip his fly, letting pop out its erect occupant, which she grasped tightly in one hand while with the back of her other forearm in one sweeping motion she sent everything atop the desk flying to the floor.

"Oh, oh, Sister Jessie, what are you doing?" Pulling the Reverend up out of his chair by his long, rigid lifeline, Jessie with her free hand and little resistance from her victim pushed him down atop the desk where he lay flat on his back while moaning, "Oh, Sister Jessie, oh, oh, oh, Sister Jessie, oh, oh, oh, oh, oh, oh, S-I-SSS-T-E-RRRRRR JESSIEJESSIEJESSIE

OOOOOOOOOOOYYYEEEEEEOOOOOOOAAAAAAHHHHHH!!!!!!!!!!!!!!!
Simultaneously with Mrs. James walking through the office door, Jessie, with all of her jawbone strength, had clamped down with her pearly thirty-twos.

Later, church officials announced to the stunned congregation that earlier that meeting Sunday morning while busily at work in his office preparing his upcoming sermon the overextended young Reverend James had suffered a sudden "attack" and been rushed by his wife to the hospital where, according to his family doctor, he wouldn't be available for services of any sort for several meeting Sundays to come. If ever again. Amen.

~ Chapter 16 ~

It was early on the very same Sunday morning of Reverend Samuel James's sudden attack that while speeding in her car, Jessie, in taking a curve leading right onto the Oconee River Bridge on two wheels and just barely missing hitting with her Mustang a young woman and child walking across the bridge, first saw the eyes. It all happened so quickly but when Jessie swung around the curve there they were...those deep, dark, wild eyes of the young, ragged woman looking from the side of the bridge right into the car straight into Jessie's as if they knew her...had been waiting out there for ages...would be out there on the bridge waiting for her...forever. Lord, Jessie was too Goddamn shook up by this sight to even curse.

~ Chapter 17 ~

Like all real farmers, Jessie worked seven days a week and was available for business twenty-four hours a day. She took no vacations—except for those every-three-or-four-months-spur-of-the-moment drives up to Atlanta to shop, dine, and enjoy a cocktail or glass of wine; or on up to the mountains, which she loved; or over to Savannah to see the ocean, another love, eat on River Street or at the Pirate's House, and later stroll leisurely about the city before moving on up to Hilton Head, Charleston, and from there back home. These treks were never more than overnighters as Jessie was always fearful something of great importance might happen at home while she roamed (her exact feelings during her brief stay in college).

As Sonny grew older, Jessie began thinking seriously of taking him with her, especially when she attended ball games—even to the beach, or selected public swimming pools, where she would teach him how to swim while he was still young—as, she was firmly convinced, her Daddy should've taught Sidney Junior.

But thus far she traveled light—alone—on these trips. Like on the sunny late spring afternoon when she felt a "spur" coming on and without a word to anyone, her wont, was gone.

But this particular spur wasn't destined for distance.

Noticing she had too little cash for comfort, Jessie, with checkbook ever present in her purse, made an immediate turn for her bank in Appalachee. Entering the bank's door she almost ran face first into, "Amos?" She couldn't believe her eyes.

"Hey, Jessie! Yes, it's 'little Amos'."

"My, oh my, I hardly recognized you!" He had been one grade below her in school, when to her only older males had mattered, yet she'd always thought of him as being the most handsome and nicest boy in school.

"It's still me." That same shyness hid behind that panty-damping blush.

"Are you out of college?"

"Graduated last week."

"You are back home to stay?"

"Yes."

"Great! What are you doing for the next hour?"

"Nothing...."

"Good! Let me quickly go in here and cash a check and then we'll go buy you a graduation drink on me." Zip!

A half-hour later the two were sitting over drinks at a table in a dimly lit corner of the local Holiday Inn's practically deserted cocktail lounge. "It certainly is great to see you again, Amos. The last time I saw you you were...."

"Sixteen."

"...And now here you are a *grown* man. Still as good-looking as ever though. Maybe even better-looking now. No need to blush. Here's to the future." Their glasses were raised, touched, drunk from, and returned momentarily to their launching coasters to await the next elbow jerks.

"You are as beautiful as ever yourself." In here it was impossible for her to see totally his warm brown blush but she was feeling it strongly where she sat.

"No counterattacking, please. Now that you are back with us what are your future plans?"

"The business."

"The family's?"

"Yes."

"It's a good business."

"I'm continually being reminded."

"You don't sound too enthused."

"Daddy is getting older so someone has to eventually take over for him."

"Why not one of your sisters?"

"Daddy doesn't believe in a woman running the business."

"Not even Estelle?"

"Not even Estelle."

"We better not start talking about your daddy here." Jessie took a long swallow of her drink. "Like I said earlier, Amos, it's simply great seeing you again. And now that you are back to stay we should make a point of seeing more of each other. What are you doing this coming Sunday?"

"Nothing that I...."

"Good! Then I'll be expecting you out at my house for dinner." The meeting was perioded by Jessie's tundra-thawing smile and a hot hand on his, thus ending her brief spur and sending her speeding like never before back home to begin preparing for that upcoming Sunday. Preparing for the arrival of Amos...nephew of Mister Randolph Blackshear.

~ Chapter 18 ~

Everybody said Amos Blackshear I was born destined to be his own man. This was no snap for a slave. But before the stench of ol' W. Tecumseh Sherman's smoke had cleared Georgia's air, young Amos was on his way to becoming his own man. In those days there were three things a southern black man could do independently of the southern white man. He could die or become a preacher (following the end of slavery white folks no longer felt responsible for getting black folks into heaven) but Amos wasn't interested in the intangible soul. He was into matter, bodies. Thus, Amos opted for the third choice and opened up on the back street of Appalachee the town's first black-owned business. An undertaker. (White folks were totally disinterested in, legally, planting black folks.)

Right following the war against the Yankees, Amos fed both black and white carcasses to color-blind earthworms. But busily burying everybody soon buried him—though not before he sired in 1872 a baby burier, Amos II, the undertaker who embalmed and dug the family Blackshear on the road to becoming, many claimed, the region's richest, and "uppiest," blacks.

It was always said that Amos I dug the first grave, Amos II built the family's name and mansion, and Amos III, an only child born in 1896, filled the house with Blackshears. Yet not wanting to create nor be the cause of too much local "upper niggerism," Amos III sent most of his children away to school, with several of them never returning home to live. One who did return was the oldest son, Amos IV, who eventually took over the, now, funeral home for old Amos II, who outlived Amos III, whom everyone accused of being more interested in producing bodies (fifteen babies he sired) than planting them.

Amos IV, Lord, had his problems too. His first four children were girls. Was he man enough to sire a boy? For eight years the family, town, and county waited. Finally, he proved himself a real man when out popped child number five, Amos V.

Growing up the only son in a house of six daughters, a mother, and a father, Amos V was babied. But he didn't grow up spoiled, just a shy loner. And, according to most of the girls, the best-looking boy in the whole town. Yet a year younger than she, in high school Amos V had been too young for Jessie. Unlike his uncle.

Chapter 19

Meanwhile, back at the farm.

"Jessie," cried an astonished Reenie, "I've never in my life seen you acting this way before! All the while we were in school with him I don't remember you ever mentioning Little Amos's name! The only Black-shear I ever heard you talk about was our teacher, Mister Randolph...."

"Amos was too young then."

"He's still a year younger than us."

"That doesn't matter now."

"Jessie, I can't believe it but you've fallen for Little Amos!"

"Reenie, honey, you should see him now. No longer little, Amos is now a *man!* The best-looking man I've *ever* seen! I invited him out here for dinner this coming Sunday."

"You what?!"

"Don't worry, I'll help you cook."

"I don't mean *that.* I mean, is *she* coming with him?"

"She, who?"

"Rachel Allen, his fiancée."

"Young Doctor Allen's daughter? Are they *engaged?*"

"I thought you knew."

"You know I don't keep up with what's going on among those younger than I. But now I guess I'll have to start."

"You think he'll bring Rachel?"

"He never even mentioned her name to me. I certainly didn't invite her. But if he does bring her it won't matter one bit."

"Why not?"

"Because, Reenie baby, dig my jive, he's now Jessie's meat, Amos Number Five."

Amos Number Five came alone.

Reenie, of course, took total control of dinner, including the dishes afterwards, giving a surprisingly excited Jessie more time for her guest. Sid and Reenie were duly impressed by the handsome and charmingly shy Amos, and Jessie took her eyes off him only long enough for them to catch a quick blink. Even Pig, while passing through, shot a couple of winks at the polite and neatly dressed young man. The day was beautiful everywhichaway, from the weather to the walk taken by Jessie and Amos around the farm following dinner.

"Why don't you take your coat and tie off. You look like an undertaker." Both burst out laughing at this remark of Jessie's before he, without breaking stride, followed her orders, putting his navy blue silk tie in the side pocket of his powder blue suit jacket, which he slung softly over his shoulder. "Speaking of undertakers, the other day you didn't sound too keen on entering your family's business."

"I'm not."

"May I ask why not?"

"It's not a profession that interests me."

"What interests you?"

"You promise you won't laugh if I tell you?"

"Promise."

"Being a veterinarian."

"A *veterinarian?*"

"You promised you wouldn't laugh."

"I'm not laughing, honestly. Just surprised, that's all."

"Why?"

"Because your family's business is one of the oldest, most established and respected in the county and it's all yours, just waiting to be stepped right into."

"But I don't want to work with the dead. I want to work keeping things *alive!*" She had never heard him raise his voice before.

"Then why not become a medical doctor?"

"I'm more interested in veterinary medicine."

"Is there any money in it?"

"I don't know and I don't care!" His voice was rising again.

"Well, what are you going to do about the situation?"

"Oh, I'm going to be the dutiful son and go into the business to help my father but if things don't work out I'll leave for vet school."

"Your family know this?"

"Not yet."

"What about Rachel?"

"No."

"Am I the *first* person you've told this to?"

"Yes."

"Is that why you came out here today?"

"No. I came out because I wanted to see you. I've always wanted to come out here to see you. In high school I had a secret crush on you. But before running into you at the bank the other day I never suspected you even knew I existed. I'm sorry to be going on this way, but I just couldn't help myself when you started asking about my future intentions."

"Amos." She stopped to look sweetly up into his shy face. "I want

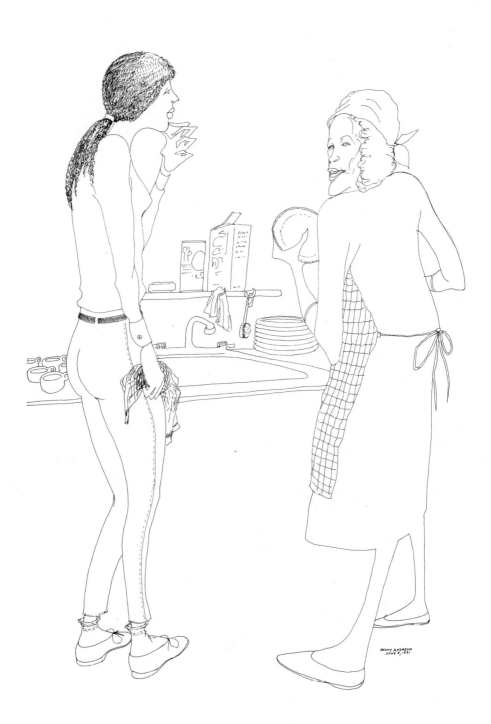

you to always feel free to talk to me about *anything, anytime.*" Then she grabbed his hand.

Even know-it-all Jessie didn't know what had come out of even-God-knew-not-where to hit her. She had never felt this way before about anybody. She couldn't keep Amos's beautiful, shy face out of her mind— nor keep him out of her sight. Nor, Lord, did she want to. Now the two of them were either together, had just been together, or were about to get together. Yes, quicker than ol' Jahweh could spot a sin, Jessie and Amos had suddenly become the hottest 'tater in Muskhogean County.

So hot a 'tater, Lord, that one sunny afternoon while sitting alone with her German shepherd, Bo, out on her family house's front porch, she looked up to see speeding down the road and on into the yard a sleek, shiny black Porsche. The door of the sports car swung open to emit a tall, slender, and shapely woman in her late twenties wearing a platinum, skin-squeezing jumpsuit and black open-toed spiked heels. Of a medium brown complexion with hair hanging off her head in long, skinny cornrow plaits, the woman slammed shut the door and behind a pair of excessive sunglasses moved across the yard with such surety of strut that Bo, out of doubt or fear, or both, stood his ground safely behind Jessie and without so much as a whimper watched this woman make her way free of his bark up to the porch.

"Hello, Jessie," said a clear-to-the-core voice, as sure of itself as had been the straight-up-to-the-porch strut, and a voice that didn't stoop to ask, instead ordered.

"Hey, Estelle."

Estelle Blackshear Crawford and her husband, Robert Lee, were the envy of blacks throughout the area for their marriage, manners, mettle, and money. Also their beauty. Neither of the mod couple ever seemed to have a hair, nor string, out of place, nor an extra ounce of fat anywhere on their forever-immaculately-dressed, tall, athletically trim, exercise-oriented bodies. "The Beautiful Black Bodies," they were known as by their many admirers.

Estelle, the favorite of her great-granddaddy, Amos Blackshear II, was at a very young age sent by him personally up North to a private all-girl school where she was the only black enrolled, and from there went to college at Radcliffe. Between school terms she spent, at her great-granddaddy's expense, most of her time globe-galloping. Graduating from college she returned to Appalachee, where it was still being talked about with envy and, among many within her Blackshear family, hatred, how generous ol' Amos II had been in his will to his favorite family member, Estelle.

Now it was being hotly discussed throughout the county, and state, how Estelle was slowly, surely, and, most of all, professionally grooming her husband Robert (owner of the restaurant chain BOB, Barbeque-On-Biscuit) for a political career. Not as a Democrat, but a Republican—whose goal was not someday becoming the mayor of Atlanta (being the figurehead of a ghetto city wasn't in the plans) but was becoming the first black governor of Georgia. And from there on to the Senate in Washington, D.C., to play international, or "real" politics. Estelle's motto was, "Always aim for the stars and your feet will clear the treetops but if your aim is only on the treetops then your ass will never get off the ground."

"Come on up and have a seat." A smiling, awed Jessie was hardly able to control her excitement at suddenly finding herself host to Muskhogean's most renowned.

"No, thank you. Please, don't get up. What I came to say will only take a minute." Estelle stopped on the top step, from where she stood looking down at the seated Jessie.

"What can I do for you, Estelle?" Jessie was puzzled.

"Stop seeing my brother, Amos."

"Why?" Now she was taken aback.

"Amos is engaged to marry his childhood sweetheart, Rachel Allen, later this year and *both* families are eagerly anticipating this wedding. And none of us in the families wants anything, nor *anybody,* interfering with these long-in-the-makings plans. Please, don't interrupt. There's nothing you need say as I came out here to tell, not ask. As I was saying, besides soon entering into matrimony with a lovely, *chaste* young lady, Amos will someday take over the family business from my father. The family is extremely interested in protecting Amos and in the process keeping its own reputation untarnished. In other words, the *last* thing we want is notoriety."

"Notoriety...?!"

"That's what I said. Appalachee is a small town and people here have not forgotten, nor forgiven, the Candy Man killing...."

"The Candy Man...?!"

"I *said* not to interrupt. Yes, the Candy Man. It's yet believed by most that it was *you* who led him on to...to his death. Also, there are those who insist *you* were the cause of the young Reverend James suddenly leaving his church and, eventually, the county. Oh, there's something else. I'm sure you know what it is I mean, but I won't bother bringing that up as that's your family business."

"What do you mean?" Jessie was no longer able to hold back.

"*Meaning* that since your brother's drowning your *parents* don't even care for you. Amos doesn't need to get himself, nor the family Blackshear, entangled in such a web. To put it simply, Jessie, stay away from my baby brother...we Blackshears don't want *your* kind!" Swiftly turning and strutting back down the steps and on across the yard into the shiny black Porsche to go speeding back up the road towards town went

Estelle, Appalachee's "Black Bitch Belle."

Stunned! Speechless! Jessie sat cemented to her seat. Of all the people she'd ever known besides her daddy, none had she respected, revered, more than she did Estelle, whom she had always looked up to as being the female's female. And now, shockingly, on this day to so suddenly and so rudely find out straight from the mouth of her idol herself that Estelle thought the absolute *lowest* of her.... *"Your* kind"! *Me!* Oh, my God! a still-in-shock Jessie sat thinking. I would do *nothing* to hurt Amos. I'm sure he loves *me* and not Rachel. Mother and *Father* don't love me? *Daddy?* Leaping up she ran up to her mother's room where, after shooing Pig out, she kneeled down beside Mildred's bed and cried. Reaching up she took her mother's hand and squeezed it in hers, silently praying for it to squeeze back. But Mildred's bony hand remained limp. Looking up at her mother, Jessie pleaded in a sobbing voice, "Mother, do you love me?" Mildred kept staring at the ceiling. Dropping her mother's hand, Jessie ran from the house in search of her daddy, whom she *knew* loved her. She found him working out at the barn...with young Sonny at his side. "Daddy, Daddy! Do *you* love me?" she screamed, running up behind her father.

"Wha'sa matter, Jessie?" A startled Sid and Sonny turned simultaneously. "Why're you crying?"

"Do you still love me like you did when I was a little girl following you around all the time like Sidney...er, Sonny here?"

"Why sho' I do. Why you ask such a silly question?"

"Because you never tell me anymore. Some folks think you don't love me anymore!"

"Don't listen to folks. I'm still yo' daddy. It's jes that you're a grown woman now and...."

"And I'm a *girl!* And Sidney was a *boy!* You *still* blame me for his drowning! Mother can't say it but I *know* she still does too!" With this Jessie turned and shot out of the barn back to the house and on up to her room where she plopped out on her bed crying. She cried until the tears began gradually being replaced by anger. Estelle's final words—"we Blackshears don't want your kind!"—kept spinning around and around in her head. *My* kind? She started to think. What *is* my kind? I know things about the Blackshear men Estelle will *never* know. That's when she picked up the telephone.

"Amos?"

"Yes, Jessie?"

"Meet me in the Holiday Inn cocktail lounge in an hour." Then she hung up...before saying aloud, "*My* kind is going to make *her* kind give me somebody that I *know* will love *me.*"

When Jessie arrived at the Holiday Inn cocktail lounge, Amos Number Five was waiting at a table that, upon seating herself, she reached under to squeeze his hand....

Before the cocktail lounge closed that night the young couple left for South Carolina, where that next day they got married. Lord, have mercy!

~ Chapter 20 ~

"The trouble with you, Amos, is that you don't have that killer instinct so necessary in every successful seduction. The ability to finish off his female partner quickly once he sees he's got her on the verge is something *every* woman, whether she's liberated or locked and chained to the kitchen sink, wants in her man. What you have instead is a bad case of conscience, and even Women's Lib ain't yet ready sexually for a stud who in the heat of the hots suffers from a Goddamn conscience!"

"But...but your chastity belt is locked."

"A Tony Quinn or Kirk Douglas type would've ransacked my purse for the key to the royal mint—then, after not finding it there, with one of his big strong hands sprouting those long powerful steel fingers would've grabbed me in back of the head by the hair and with gritted teeth glistening twisted my smooth beige neck until I told him in a soft pleading voice that the key to the cookie jar was kept in the right front pocket of Daddy's trousers. After slinging me across the room, Tony would've wrecked the apartment in his frustration at not being able to get to the crown jewels, while Kirk would've sat right down and boo-hooed like a baby. Now what are *you* going to do? Let your conscience be your Goddamn guide?"

"No! I'm going to go and steal your daddy's trousers!"

"DADDY!!!!!!"

"Jessie! Jessie! Wake up! Everything's all right! You are just having a nightmare. You are here in the hotel with me, Amos, your husband."

"Oooh, Amos, sweetiepie, I just had the weirdest dream!"

"You shouldn't watch TV on your wedding night."

"I would not've if you hadn't fallen asleep so fast. Are you awake now?" Jessie reached out for her favorite part of her new husband only to have a snore greet her groping fingers, which paused disappointedly before walking on across his sleeping body to the night table to fondle the *TV Guide*.

~ Chapter 21 ~

Appalachee, Lord, went into shock. Jessie brought her brand new husband back home to live on the Mitchells' Dairy Farm, moving him into her room where her single bed was immediately replaced by a king-sizer. Amos IV, whom it was said adored young Rachel enough to marry her himself if he hadn't already been married, disowned his only son. Thus Amos V, "Mister Jessie," as many now called him, went to work at the dairy, concerning himself mainly with the health care of the farm's livestock, a job he quickly came to love. Sid and Will, despite thinking him "city soft," gradually took to Amos. Reenie just loved him and was so happy for her best friend Jessie—although she did feel a pinch guilty about all of her good feelings whenever she thought of poor Rachel, whom she always tried her darnedest not to ever think about but couldn't help but always think about. Sonny loved Amos too but most of the youngster's time now was spent following Sid around the farm. Pig's winking at both Jessie and Amos became even more frequent. And Jessie just dared the return of Appalachee's Black Bitch Belle, Estelle.

"Reenie, guess what!" An excited, just-from-town Jessie burst into the kitchen three months later.

"I won't try because I never guess right," said Reenie, up to her armpits in soapsuds.

"The *greatest* thing that could ever happen to me!"

"You just bought the county."

"Seriously!"

"I don't know."

"Oh, you give up too easily. What's the greatest thing that can happen to a *woman?*"

"JESSIE!!!!!!!"

"YES!!!!!!!" Hugs and soapsuds mixed with tears—Reenie's and Jessie's.

"Oh, Lord, Jessie! Are you sure?"

"I just left the doctor. I hate false alarms so I didn't want to say anything until I was one hundred percent sure."

"Oh, Lord, Jessie! I am sooo happy for you!" Reenie hugged tighter and cried harder. "Does Amos know?"

"Not yet. I wanted Daddy and you to know first."

"Then go right out and tell him *now!* He'll be so happy! Oh, I'm so glad for y'all it happened right away!"

"It had to've been on the first night. I just hope she doesn't come out clutching *TV Guide.*"

"What do you mean?"

"Oh, nothing."

"You want it to be a girl?"

"Of course! Didn't you?"

"Er...no...."

"You *wanted* a boy?"

"What's...what's wrong with wanting a boy?"

"Boys can't be trusted to love you. A girl always will."

"Sonny loves me."

"Then why doesn't he follow you around? I only see him following behind *my* daddy all the time. A little girl will do that for you. I did. Now I want someone to follow behind, and *love,* me."

"I didn't know you followed Miz Mildred around like that."

"Reenie, sometimes you don't understand shit!" Jessie stalked out of the kitchen.

Jessie's period of pregnancy was the happiest time of her life—topped off by the birth of the baby. A girl. Lisa. Named by the mother. Now Jessie spent practically every minute of her day with Baby Lisa, whom she insisted was going to grow up being to her mother both a daughter and a buddy—but most of all, someone to *love* her.

The coming of Lisa all but shut Amos out of Jessie's life—though truthfully, Amos had started to leave Jessie's life the instant she discovered she was pregnant. At that moment she realized that, finally, she *had,* in her belly, somebody who belonged to *her*. Someone who was going to love her. She still felt Amos loved her, as he was still as sweet as ever to her and the baby—in fact, for Jessie's taste, too Goddamn sweet! He *never* got angry, never even raised his voice, argued, nor pressed too hard a point of view of his. Rather than argue he would either agree, change the subject, turn silent, or just walk away, not angry, just not wanting to argue his point nor even listen to someone else arguing theirs. His passive stance infuriated Jessie, the battler. All it seemed to his wife that Amos ever wanted to do was to take care of the farm, or any other, animals. Yet he did love Lisa, even though Jessie didn't want him to spend too much time around the child for fear that Lisa might pick up too much of her father's passiveness. True, Jessie wanted her daughter to grow up a lady, but a lady who knew how to handle herself and not get pushed around by *anybody*. Grow up to be a lady like...her aunt. Aunt Estelle.

While Jessie didn't want Lisa to grow up possessing her father's nonaggressiveness, she had wanted her daughter to inherit Amos's physical features. Indeed, looking back, Jessie realized that perhaps her main reason for wanting to marry Amos was for his natural beauty. Although at the time she had secretly thought, and hoped, that he could fuck as well as his Uncle Randolph, that wasn't all there was to it. Amos was so good-looking that something deep within her subconscious soul had screamed the message for her to marry this beautiful man in order for him to plant a seed of beauty into her womb. Thus the seed was planted and from it sprouted her beautiful baby, Lisa. And now, Lord, Jessie no longer needed Amos.

In fact, as far as Jessie was concerned, besides the miracle of the pregnancy itself, nothing ever really happened between her and Amos. Particularly in bed. For Jessie's taste, wants, and needs, Amos was just too nice—too sweet and too tender for her. She always ended up being the aggressor, the stalker, the killer, while he lay purring. Starting out making love tenderly and softly was all right, but GODDAMMIT she didn't want the act to *end* that way! She wanted her aggression met head on, wanted to be held tight, wanted to be *crushed,* fucked to exhaustion! Like...like Mister Blackshear had fucked her! She didn't like being purred over throughout each fucking and ending up smelling like the perfume she entered the arena wearing. She wanted to ring down the curtain wearing the pungent musk of sweat and sex! Dammit, she didn't want to *always* have to take the lead. She, too, sometimes, wanted to be subdued! To feel *fucked!*

She remembered the only time she orgasmed with Amos. It happened during their first sex following Lisa's birth when Amos lay atop her employing his customary short, weak, unrhythmic, and unimaginative strokes and she lay in such desperate want of a real manhandling fuck that her mind went fantasizing back to that long-ago high-school day when Mister Randolph Blackshear had nearly squashed her in between his broad shoulders while his lips pried open her mouth and proceeded to nearly suck her tongue out by its root! God! Never before in her life had she felt the feeling he made her feel with that kiss! Then he had spun her around and before she knew what was happening she was leaning face down with elbows propped atop his paper-filled desk feeling the hem of her skirt sliding up her protruding buttocks, then her panties being ripped off, automatically causing her to spread her legs in anticipation of, God, the Bulge! Quickly recovering from the initial abrupt, sharp pain, she was soon moaning, groaning, moving, and gyrating, battling the Bulge faster and faster and faster and faster until she began to feel something happening to her she never in her farthest-out fantasies imagined could possibly be felt by body and soul, causing her to start hollering and he to reach around to cover her mouth with his hand, which she bit hard into while trying to still holler and shove her body back and forth faster and faster and fasterfasterfasterfaster and biting and hollering and shoving until—God!—starting to COMEANDCOMEAND COMEAND....

She lay exhausted while Amos, having miraculously held on during her fantasy, was still atop, sweetly pushing and pulling until quietly coming.

Minutes later, while lying beside her, Amos asked, "Who is Randolph?"

"Who?" Jessie was rudely snatched back over to this side of the rainbow.

"Randolph. You hollered out the name just now when we were having sex."

"Did I?" Oh, my God, Jessie thought, I *did?!*

"Yes."

"Who knows? In the battle of heat anything's liable to come out of the washer."

"Do I know him?"

"Know who?"

"Randolph."

"Are you picking?" This was so unlike her sweet Amos.

"I'm curious."

"Just forget you heard anything."

"I can't."

"It's best if you do."

"Why?"

"Because if you keep this shit up I might just tell you."

"Tell me."

"Look, sweetiepie, let's just say I didn't know what I was saying and leave it at that. Okay, honey?" She reached over to grasp a piece of him in her readiness to forget and fuck.

"Let's not." He pushed her hand away. "Tell me who Randolph is." She had never before seen him acting this way.

"No."

"Why not?"

"Because you can't take it."

"Try me."

"Not with this one. Honey, that happened a long time ago and has absolutely *nothing* to do with us now. Come on, let's do it again!" And this time, she promised herself, I'll holler out "AMOS!"—come or no come.

"If it was so long ago then why is his name yet so fresh in your mind?"

"I didn't even know I hollered out any name."

"You did. Now I want to know who he is, or was?"

"Okay, then! But don't you *ever* say I didn't warn you!" Jessie was getting a bit annoyed.

"I won't."

"How many Randolphs do you know?"

"None."

"So why can't we just leave it that way?"

"Now I've *got* to know."

"When you gotta know, baby, you gotta know. Think hard about how many Randolphs you *really* know."

"None, I told you."

"Shut up and think so we can get this over with!"

"Humm.... I can't think of any, except...except for Uncle Randolph." The long silence suddenly dropping over her side of the bed finally reached out and slapped him. "UNCLE RANDOLPH?!!!" He sat straight up in bed and turned to her. "*You* and *Uncle Randolph?! My* wife and my *favorite* uncle?! Is *that* why he's the only member of my family who's ever been out here to see me?! Coming to see *you, my wife,* on the sly?"

"NO! I've had *nothing* to do with him nor anyone else since you and I met at the bank that day! *All* of that is in the past! It's got nothing to do with us *now!*"

"Are you *sure?*"

"I *said* so, didn't I?" Now she was angry.

"Then tell me why you hollered out my uncle's name here tonight in bed while having sex with me, your husband?"

"BECAUSE IT WAS THE FIRST AND LAST GODDAMN TIME I'VE HAD A GOOD FUCKING!!!!!!"

Oh dear God, she hadn't wanted to do that to her sweet little Amos but he laid there asking for it! Even then she lay wanting him to grab, *man*handle her while hollering out that he would prove to her right there on their bed that very instant that he could fuck her better than his Uncle Randolph did! At least, *fuck* her, Goddammit! Or even get up, cuss, holler, and stomp madly out of the bedroom, slamming the door loudly behind him! Something, *anything,* assertive, noisy! But, no. Hell no! At this blunt outburst of hers his only reaction was to, without mumbling a single syllable, just turn away from her to lie over on his side of the bed and pout. That, Lord, is when Jessie gritted her teeth, balled up her best fist, and with all of her might and a loud "GODDAMN SONOFABITCH!!!" hauled off and hit him right smack dab in the middle of his back so hard that she farted.

~ Chapter 22 ~

Early that next morning when Will entered the barn to begin setting up his milking he was fully awakened by the sight of an object slowly swinging in the breeze while hanging from a rafter on a rope by its neck, dead. Amos Blackshear V left no forwarding address.

Upon learning of her husband's death, Jessie was saddened. Then maddened. Mad because of Amos leaving her daughter fatherless and she herself looking responsible for his suicide, which she knew good and Goddamn well she was not the cause of yet knew everyone for sure would accuse her of, like at the funeral, where she took Amos's baby, whom the Blackshears weren't demanding as being rightfully theirs only because it was a girl and they already had enough of those, and where, led by Appalachee's Black Bitch Belle Estelle, the family didn't so much as once look her direct in the eye—except for Randolph, who never stopped trying to. But, Lord, she needed no one else because she now had all to herself, Lisa.

Chapter 23

On the way home from the funeral, while driving around the bend in the road leading onto the Oconee River Bridge, Jessie looked up and right smack dab into those deep, dark, wild eyes of the young ragged woman standing on the side of the bridge holding the hand of her little ragged boy.

Jessie hated people on the road who weren't driving. They didn't belong on *her* road. From behind the steering wheel she always felt like...like hitting...SMASHING them! Especially, for some sudden, eerie reason, these ghost-like figures.

Chapter 24

Everywhere Jessie now went, riding or afoot, went Lisa. In her daughter's presence, some said, the momma was a mite more mellow. But most felt Jessie was still a mean momma who let nothing nor nobody worry her. But this wasn't quite true, as one day back in the Mitchells' kitchen, her best friend was to find out.

"Reenie."

"Yes, Jessie."

"You ever felt followed?"

"What?"

"Ever felt you were being followed, or watched?"

"No. Is somebody looking in here at me?" Reenie stood up straight from the sink to look around the kitchen.

"No, not you. I think I'm being watched. I *know* I am."

"I don't see anybody." Reenie's eyes went now to the back door and then the windows.

"Not in here, sillyass!"

"Where, then?" Reenie turned to look back at Jessie.

"The other night before going to bed I happened to glance out of my window down at the pecan tree in the front yard and saw someone standing back under it. I didn't want to wake Daddy so I got a flashlight and the gun and went out myself. By the time I got down there whoever it was had gone. Now I'm worried that someone is watching me nightly."

"*Every* night?"

"It has to be someone coming there often enough to've gotten familiar with Bo, who last night I didn't even hear bark. When I got to the pecan tree with the flashlight Bo was under it happily wagging his tail. All of this automatically makes me think back to a few years ago. I was in high school at the time, when in the middle of the night I would be awakened by what sounded like a baby crying. The sound always came from the direction of the barn. Real eerie. I was always too scared to go out in the middle of the night alone to investigate and didn't dare wake Daddy, whom I knew would've told me I'd just been dreaming. Right after dawn on the mornings following these cries I would go out to the barn to look around. But by this time of the morning Mister Ingram would be up and out getting the cows milked. And you know your daddy. He didn't, and still doesn't, like *anybody* getting too close to *his* cows. Especially during that time when ol' Mag was sick. He wouldn't even call the vet, took care of whatever ailed her himself. But he didn't want humans, especially children, anywhere inside *his* barn where he said they'd give the cow a child disease, a sure animal killer, he let me know. Anyway, I was always too sheepish to ask him had he seen or heard a baby crying anywhere in or around the barn. I never told anyone, not even Daddy or you, about any of this. That baby-crying sound I continued hearing off and on for several more weeks and then I never heard it again. It just ended, like that. And now this."

"You think maybe it's a man...a peeping Tom?"

"It's not a man. *Men* don't scare me."

That night Jessie sat in a chair in the darkest corner of the unlit front porch with Bo by her side (Lisa was upstairs asleep). Sid's five-shot automatic shotgun lying across her lap, she sat waiting, watching, and listening. But that night nobody came to stand under the pecan tree. Nor did anyone come the next night. Or the next. After a week went past with still no late-night visitor, Jessie became convinced that somebody *knew* she was sitting in the dark of the front porch nightly awaiting them. Thus she became more puzzled than pissed—puzzled enough to get behind the wheel of her Mustang and begin driving the back roads of Plain View at night, slow and watchful.

At first she found nothing back there. Then on one of these late nights while en route back home and just before reaching the Oconee River Bridge, she pulled her car off to the side of the highway and turned off the lights. There was no sign or sound of any other car out on the heavily wood-lined highway on this starless, pitch-black, and still night. Jessie sat waiting without lighting up a cigarette or turning on the car's radio until about three that morning, when she finally thought she heard something out there. Straining her ears...she *did* hear something. Something crossing the bridge...slowly. It sounded like somebody walking. Slowly. It was somebody walking...slowly...getting closer. Now it sounded like two people walking. No talking...just walking. Getting closer...almost, Jessie could all but feel them, up to the nose of the car. THEN! Jessie quickly switched on the car's headlights! Stone still in the sudden glare of the bright lights stood the figures of the young ragged woman and the ragged boy. Shotgun in hand, Jessie threw open the car's door and leapt out. Out to an empty road. Like spirits, the two ragged creatures of the night had vanished into the darkness. Stunned... baffled...Jessie, with shotgun pointing, ran around the car to the edge of the woods and screamed into the ghostly lined trees, "WHO ARE YOU AND WHAT IN THE HELL DO YOU WANT FROM ME?!" The death of the echo of her voice quickly gave back to the night its stillness.

Chapter 25

"Daddy," a red-eyed Jessie asked Sid later that morning at the breakfast table, "do you remember the old white woman people used to talk about roaming the countryside at night with her black baby?"

"Ol' Gal, you mean. Sure I remember," he answered cautiously.

"Whatever happened to the daughter?"

"Why all of a sudden you want to know about her?" Sid stopped his eating as that subject, or anything connected with the Candy Man, had never been brought up between father and daughter since the day of the tragedy.

"Just curious, that's all."

"Curious about *what?*"

"Nothing but what happened to the girl."

"She left town a long time ago and ain't been seen since."

"Oh? Did she have a child?"

"Not that I know of. Why?"

"Just asking." Slowly, Sid went back to eating while Jessie sat, mouth open, space-staring.

Twenty-four hours later, Jessie had granted Sid permission to run the dairy alone until her scheduled return shortly before that upcoming Thanksgiving from a few weeks of what she suddenly and deeply felt was a much-needed vacation in New Orleans, where Jessie had always wanted to visit. Before the surprised father could ask why the vacation, so unlike his daughter, Jessie and Lisa had Mustanged their way on out of Plain View, speeding west, the opposite direction from the Oconee River Bridge.

Lord, Jesus was stumped! What in the world had she done to bring out the "shotgun" in the Pretty Girl? Had the Pretty Girl wanted to kill her? Why was the Pretty Girl mad at her? It was enough to make her cry—later. Right now she was too baffled to boo. She wanted to be the Pretty Girl's friend—even though she'd been told on that long-ago and sorrowful day that the Pretty Girl had been the cause of her Candy Man getting killed. She hadn't understood why anyone would've wanted to kill such a good person—a person she hadn't been able to imagine doing anything to make someone even think of killing him. And then, the idea of someone as pretty as the Pretty Girl doing such a thing, or being the cause of it, she, as the years went past, found harder and harder to believe.

These passing years found her back following many of the same trails she and her ma had blazed throughout the area much earlier. Out on the trail again, she, in the very beginning, had often thought of going up to knock on someone's door and ask for work and a room. But she was deathly afraid of people. Her ma and the Candy Man had been the only two souls she'd never been afraid of and now they both were dead. After taking her in following her ma's death, the Candy Man had at first wanted to turn her, who had nobody and nowhere to go to, over to the authorities whom, he tried his best to assure her, would see she got a good home. Her answer to this was to head back to the trees...a move stopped only by his letting her stay with him, the only person once her ma died (and whose burial he personally saw to) that she felt she could trust.

In the beginning, the Candy Man had wanted her to meet and associate with children in her own age group, she being fifteen when she came to live with him. Lord, she tried. But everybody just laughed at her because of her name and because of the facts that she'd never before lived in a house or been inside a school. But in much less time than a year she'd learned to cook, clean, and care for the Candy Man's house, he'd told her, just as good as or better than any other house was taken care of in the neighborhood of Thompson Town, where they lived. And as far as school was concerned, her ma had taught her how to read from her frazzled old romance magazines, and she felt she was just as good or even better at reading than anybody in her class or in the school. But most of all everyone had made fun of her because of who her ma had been. "Gal, the ol' crazy cracker chick with the nigger baby," she'd often heard her ma and herself referred to as. She'd loved, and deeply missed, her ma, who'd been a good ma who had loved her right back. Her pa she hadn't known but her ma had often told her he was the first man who had ever been good to her and always referred to him as being "a nice colored gentleman." She hadn't wanted to be around any of these hate-minded people, and thus her whole life at the time came to center on the Candy Man and on doing for him—up until the day she'd gone to the doctor, where she found out she was pregnant with his baby and hurried happily back home to find the law...and, Lord, a dead Candy Man.

She'd cleaned up the Candy Man's house and left, carrying her few belongings in a plastic bag and wearing the pretty new winter blue dress he had just bought her the day before his death—the one she wore to the doctor when she found out the happy news about the baby and the one she'd worn ever since. She'd also left crying, wanting, needing to talk to the Pretty Girl, whom Thompson Town folks had told her he'd been with when her pa killed him. She'd wanted to know from the Pretty Girl why did her Candy Man, the only person besides her ma who had ever treated her kindly, have to be killed? Or she'd just wanted *somebody* to talk, or cry, to. But after walking all the way from Appalachee out to the country and seeing the big pretty house the Pretty Girl lived in, she knew she wouldn't, didn't, know how to talk to such a person living in such a house. That, Lord, is when she came back home to the woods.

She didn't go to the Candy Man's funeral because she felt even his family hadn't liked her. On the day of the burial, she stayed in the woods...not coming out until sundown to go to the cemetery, where she slept the night and cried on the Candy Man's grave.

During her first year back to the woods she'd kept pretty close to the Mitchells' Dairy Farm because of her expectant baby. Here at night she could leave the forest and walk just a few yards to gather and eat fresh, raw vegetables from the family garden of the Mitchells' farm helper—the "Milking Man," she called him—and fruit from the trees making up the orchard in back of the dairy's huge barn. And, of course, pecans from the big tree in the front yard. All healthy food, she felt, to nourish her and her coming baby. Besides, she deep-down believed, because of the Pretty Girl and her pa being responsible for her Candy Man's death, his son had the *right* to eat free from the family Mitchell's land.

When that first winter of her being back to the forest came and all the vegetables, fruits, and nuts were no more, she lived solely off the dairy cows' milk, drinking it straight from the teat. To ensure her baby good health, she refused to eat out of the garbage, even though she just knew the Pretty Girl's garbage was better than most. Nor, when in the woods, unlike her ma, could she bring herself to kill and cook any of the forest's wild game. She considered them all, from the harmless fish to the poisonous snakes, to be her friends who just like her were just trying to survive. Nor did she steal farmers' animals or fowl for food—only (the Mitchells') vegetables, fruits, and nuts, and always only a few at a time so that she felt they wouldn't be missed. Soon she'd become such a familiar nighttime figure moving through the garden and orchard, beneath the pecan tree, and around the barn that the Mitchell Dairy Farm's two families' dogs became her friends, their barks at her quickly replaced by wagging tails for her. If the Pretty Girl's big and nice German shepherd didn't come meet her at night out by the barn upon her exiting the forest, she automatically suspected the animals of being somewhere close to the Mitchells' house with its owner. Thus she knew these weren't the nights to go gather pecans from beneath the big pecan tree in the front yard.

It was in the barn's big, fodder-filled hayloft where her baby was born that spring. The birth occurred sometime between midnight and daylight, she in the dark of the loft delivering the baby herself, with her teeth chewing through the umbilical cord. Having spanked a cry out of the baby and yet unable to see it in the dark, she slowly and surely ran

95

her hand all over its tiny body, caressing and exploring its head and face, counting each finger and toe to make sure they were all there, checking between its legs where she felt a penis and sac, and rummaging around back to make sure the butt had its hole. Satisfied that everything was accounted for and in place, she left her baby temporarily to descend the ladder to the ground floor with the empty quart tin she'd kept among her belongings for this special occasion. No warm water being available in the barn, she roused awake one of the cows down there and after getting it on its feet and eating the feed left in the evening before, began milking it until her can was nearly full. Returning to the loft, she washed her baby in the warm milk, dried it with the lone towel from her plastic bag of belongings, and nursed it from her breasts for the first time before, finally, wrapping it in the towel to sleep. Then she went back down the ladder to bathe herself with cold water from the faucet located inside the barn. Climbing back up to the loft, she had the intention of resting awhile to regain her strength before taking the baby to her day place in the woods, thus leaving just ahead of the Milking Man, who arrived at the barn before dawn each and every morning. Instead, exhausted and still weak, she fell quickly to sleep.

Then, suddenly, her eyes popped open to stare right smack dab back into a bigger pair looking out of a head peeking over into the loft at the now-wide-awake mother and still-sleeping baby on their haybed. She and the Milking Man just stared at one another wordlessly for several long moments until, finally, his head popped down out of sight. She lay listening to his feet descending the ladder, waiting until they cleared the last rung before making her move. But before she, yet-sleeping baby in one arm and plastic bag of belongings looped around the other, could reach the loft's opening to escape the barn, she heard someone coming up the ladder. The sound froze her in her tracks. The Milking Man's head popped back up through the opening—followed by his right hand...carrying a gallon waterbucket nearly half-filled with fresh milk and holding a tin dipper. Setting the pail down gently over into the loft, the Milking Man didn't say a single word but gave her a look telling her she didn't have to run and that it was all right for her to stay. Then he was gone back down the ladder. Only to return about a half-hour later. This time he brought and left at the edge of the loft's opening a large cardboard box before disappearing from view again. Walking over slowly and looking into the box, she reached in and began taking out still-warm containers of food: biscuits, grits, scrambled eggs, fried ham, coffee, butter, jelly and sugar, along with salt and pepper shakers, a fork, knife, and spoon. Lining the bottom of the box were several items of baby clothing, diapers, safety pins, and a quilt. Later, while enjoying her first home-cooked meal since returning to the woods, she sat that early morning crying in her grits.

Every morning before the crack of dawn, the Milking Man would

climb the hayloft ladder to leave a cardboard box containing enough food for her for the day, at the same time taking away the box from the day before with its empty containers washed the previous night by her in the dark under the barn's water faucet. The two never spoke to one another, but every morning when the Milking Man's head popped up into the loft she would be awake with a smile for him and the look in his big warm brown eyes told her he knew she appreciated and thanked him with all of her heart for everything he was doing for her and her baby. When the weather was nice, which it was most of that spring, summer, and fall, immediately after eating and while the Milking Man was busy at his work, she would descend the ladder with her baby and belongings and sneak out the barn's back door, walk through the orchard, and reach the woods before sunup. Here she would remain until the lights went out in the Mitchells' house that night, whereupon she would return to the loft. When the weather was too bad for the baby to go out into, she would remain as quietly as possible in the loft. Fortunately for her, during this period her baby had been one who didn't cry very much. At first she was deathly scared he just might be too noisy and the two of them would be discovered by the Pretty Girl or her pa and thrown out of the barn, especially if they found out her baby was the Candy Man's. Or, worse, they would be arrested and turned over to someone she would be afraid of. But during a brief period that first year the baby did cry quite often at night. Whenever this happened she always tried to make sure the morning after that she was out of the barn and back into the woods before the lights in the Mitchells' house went on. One morning she didn't quite make it.

The baby had cried most of the night and didn't fall asleep until just shortly before dawn. Not wanting to interrupt his sleep by picking him up, she decided to chance staying in the barn a bit longer than her usual time that morning—Lord, long enough to hear and then, through a crack between the floorboards of the loft, see the Pretty Girl come into the barn early that morning. Hardly breathing from fright, she watched the Pretty Girl walking around down below looking all over the barn as if in desperate search of something...or somebody. Not finding it down there the Pretty Girl looked up at the loft...then started up the ladder. Here the Milking Man stopped his work to holler out at her to leave the barn right away because he had a very sick cow on his hands and no one, especially young'uns who were full of all kinds of children diseases, was to touch *anything* the cow ate...even the hay up in the loft...but himself. At this bit about the hay, the Pretty Girl stopped halfway up the ladder...but started back down only when the Milking Man told her the name of the sick cow. Yet after reaching the floor and pleading with him to let her back to see the sick cow, whom they called "Ol' Mag," he refused her and the Pretty Girl left the barn pretty mad. The Milking Man went back to his cows and she quickly got her baby and belongings and left out the back way for the woods.

She was concerned about the sick cow herself, but she didn't know, nor could she tell, which one ailed. Nor from her view through the floorboards over the next several days did she ever see the Milking Man below attending to a sick cow.

The older her baby got the less time she spent in the barn, preferring the pine-needled beds of the forest during the warm months over that of the hot hayloft. The Candy Man had once told her that while he was in the Army and stationed overseas in France, a Frenchwoman, upon learning the name he was best known by among his friends back home, began calling him "Le Bonbon." So sweet did this name sound to Jesus that she decided immediately to give it to her Candy-Man baby the day she found out she was pregnant.

Le Bonbon was her whole life. The older he grew the more he looked like his pa—the hair of the same generous-sized curls, those dimples ever teasing the corners of his mouth into a smile, and, Lord, those green eyes. He didn't at all look like her, whose skin, according to her ma, was the dark color of her pa's and whose thin, tight features she got from her ma. And like her pa was supposed to have been, she was all seriousness, with no sense of humor whatsoever, unlike her ma, who knew how to laugh. There came those times when she thought about whether or not she should put Le Bonbon in a schoolhouse where he would grow up and have a life more like other children. But remembering how she had been treated by those "normal" children and knowing how mean and hateful they would be to her son once finding out who his ma was made her feel extremely protective and not want to think about his ever leaving her. Meanwhile, from books the Candy Man had bought her, which she still kept among her few belongings, she, like her ma had done her, taught him how to read.

The older the Pretty Girl got the more time she seemed to spend at home, especially in and around the barn and farm—a situation eventually ending Jesus's and Le Bonbon's barn days and sending them to live full-time in the woods. However, unlike her ma had done with her, she didn't roam throughout the region with her child. She never strayed too far from the Mitchells' land, from whose garden, orchard, and dairy she deeply felt her son had a right to feed. So strongly did she feel about this that she refused to take anything from any other farm, or house, in the area.

Then, Lord, came the day of the Pretty Girl's husband's funeral. When the burial services ended most of the cars left the church early, going back towards town. Thinking all of the funeral cars had gone, Jesus, holding Le Bonbon's hand, had just exited the forest at the Oconee River Bridge and the two of them were about to cross over to the other side of the road and into the woods when, suddenly, a car shot around the curve leading onto the bridge. It was the Pretty Girl's car. This was the second time she'd been on the bridge when the Pretty Girl came speeding by. The first time she hadn't been able to take her eyes off the Pretty Girl's face as she shot past. But this time her eyes were able to catch a fleeting glimpse of the face of the child sitting beside the Pretty Girl on the front seat of the car as it blurred past...but not so much of a blur that she wasn't able to see the child's face and tell that it was even prettier than the Pretty Girl's. Lord, that's the very instant it struck her that she knew now what in life she wanted for her son, Le Bonbon. Long after the car had gone she yet stood on the bridge staring after it while holding her son's hand thinking that, having been the cause of his pa getting killed, the Pretty Girl now *owed* her son. *Owed* Le Bonbon her pretty little girl.

But, she knew, first she had to ready her son. He was a good boy but despite his obedience she, as the years slipped past, could strongly sense beneath his quiet and calm facade a growing curiosity about life other than the way they lived it. She now, convinced of not wanting her son to roam the woods with her until she died like her ma had done with her, right away started preparing him for his future. She began by attempting to teach him the ways and habits of the world of the "normal" people. Thus, for the next two years the two of them competed with the local raccoons and possums throughout the area in raiding garbage and trash cans and dumps. But instead of looking for food for the belly, they were searching for fuel to feed Le Bonbon's mind, printed matter. Few books were ever found but newspapers, magazines, and, Lord, *TV Guides* were plentiful, all of which she fed her son to read and study to learn to be "normal." When not reading he would be brought by her out of the forest up to the edge of the trees where, without their being seen, she would point out to him the Mitchells' big house and barn. Occasionally the Pretty Girl would be spotted and, Lord, she just *loved* looking at the Pretty Girl, who was always so immaculately dressed. Not a hair or string did the Pretty Girl ever have out of place, even when she wore overalls. Her slender and shapely body carried clothing like it had been painted on her. Jesus wished she was as beautiful...and as important... as the Pretty Girl.

Then whenever she and her son saw the Pretty Girl's Pretty Little Girl she would whisper sweetly to Le Bonbon, "If you keep reading and learning all them books and papers we keep getting for you, then one day you'll be jes as smart as the Pretty Little Girl there." Without a word he would squeeze her hand and just keep staring at the big house and barn...and the car, and most times two of them, sitting in the front yard. He, she knew, was a good boy and would someday do what his ma wanted for him.

Now, Lord knows, she didn't want the Pretty Girl mad at her. Especially not mad enough to come after her with a shotgun again. She was sure the Pretty Girl was mad at her because of how she was always dressed. She had some other clothes, given to her by the Milking Man (though she couldn't help but feel the good man's wife, whom she'd seen only once and at a distance, was the one chiefly responsible for him giving her and Le Bonbon all the food and clothing he'd given them without a single word of complaint at her over the years) but didn't like not wearing the last dress the Candy Man had bought her. Now, though, she would change that by wearing around her body the beautiful, colorful quilt given her by the Milking Man, and dress, she felt, in a manner more befitting the ma of Le Bonbon.

Tomorrow, Thanksgiving Day, would be the tenth anniversary of the burial of the Candy Man. She and Le Bonbon would, after dark, go and put flowers on his grave. Then, she had firmly and finally decided, on the day after that she would take her nine-year-old Le Bonbon out of the woods to the Mitchells' barn before daybreak to see the Milking Man who'd always been so good to both of them and ask him would he let her son help him do the milking. (The little boy who looked to her to've been near Le Bonbon's age and whom she'd seen at the dairy from afar was always in the company of the Pretty Girl's pa and never seemed to help the Milking Man. She was never quite sure who this little boy belonged to.) This way, she figured, her Le Bonbon would eventually get to know the Pretty Little Girl...who, when they got old enough, he would court...then *marry*...then live with in the big pretty house...then she and her son wouldn't have to live in the woods any more...because he and the Pretty Little Girl would let his ma live in the barn.... Yes, Lord, the Pretty Girl *owed* the Candy Man's Le Bonbon her Pretty Little Girl....

Chapter 26

"Happy birthday, Sonny!" Jessie opened the door for the just-turning-eight-years-old-that-Thanksgiving-Day youngster and his grand-parents, Will and Mattie, all invited to eat their holiday dinner with the family Mitchell. "Give Auntie Jessie a BIG kiss! Ummmuuh! Good!"

"Sonny, thank Jessie fuh the new suit she bought you fuh yo' birfday," Grandmother Mattie coaxed.

"Thank you for the new suit you bought me for my birthday," parroted a buck-toothed, bright-eyed, handsome lad.

"Thank *who?*"

"You...*Aunt*Jessie." His beautiful dusky face lit up with a white grin.

"That's right, I'm your aunt now but one day I'll be your mother-in-law. You are most welcome for the suit. My, it looks fantastic on you! Makes you look like a little man. *Lisa's* little man! Good afternoon, Mister and Missis Ingram." Jessie swiveled her smile onto the grandparents. "And a most happy Thanksgiving to both of you! Please, come on in. Daddy, our guests are here!" she called, leading the visitors into the living room where in his rocker sat Sid holding his two-year-old grand-daughter, Lisa, a miniature replica of her late daddy. Freshly shaved and bathed, Sid wore a heavy green-and-white-plaid checkered shirt tucked into the top of a pair of thick dark brown corduroys held up by a set of wide tan suspenders with the trousers rolled up, cuffs resting atop two black heavy-duty brogans.

"Hi yawl?" Sid rose with Lisa for the greeting.

"We's jes fine, Sid. Hi you?" they said together. "Hey, Lisa," waved a smiling Mattie.

"And, as you can see," Jessie's eyes guided those of the guests deeper into the room, "we brought down Mother who will be eating Thanksgiving, and *your* birthday"—turning to beam down at Sonny for a second before looking back at Mildred—"dinner at the table with the rest of us. Right, Mother dear?" Jessie lighted up the room with a quick flash from that sparkling, tundra-thawing smile. Not seeing the light, though, was Mildred, sitting in a wheelchair dressed in a bright-yellow, neck-high, wrist-reaching, and ankle-length dress hanging loosely off her big-boned, no-longer-robust frame. What the dress tried to hide of her dissipated body her face shamelessly gave away. Once striking, this face was now old, ashen, sunken-cheeked, and wrinkled, and on its left side carved with a perpetual wink. In a chair alongside the sick woman wearing (on Jessie's order) a crisp white nursing uniform topped with cap was Pig, holding a copy of the *National Enquirer* while smiling from ear to ear beneath the long, flowing, blonde strands of her "Sunday" wig.

"Happy Thanksgiving, Mildred!" chorused the guests in unison. The invalid's fully opened right eye stared off into a nonexistent world beginning just beyond the visitors' shoulders. "Such a pretty dress you got on!" Mattie said in a small but loud voice as if all Mildred needed to come back to this world was a good hollering at.

"Thank you, Missis Ingram!" Jessie kindly took the shy little woman off center stage. "I brought it back from New Orleans for Mother especially for today, *your* birthday, Sonny." She turned to beam down once more at the youngster wearing the confident grin. "Mister and Missis Ingram, please, sit down." The two, dressed for the occasion in their finest wear, sat down timidly side by side on the sofa like a young couple out on their first date together.

"You have on a beautiful dress yourself, Missis Ingram. Purple certainly does suit you nicely," Jessie complimented the petite, graying Mattie, whom everyone agreed that of all her children Reenie resembled more in both appearance and temperament than did any of the rest.

"Thank you, Jessie. It ain' nud'n much." Mattie looked shyly down at her lap, unable to handle such flattering exudings.

"To be 'nud'n much' it sho took you a lon' time to put it on befo' we could leave the house to git heah." Will's thoughts on the purple dress brought laughter, including a smiling blush from Mattie—but not Mildred, who continued to stare at something not of that room.

"If we women didn't take the time to fix ourselves up, you men would complain even more than you already do," said a jovial Jessie, rushing to Mattie's rescue. "Missis Ingram, no matter how long it took you to get ready, Daddy, myself, and Lisa...and, of course, Mother dear," shining her smile upon Mildred's blank face, "are so pleased all of y'all were able to come join us today for dinner and, most importantly, Sonny's *birthday*." Jessie smiled over at the grinning-back youth standing alongside Sid in his rocker. "Your buddy Daddy got you now but in a few years you are going to belong to Lisa. You are going to be *her* boyfriend and she will get the last say-so, not Daddy. Right, Lisa baby?" Jessie looked at her daughter, staring from her nest in her grandfather's arm out of two huge, sad brown eyes, then switched back to her guests. "Being the guest rather than the hostess, or cook, on Thanksgiving must be quite a change for you, Missis Ingram?"

"It sho is. I don' know the las' time I din' cook on this day. It's mighty nice of y'all to invite us ovah to eat." The untalkative Mattie was winded.

"Only too glad to have you. But as you know you are still going to be eating your own family's cooking. Reenie's. She started in the kitchen last night and won't let a single soul back there to help her."

"Tha's Reenie fuh you," said a proud Mattie.

"Sugar Dumpling, I don't see you trying to break the door down getting back there to help her." Everyone laughed. Normally a comment such as this bit bouncing off Sid's lips would've sent Jessie springing toward the source with all four feet and tail. But surprisingly to all present, perhaps even Mildred too, on this day of thanks, she smilingly replied,

"Oh, Daddy, I'm well aware of my limitations. This is one meal I want us all here to enjoy and *never* forget and I know that for this to happen it's best I stay out of the kitchen and wisely leave the cooking to Reenie. But, Daddy, I baked Sonny's birthday cake and *did* help clean the house."

"The baking I didn't see, but I did see you cleaning those few small spots Reenie didn't have time for." More laughter.

"Maybe I oughta go back 'n help," offered a serious Mattie.

"No! Missis Ingram, you sit right where you are. You are our guest. Daddy, you've got everyone here believing I'm lazy, which you well know isn't true. And to prove my point I'm going back to the kitchen right this minute and offer Reenie my services, again."

"Reenie." Wading into a world of cooking sights, smells, and sounds, Jessie asked, "Can I *please* be of some, *any*, help to you back here? Out front Daddy is dragging my ass through the ashes for not helping you."

"You can set the table." Reenie materialized from a gust of steam.

"'Go set the table' is your way of telling me to stay out of your way. You've told me that three times already today and I can only set it once, which I did right after lunch."

"Everything's about ready. You are in charge of what everybody's drinking. Just please don't give Daddy too much wine."

"Don't you worry about your dear daddy, Reenie sweets, I'll personally take good care of him. Oh, Reenie, I just wanna say I'm so happy your parents could come today!"

"Me too!"

"Over the years I've not seen enough of your family. Starting today I'm changing that. Now I can see what everybody's always talking about when they say your mommy and daddy never stopped courting. They look so cute...and happy...sitting out there on the sofa holding hands. Is it really true they are like this all the time?"

"*All* the time. I never have seen nor ever heard of them ever fighting. Nor has anyone else. Lord, nobody, *nothing,* could ever come between them."

"You really don't think so, huh?"

"I *know* so! Momma and Daddy are...are...just different."

"We are all different."

"Not like them. Daddy, as everybody knows, sometimes drinks a bit but all he ever does then is try to hug and kiss Momma in public, which embarrasses her and which I don't want him doing to her here today."

"Drinking makes him horny, huh?"

"I didn't say that!"

"Most men, especially his age, alcohol has the opposite effect on."

"Yes, *that's* the truth."

"How would you know?"

"From...from what I...I hear...and...and read." Flustered, Reenie turned her back to Jessie to work over the stove.

"You read *Playboy* now, huh? Truthfully, Reenie, how long has it been?"

"How long has *what* been?" Suddenly Reenie was frantically lifting and lowering lids of pots atop the stove.

"Since you last had it?"

"Since I last had *what?*"

"Sex. Not since that *one* time with Samuel?"

"How did this talk suddenly get off onto *me?*" Clang, clang, the stove top pots' lids rang.

"Reenie sweets, one of these days soon I'm gonna throw you in my car and drive off somewhere and get you fucked."

"JESSIE!"

"Reenie, we *all* need it once in a while. It's natural, *normal.*"

"I don't *need* your damn pity!" CLANG!

"Where are the youngest children eating today?" Jessie knew now was subject-changing time.

"In town with my oldest sister, her husband and children," Reenie said softly, following a brief stirring-the-pot pause.

"I was just going to say they could eat here with us. There's plenty of food, as *you* so well know."

"Thanks, but they wanted to go into town to eat." Then, following another pot-stirring pause: "Jessie, I didn't mean to holler at you, I'm sorry. You only meant well. You always do. Sometimes it's just how you say things that always gets my goat. But what I really want to say is that for the last week or so you've been acting so different. Like you are finally getting over what happened to Amos. You've been showing more concern for others. Like my folks...and Missis Mildred. You've been acting so nice. So *happy.* And today you look just too pretty for words in your new outfit. I wish to God my clothes would fit me just half as good as yours fit you. If that's how the women dress in New Orleans then it's no wonder men are always wanting to go there. Oh! You aren't wearing a bra?"

"There ain't much hanging loose. I would trade with you any day."

"As far as I'm concerned you can have 'em. They ain't done nothing but cause me trouble. But, Jessie, at the family dinner ought'n you wear a bra? Are you *high* on something?"

"Yes! High on *life!* It wasn't Amos's death that had me feeling low just before I left. I got over Amos at his funeral—the moment I detected the Blackshear family wasn't interested in his child, Lisa, because she was a *girl*. That attitude I know too damn well and after finding that out, I don't want anything else to do with the family Blackshear. After the funeral I got sort of down upon learning about the poor homeless woman roaming the woods around here."

"What poor homeless woman?" Reenie almost stopped her preparation of some Thanksgiving something.

"We'll talk about her later. That New Orleans vacation was just what I needed. It made me feel much better about everything and everybody. You know, Reenie, New Orleans got some *interesting* men."

"Jessie, Amos...."

"Shut up, Reenie! Anyway, this morning I woke up feeling great. I knew today was going to be special—special to me because I'd be with the people I love. Lisa, Daddy, you, and your precious little Sonny, whom I love as if he was my own. And, of course, I love Mother. And I do plan to get to know better and love your folks. Yes, Reenie, it suddenly dawned upon me after seeing that poor homeless woman that I have a lot to be thankful for...."

"What poor homeless woman?" This time Reenie did stop her stirring of some Thanksgiving something.

"We'll talk about her later, I said. There's not enough laughter in my life. Even with Amos, we didn't laugh. I want to laugh more! And teach Lisa how to laugh. Like your family does it. That real 'git down' *gut* laughter! No more of this standup *lip* laughter! Laughter is not only healthy for the body and the soul but for the head, heart, *and* the home. Oh, Reenie sweets, I'm sooo happy! Please, God, bless this house and these very happy families here on this special Thanksgiving Day." The two dear friends were now hugging one another and crying amidst the kitchen's sights, smells, and sounds. Their tears were briefly interrupted by Jessie's sobbing, "I love you, Reenie sweets, even if you *never* again get fucked!"

Treetop tall and snapbean lean, Will owned a solemn, almost pious face this day, matching his aged brown suit. But most noticeable about the man were his hands. Big. Everybody said he grew such big hands because of milking cows from the time he was old enough to hold onto a cow teat. While growing up he became very self-conscious of his huge, long-tapered-fingered hands, not knowing exactly what to do with them. When not in use, mainly for milking, he tried to keep these oversized hands out of sight behind his back or in his pockets. When the milking machine came and stole away the cow's teat from his long fingers, he took up smoking, trying to find more use for his suddenly unemployed hands. But after the cigarette was lit, smoking only involved the use of one hand, the extra one hanging useless by his side, hiding behind his back, or pocketed, self-consciously awaiting the lighting of another cigarette. That was the reason, cynics claimed, why he often hid one of Mattie's tiny hands in one of his in public, giving it something to do. That's what it was doing in the Mitchells' parlor on this Thanksgiving Day while the other one held a cigarette and their owner waited to attack the dinner table, where for the first time Jessie saw close up these huge hands. She sat wordlessly watching them pick up drumsticks, slices, and slabs of turkey and like a stevedore dunk the chunks in their owner's mouth. But rather than feeling disgusted at this sight a slowly, etiquettely chewing Jessie found herself sitting totally awed by Will's table manners, or lack thereof. With grease smeared around his mouth, atop his nose, and down his chin, he ate the food the way, she kept digging, God meant man to eat pussy. Sloppy. Slurpy! But at the same time she thought, *if* Will ate pussy he probably did so the wrong way. Politely or timidly. The more wine she sipped the less she could keep her eyes off those big, greasy hands.

Reenie had so crammed the big dining room table with food that there was hardly room left for the day's devourers. But all managed to find a toothhold around the rim of the feed. Sitting at the head of the table was Sid, who after blessing the food, along with expressing a special prayer of appreciation for Momma Mildred's presence at the table of thanks and carving the turkey, sat about knifing and forking it off his plate on down his drain. At the foot of the table in her wheelchair sat Mildred being slowly fed and softly talked to by a sitting-alongside Pig, who took two large mouthfuls of food for every small one she gave. Reenie, finally forced by Jessie to sit down, sat on the edge of her chair on the alert for the first hint of a want from anywhere around the table. Next to her was Sonny, next to Jessie, sitting near the head of the table directly to her daddy's right. Lisa was upstairs napping. Eating through from the other side of the table was Mattie, munching delicately with eyes glued to her plate. To Mattie's right, on Sid's left, was Will, whose hands Jessie, directly across from Will, couldn't keep her eyes and mind off.

"Daddy! You *promised* last night you would eat with your knife and fork here today," reminded Reenie.

"Don't bother Mister Ingram, Reenie. Let him enjoy his food." Jessie took a big sip of wine while near-breathlessly watching a big, thick vein crawling along the back of Will's big, long right hand standing with a load of food poised outside a pair of stretching-wide lips.

Ice it! Jessie quickly told herself. Don't end up doing exactly what you don't want to do on this special day and what you can do so well—fuck up everything for everybody! But, her strong mind countered, I can think, can't I? Surely I'm not sitting here contemplating having a rendezvous with Mister Ingram, my best friend's *daddy?* Imagine! No, I could *never* do that to you, Reenie. *Never!* Or could I? You know *never* to say never. Yet Reenie, and everyone else, believes nothing, *nobody,* could ever make Mister Ingram unfaithful to his wife. Bullshit! I'll bet with just one wink of my eye I can have him crawling behind his dick on all fours, begging. But he's definitely not my type. Rarely talks and when he does what I've heard of it has been of no interest to me. But who needs talk? Action, baby! No, don't you worry, Reenie sweets, our friendship means much too much for me to fuck your dear daddy. But he most certainly is a good-looking man. Horny when he's high? And, Lord, Lord, those *hands!* Jessie momentarily closed her eyes to backlid-visualize them moving all over, up, down, around, and *into* her body. God! She'd often heard it said that one could tell the shape and size of a man's penis by his fingers.... It was while staring intently at Will's ring finger that she suddenly felt herself being watched and turned her eyes down the table, where they fell directly upon those of a grinning, mouthful-of-food Pig, who winked.

Accustomed to table conversation, Jessie, in an attempt to keep her eyes and mind off her best friend's daddy's hands, abruptly began talking. She gave little thought to what she was saying or how long she talked until she got to "Mister Ingram"...all five fingers of whose right hand were spread out in front of his mouth while one at a time being slowly and slurpingly sucked free of gravy.... "Daddy tells me you do good carpentry work. I need some wall shelves made for my office and if you could find the time to do the job we can discuss a price." Then: "After we finish eating here...and if you don't mind so terribly much...I'd love to show you exactly where in my office the spot needs shelving." Then, without looking at Reenie, she reached across the table with the wine bottle to refill Will's glass. Nor did she look down the table...just kept her eyes on those long, being-slowly-licked fingers, wondering, was it true?

Later, in her office, she showed a slightly-tipsy-and-smiling-amorously Will the exact spot to sit on the edge of her desk where she felt he could get a better feel of the space she wanted him to work and suddenly but gently took both of the man's huge hands and placed them beneath her white silk blouse over a braless breast each, where they instantly snapped hold, permitting her now-free hands to reach down and rip open his buttoned-fly ancient trousers, where out popped the TRUTH. Gasping, "Sorry, Reenie sweets," Jessie hurriedly straddled the mountain and...slowly...slowly...slid down....

Looking at herself in the downstairs bathroom mirror, Jessie felt no remorse whatsoever about what had just taken place out back in her office (the old, since renovated, tool shed where the "changing of the guard" had taken place that long-ago day when three-year-old Sidney had replaced nine-year-old Jessie by her father's side). Reenie, she was firmly convinced, would not only never find out but wouldn't believe it even if she did find out. About Mattie the meek Jessie never thought one way or the other, except for imagining Will crawling back to her "tainted." But in proving the day special like she'd awakened early that morning knowing it would be, she'd fucked her best friend's father. Her best friend's daddy? He'd had something to do with it, too, though; I didn't *rape* him, she thought. Not that Will, having been about as shocked and surprised over what was happening as Reenie would be, had done anything so great on his own. It had been her taking those huge hands of his by the wrists and raking them with their hardened calluses all over her soft, quivering body that, combined with her fantasizing about the day she lost her virginity while scaling and descending the mountain, had sent her flying and screaming over the top. But immediately upon landing back on both feet (which she had a talent for doing), Jessie quickly realized that despite her coming, this was going to be strictly a one-time thing when Will spoke the only words he'd uttered the whole time: "I guess Sid 'n me 'bout tit fuh tat now"—to which she right away set him straight.

"This, Mister Ingram, was done purely out of curiosity on my part. *Nothing* more! And now that I've satisfied that particular whim of mine please don't jump to the conclusion that you've found yourself a 'permanent piece' here because you sure as hell haven't. You are still in the employment of my father, whom you are *not,* and never will be, a 'tit for tat' equal to. Now let's walk back to the house like we left it, together *and* talking. But first, Mister Ingram, here's a safety pin for your fly."

Upon their arrival back into the living room, she busily discussing wall shelving and he mum, Jessie sat down and was immediately greeted by Bo. Placing his head in her lap while she still talked to Will, now sitting back on the sofa holding Mattie's hand, the dog commenced to sniff, whimper, and, finally, salivate while burrowing his snout deeper and deeper into Jessie's crotch, where beneath her thin skirt she was yet damp from her recent trip atop the mountain. Roughly pushing the whimpering dog aside, Jessie stood up and announced she was going to freshen up for the cutting of Sonny's birthday cake and headed for the downstairs bathroom. The whimpering Bo followed. Pig, still sitting at the dining room table eating, gave Jessie a wink.

110

A jubilant Jessie began gathering everyone together for the cake cutting and present presenting. Lisa was still sleeping. The birthday boy and his grandparents were all in the living room (Will sitting on the sofa sneaking a snooze with head kicked back and mouth open) along with Mildred. Sitting next to the sick woman was Mattie, talking in a loud voice in an attempt to holler over the top of the fog to the "real" Mildred she was sure was on the other side just waiting to hear, "SUCH A PRETTY DRESS YOU GOT ON!" Pig was missing.

One look at her sitting and appearing-exhausted mother without her nurse at her side instantly irked Jessie. Finally having had it up to the other ends of her nose hair with Pig, a highly pissed Jessie quickly went in search of her mother's nurse. The kitchen? Empty! The bathroom? Empty! Why did she, dammit, have to take care of *every* little thing?! Because right now she was damn determined to make Sonny's birthday party a memorable event for *all* present!

Then, Lord, screaming from out of only-You-know-where to hit her hard, hot, and heavy dead center of where she did her living came something that sent her tearing out the back door to her office before rapidly returning and heading straight upstairs for her daddy's room where, flinging open the unlocked door and with murder in her voice, she screamed, "TAKE YOUR GODDAMN HANDS OFF MY DADDY YOU GODDAMN SLUT" at the bare back of Sid, who turned to look smack dab down the bulldog nose of a .38 caliber revolver pointed by Jessie, whose mouth was poised to holler out a real-mean-and-low-down-dirty-dog-nasty-yo-momma piece of Pig slop before pulling the trigger on the woman lying spread-eagled naked beneath her daddy on the bed—but, Lord, absolutely nothing came up and out of her wide-open mouth nor from out of the barrel of the pointing gun. The woman was Reenie. Jessie fainted.

"Jessie, can you hear me? The doctor is on his way. You are gonna be all right." Lying motionless on her own bed while staring blankly up at the ceiling, Jessie didn't answer Reenie, sitting alone in the room with her friend whose listless right hand she was holding tightly in both of hers while sobbing out the words, "I wanted so badly for so long to tell you but I knew if I did tell you it would end our friendship forever and I *never* wanted that to happen. You've always been the best friend in the world to me no matter what everybody else might've thought about me. But now I know you don't want to ever again be my friend and I won't blame you. Yet I will *always* be your friend. I did what I did because it was *my* fault that Mister Sid's only son, Sidney, drowned. I *had* to give him another son. Mister Sid, too, never wanted me to tell you about us. He wanted to wait until it was 'safe,' he said—when Sonny was older...and could take care of himself. He...we...didn't want anything to happen to our Sonny. Mister Sid was going to tell you someday that Sonny, who everybody says looks more and more like his daddy every day, is his son. A *Mitchell*. Your *brother*. Lisa's *uncle*. And...and...the family's *legal* heir." Lord, here's when Reenie felt Jessie's hand stiffen in hers.

~ **Chapter 28** ~

"Where's Jessie?! She's not in her room!" A frantic Reenie ran downstairs to Pig, in the kitchen fixing a snack, later that same evening.

"She jes lef in her car."

"In her *car?!* The doctor said she shouldn't be outta bed!"

"Go tell 'er."

"Where did she go?!"

"Swim'n, I heah'd her tell the chil'."

"Swimming?! She's out of her head! And she took Lisa with her?!"

"Her too."

"And *who* else?"

"Sonny."

~ Chapter 29 ~

It was pitch dark that Thanksgiving night when the young woman—wrapped in a bright, colorful quilt, just having visited the grave of the Candy Man—and her son were walking across the Oconee River Bridge when just ahead of them a car with headlights flashing suddenly shot from around the curve. The woman and the boy froze in their tracks up against the railing midway of the bridge. Then, Lord! Following what sounded like a scream piercing off the lips of the person driving, the speeding white Mustang suddenly swerved sharply and ran right smack into the colorfully quilted woman against the railing before spinning crazily over the top and down into the river.

~ **Chapter 30** ~

The driver of the white Mustang—twenty-six-year-old Jessie Mitchell Blackshear, heard crying out the name "Sidney!"—did not save her eight-year-old half-brother, Sonny Ingram Mitchell, who drowned.

Killed instantly by the car was the colorfully quilted woman on the bridge, twenty-six-year-old Jesus...*nailed* to the railing.

From the river yet alive was dragged two-year-old Lisa Angelina Blackshear by nine-year-old Le Bonbon...the Candy's kid....

Jessie's body was never found.

COUSIN CLAIRE

~ Chapter 1 ~

WHEN THE DOCTOR TOLD HER THERE WERE LESS than six months of life left in her body she, figuring she could deal with death better from her house than from the formality of the hospital, told him she wanted to go home and die in her own bed. Thus in late winter of 1980, Luella Hemphill left the Muskhogean County Hospital to come home to die informally.

Luella felt guilty about dying—guilty because she didn't think she was feeling sad enough to suit God about leaving the life He'd been good enough to give her free of charge without her even asking Him. Maybe, she hoped for God's sake, the longer she lay dying, the more sadness would gradually creep over the whole of her soul and end her feeling of guilt. But until that time came she lay abed looking forward to leaving behind this dirty old disorderly world with all its pain. She of course told none of this to those long faces coming to hover over her bed because she didn't want them thinking she was already dead in the head because of her wanting to exit laughing. She decided to just enjoy her dying in silence.

Life hadn't turned out quite the way Luella felt she'd been promised (by God? her parents? her minister? whom?). She had gone through life expecting something extraordinarily wonderful to happen, with renewals at timely intervals, to her. Now, at forty-two, here she was dying. Was this, *death,* it? The BIG life happening she popped out of her mother's womb crying to experience? Maybe, she lay thinking daily, there's truly something awaiting the other side of death for all those having been missed by that something extraordinarily wonderful during life. But secretly she hoped, God forgive her, there was no such reward because if whatever it was did not come up to her high expectations, then she surely wouldn't want to be stuck with some unwanted prize for eternity. In life one could die and leave all the disappointments behind, but from what she understood of heaven, it provided no such out. Heaven was forever. For example, she'd heard all they drank and ate up there were milk and honey. Ugh! Not wanting to chance another big disappointment, especially the after-death diet, all she now asked of God was to let her drop off into a deep, dark, warm, and painless sleep where the alarm clock never goes off and where nothing was expected of her and she expected nothing in return and no one would ever be disappointed.

Luella came from a family of short-lifers. She was only six years old at the time but remembered vividly the day the long envelope came in the mailbox and her mother opened it and screamed. The only thing she could ever recall about her daddy, who was thirty years old when World War II came to kill him, was the strong smell of his brown Army uniform and the gold tooth smack in the middle of the big smile he always had for her. Her mother never married again and with the money she got from the government in exchange for her husband's life she had built, right after the war, there in Appalachee, the county seat of Muskhogean, Georgia, for her and her only child, a house next door to her only sister. Her sister and husband also had just one child, a boy. Luella's first cousin. Cousin Clarence.

Cousin Clarence was three years older than Luella and was what the grown folks called "mannish." A brat. But, Lord, Luella loved him. Better, *worshipped* him. Cousin Clarence liked her well enough to teach her how to ride a bicycle, roller skate, throw a rock through a window pane, and strike a match and set fire to one's own fart. He also promised to teach her a medical game called "doctor." But before getting around to this operation, Cousin Clarence moved with his folks to Atlanta. Nine-year-old Luella cried. Now she was all alone. Except for her daydreams. Wherein Cousin Clarence never left to move away to Atlanta. Wherein they both were grownups, he in his white "doctor" uniform and she his nurse. And they were married...with a pretty little baby. When she told her mother this the older woman told her that it was against the law for kinfolks to marry one another. Luella was so fearful of breaking the law, even with Cousin Clarence, that the male in her daydream instantly took on a blank, law-abiding face, though yet remaining in his white doctor uniform. This male face in Luella's daydreams remained blank throughout her high school years. Not that males weren't attracted to her. Quite the contrary. Many fell for her cute doll face, beautiful manners, and petite, shapely body. But in her mind none of them could ever replace Cousin Clarence.

When her cousin first moved, Luella wrote him a letter a day; then a letter a week; followed by a letter a month; thereafter a letter a year—until, finally, she stopped writing him altogether. Only because he never answered a single one of her letters.

Chapter 2

After seven short years of marriage, Emma Lou Walker was still madly in love with her husband Henry, and when the war killed him she grew even madder in love with him. She hadn't wanted to go on living but because of Luella she knew she had to wait until her only child grew up before flying off to join her Henry atop the clouds. Before leaving earth she wanted to make sure her Luella had a Henry of her own— though she was more concerned that Luella's Henry be someone to take care of her rather than merely take her away. Emma Lou's physical and mental health both had begun slowly deteriorating the instant she opened the long envelope sent from the war, telling her it was keeping her Henry. Thus, by Luella's last year in high school, Emma Lou, a diabetic to go along with her broken heart, was about to take off to the top of the clouds. But she stubbornly taxied on life's last runway long enough to decide which man she felt was most fit to take care of her only child till death did them part. Luella remembered that day all too well when she walked into the room of her bedridden mother, who lost no time in saying to her, "Honey, come and sit here beside your ol' momma. I want to talk to you."

"About what?" Luella said.

"We never know when I'll be leaving you here alone to go and join your daddy...."

"Momma, you've been saying that ever since Daddy died. You've got plenty more years to live."

"...And you're almost eighteen, soon a grown woman. With you finishing school this year it's getting time we started thinking about who's going to take care of you when your ol' momma is gone to meet your daddy."

"I can take care of myself." Luella rose.

"Every woman needs a good man to take care of her."

"I don't." Luella walked.

"Of all the boys coming here to see you all the time there's just one of them who would be a good provider for you."

"Which one is that?" Luella stopped.

"Oscar Hemphill."

"OSCAR HEMPHILL?!" Luella spun around.

"Yes, honey. Oscar Hemphill."

"Momma, you don't know what you are saying! Oscar Hemphill is the BIGGEST BORE in Muskhogean County!"

"Sugar, he just might be but he's the only one of all those boys coming here to see you who can provide for you right now."

"Momma, Oscar Hemphill doesn't even dance, doesn't like to read, doesn't like the movies, radio, nor television. All he ever wants to do is sit and talk about his silly ol' job, which is *nothing!*"

"He's got every right to talk about his job. And it *is* something. Working for Singleton Seed Company is the best job a colored man working by the day can have in Muskhogean County."

Chapter 3

Thus, shortly following her graduation from high school in the year of our Lord 1956, it came to pass that the blank male face in Luella's daydreams was filled in by the sober, practical, down-to-earth, reliable, dependable, common, two-feet-flat-out-on-the-ground, unimaginative, unpretentious, predictable, dull, and boring Oscar Hemphill, the provider. The white play-doctor uniform in her daydreams had suddenly turned into a pair of blue denim overalls. When Luella announced her engagement to her female friends they all heartily congratulated her but once alone among themselves heaved a mutual sigh of relief, pleased to know that their respective mothers would now be off their individual backs about any of them catching Oscar, the prize bore.

Less than a month following the wedding, Emma Lou's soul sailed out of her thirty-nine-year-old body for the top of the clouds to meet with her Henry, leaving behind for Luella the house where she and Oscar still lived.

Despite not having wanted to marry Oscar, Luella, feeling she had done the daughterly thing by not letting her mother die worrying about her only child's welfare, wanted to be a good wife. She believed God just might possibly teach her to love Oscar if the marriage itself got off to a good start. Like, Lord, on the wedding night.

On this special night that every female is supposedly born looking forward to, Luella lay on the bridal bed nervously hoping and praying that her Oscar, a grown man of twenty-one, would know exactly what to do to and for her, his young virgin wife. She lay anticipating her husband beginning this created-personally-by-God-Himself-in-heaven night by whispering softly and sweetly in her ear how much he loved her before tenderly kissing her lips, and, Lord, her breasts....

Of all her bodily parts she, secretly, was most proud of her breasts. Her mother, along with many of her girlfriends, had often complimented her on how beautifully her bust fitted her dresses, blouses, and other tops, especially bathing suits. Not too big was her bust, size thirty-four, yet shapely and perfect for her petiteness. She'd always had the secret desire to bare her breasts in public like many African and Island females she'd seen pictured in *National Geographic* magazine. She wanted to bare them herself on this special night but instead waited, granting her

Oscar this pleasure, as she wanted to witness his facial expression, especially his eyes when they lit up the bedroom upon seeing her beautiful breasts for the first time—spongy firm, acorn smooth, upturned, and topped off by readily excitable burnt-almond nipples on this night of nights standing as hard and as erect as two thimbles, naked and straining beneath her gown to be freed and kissed...and kissed...and sucked.... THEN!

The light in the room went out and the hem of her new silk nightgown she'd spent hours selecting especially for this intimate evening was suddenly yanked up above her navel, followed by her legs being roughly pulled apart, then rudely stuck up into the air and furiously swung every whichaway before she was abruptly rammed right down her middle by what felt like a sledgehammer, then immediately afterwards pried open by a crowbar! WHAM! BAM! CREAK! WHUMP! WHUMP! WHUMP! Lord, before she realized what had hit her the sudden, rude attack on her body was over and she lay in the dark crying, bleeding, and hurting while Oscar lay beside her snoring loudly. God! Was this it? Love? She felt vile, violated. Raped? Had that man who just a few hours earlier had vowed before her minister and her mother in her church to protect her been her Oscar, her *husband?* Lord, all during that...that *invasion* of her body...he hadn't even uttered one single word! Just suddenly and without the least bit of warning he'd turned out the light and jumped her in the dark like a bull jumping atop a cow. Instead of sweet, reassuring whispers, coming out of him were nothing but snorts, grunts, groans, moans...and all that sticky stuff she now lay in. And when it was all, finally, over and he'd evidently gotten what he'd married her for she received not even so much as a thank-you from him before he rolled over and immediately broke out in a snore. Worst of all about the whole horror show, she lay sobbing, was that he didn't even *see* her breasts, much less kiss or touch them. GOD! She felt used...and, Lord, sticky! Oh, she wanted her mother as she began crying harder and Oscar snored louder.

Oscar, Luella quickly learned, was definitely not a breast man. Other than occasionally giving her ever-fervid nipples an indifferent tweak, he paid no attention at all to his wife's bust in the bedroom, or outside of it. Yet this slight never stopped Luella through the years from fantasizing about taking her husband's hands in hers and placing them on her proudest bodily possessions. But she never proved brazen enough to do this, forever believing it was a man's duty, and not that of a lady, to take the initiative in all things sex, whether talking or doing. Thus each of their bedroom romps (no hanky-panky outside of this door for the Hemphills) always started with Oscar frantically grabbing and 'rassling Luella down into his favorite position of her heels over her ears. Other than her having stopped crying for her mother, these moments of togetherness for them never significantly varied from their wedding

124

night.

Two things saved Luella from her marriage. First, she eventually learned to close her eyes and pretend that the snorting, grunting, groaning, and, finally, moaning bull banging away atop her was Cousin Clarence (although she just *knew* Cousin Clarence didn't make love in such a crude, unromantic, and obscene manner). Next, she believed (prayed) that all of this pounding of her body would eventually lead to a baby. Which, a year following their wedding night, it did. A boy. Whom Oscar wanted to name after him, as he'd been named after his daddy. But here, Lord, little Luella stomped down her front foot and got in the last word. And that word, Lord, was "Clarence."

Luella no longer needed Oscar to kiss her breasts. She now had her baby Clarence to suck on them *anytime* she wanted them sucked—even in public, where at long last, like the African and Island women of *National Geographic,* she could bare a breast to nurse her baby. Lord, no bottle for her Clarence. She gave her baby the *real* nipple. Long after there was no milk left in her breasts she continued to dry nurse little Clarence before finally weaning him almost a year past the norm for such. Thus ended the most sensually satisfactory years of Luella's married life.

Oscar had wanted a house full of children but all Luella had ever really wanted from her husband was one, boy, child and once she got him she had no desire whatsoever to birth another Oscar baby. But she remained convinced that if the law had permitted her to marry Cousin Clarence she never would've tired of birthing his babies. Such feelings she of course never expressed around anyone else, as her undying, even while she lay dying, love for Cousin Clarence had always been her very own secret. This, her sweet secret, and her son were the only two things that had kept going any real interest in life for her once she married Oscar.

She and Oscar continued to have sex every Friday night, his Singleton pay day, up until she got sick the last time. But she'd long ago gotten all she'd ever wanted from their congresses, her baby Clarence, thereafter just lying beneath her husband fantasizing about her Cousin Clarence.

Luella never did completely cut the cord with her son Clarence. Never really wanted to. She kept it attached so that at the first sign of danger to him she could quickly reel her flesh and blood back into the safety of her womb. As a youngster, Clarence hadn't been allowed to play any "rough" games with his peers like football, boxing, wrestling, or even basketball. Luella did permit him to play baseball, providing he didn't play with too rough a group or get hit by the ball. While the boy was in his early teens his father had wanted to teach him to hunt but Luella immediately vetoed the thought. Not that she was against animals getting killed for the table. She was against her young Clarence getting shot by some other hunter. She did let him fish. But Oscar didn't fish. Even more than going hunting with him, Oscar had wanted his son, once finishing high school, to join him at Singleton like he had his daddy. But once again, Lord, Little Luella with her front foot stomped out a loud "NO!" No Singleton "sweat shop" for her Clarence, she vowed. Not even during his summer months out of school would she allow him to work at the seed company, or any other similar type of job. Instead she'd seen to it that during the summer her son had gotten the less toilsome job of delivering locally the two Atlanta major daily, morning and evening, newspapers. Upon his completing high school, Luella had plans for her

son to attend the college where she'd heard her Cousin Clarence had gone. Morehouse in Atlanta. Oscar and his son Clarence never got to do very much together.

Oscar and Luella, once the baby was born, didn't get to do very much together either. Oscar's idea of socializing was to take Luella and Clarence with him to church and afterwards go spend the rest of the day at the home of his parents, the husband figuring that the wife, having no living parent of her own, needed to be in the presence of someone else's folks. In the beginning Oscar's family adored the beautifully mannered and prettily petite Luella. (So tiny was she in comparison to the oversized Hemphills that among themselves they accused her of having worms.) But as time passed they started to feel she was a bit too proper for their tastes—especially when they weren't able to see their first grandchild, Clarence, as often as they felt was their due, at least every Sunday following church. Luella hadn't wanted her son spending too much time in the company of her husband's folks, or his friends, lest the child pick up too many of their bad habits, particularly poor grammar and ill manners. Oscar accused her of always trying to "talk just like the white folks" while teaching their son to do the same. But she didn't pay her husband, his folks, nor his friends any mind, as she was determined that her son was to grow up to become a gentleman and not some seed warehouse worker. Oscar's coarseness riled Luella's roots. Oftentimes at the dining table he would let go with a belch without so much as covering his mouth or, if she didn't remind him to do so on the spot, excusing himself. But what really got her back up around her neck and even made her hate the man for it was when he would frequently and thoughtlessly break wind right next to her and the child just as if they weren't even in the room, or the house. Lord, she was *determined* her son Clarence wasn't going to grow up to be like his daddy.

~ Chapter 5 ~

   Luella still remembered the day, the very instant, less than three years earlier, when she first felt the pain. It was ten times the pain of her wedding night of the sledgehammer and crowbar. The lump was there earlier but she'd thought, prayed, it would go away. It didn't. It just got larger. She didn't tell anyone, not even Oscar, who wouldn't have noticed it anyway. Nor did she want to go to the doctor, whom she knew would want to operate. When the pain became too much to bear she finally went but told the doctor he could operate only if he thought it could be saved. He promised her it would be saved. She believed him. But when she awoke following the operation, gone was her left breast. She cried and cried. Before she left the hospital the doctor promised her everything now was all right. She believed him. Until, even before the operation had time to heal, she found the lump in her right breast. This time she *pleaded* with the doctor to save this one. He promised her he would save this one. She wanted to believe him. When she awoke this time to find her last breast gone she didn't cry. Just didn't understand why God would want to take away her body's most beautiful feature. The doctor told her this time everything for sure was going to be all right. She no longer cared. Then, weeks later, in the middle of the night, she was unmercifully awakened by a lightning shot of pain rooting around in her chest. Back to the hospital where, her not having another breast for them to chop off, they could do nothing to stop the cancer submarining beneath the scars mapping her chest. That, Lord, is when Luella came home to die her way.

~ Chapter 6 ~

"Hi ya feel?" Oscar walked into his wife's sickroom.

"Pretty good, right now." Luella was sitting up in bed, her back resting against pillows propped against the headboard. Her soft, baby-blue cotton gown, like the color of the bedclothing and the room's decor, matched the brightness of spring radiating through the window that Sunday afternoon. "How was church?"

"Righ' nice. Kin I gitcha some'n?" Oscar stopped at the foot of the bed.

"No, thank you. I just had lunch. Many people at church?"

"Hadda righ' good tun'out t'day. Momma say she will be com'n by to holla at ya."

"Just as long as she doesn't holler too loud and too long." Luella gave a half-and-half smile and snicker. Even during her last days here she still hadn't gotten used to Oscar's slang. "The roof is not leaking today so you can take off your hat." Taking off his blue felt hat to reveal a head of steadily-sliding-backwards hair, Oscar, for lack of knowing what else to do or say, moved around to sit in the straightback chair alongside the bed.

"Ya look good t'day."

"Thank you," Luella said, closing her eyes, almost as if sighing.

Dressed in his dark blue suit (Luella liked light colors against her husband's dark brown skin), Oscar of the soft brown eyes and warm smile was well known for weighing, many felt too long, his every word before dropping it off his tongue. Sitting there beside his wife he, like always, felt very self-conscious, even now, when he knew she was dying. He'd felt this way even when they were young and in Sunday school together. Even back then he was always listening and she talking—though not talking to him because, he figured then, she never even knew he existed. Until that Sunday at church when at the age of nineteen he somehow got up the nerve to ask her, sixteen, could he "Come ovah sometimes?"

"Come over where?"

"To yo' house?"

"For what?"

"To...to...to see ya." For what seemed like both their lifetimes she just stood staring at him and his self-consciousness as if he'd asked her the most stupid question imaginable before confidently throwing back her head, automatically shooting out her chest, and saying,

"If you behave yourself."

He did. That's why he was so surprised, stunned, two years later when after numerous courting visits to her house without so much as touching her, *anywhere,* even once, she suddenly started acting toward him as if she knew he existed, even liked him. Less than two months later they were married. His folks, all uneducated but hard workers, were so proud of their son and happy for him for having made what they, and everyone else, felt to be a real catch. Besides being one of the county's prettiest and most beautifully mannered girls, Luella at eighteen became sole inheritor of her late mother's seven-room house and its acre and a half of land. Oscar hadn't understood why out of all of Luella's many male admirers he'd been the lucky one, especially after so long when she never appeared the least bit interested in anything he did or said. In fact, she'd never seemed to stop long enough to even listen to anything he'd ever had to say. She was one of those very much interested in school and educated folks and things they had to say and do. Meanwhile, he had dropped out of school in the eighth grade and gone to work at Singleton Seed Company alongside his daddy, who had never even gone to school. It was due to this "miracle" marriage that Oscar began believing strongly in God, thus starting him attending regularly his family's church. But not for long.

"Let's change churches," Luella suggested to him one Sunday the summer of their marriage while they were en route home from their house of worship, Bethel Baptist, Muskhogean's biggest black church.

"Change churches?" Oscar was bewildered.

"Yes. Let's try a new one for a while and see how we like it. If we don't like it we can always come back to Bethel."

"But why leave? Wha's wrong wit' Bethel?"

"There's too much hollering and shouting going on all the time. Let's go to one a little more quiet...and more refined."

"Go wheah? All churches is 'bout the same."

"Not Wesley."

So Luella led him "up the tracks" to Wesley, of the Methodist faith, located in the small elite black section of Appalachee and supported primarily by this compact group. This bold venture by Luella started the early rift between her and her husband's family. For having carried their Oscar up the tracks to Wesley, the Hemphills immediately accused her publicly of "putting on airs." From his very first visit, Oscar never felt comfortable in the less populated, much quieter, and, according to Luella, more "refined" atmosphere of Wesley. After sitting a few Sundays in this new, calm and composed, religious environment, Oscar realized he much preferred the get-down-with-God feeling slapped on his soul

weekly "down the tracks" at Bethel. Soon, and despite his own low-keyed style, Oscar found himself unable to sit through another one of what he felt were Wesley's "silent" sermons and one day said to his wife, "We done changed churches fuh awhile now, ain' it 'bout time we got back to our real one?"

"NO!" Luella quickly shot back. "Wesley *is* my real church!" And, Lord, she proved this to her husband that very next Sunday by up and joining the Methodist church! Now, again, Lord, this put Oscar right smack dab in the middle in between his wife and his family and friends (and You too, Lord, because You knew Oscar wanted badly to someday be a deacon in the church and You and he both knew You weren't gonna let him be one up the tracks at Wesley), who all talked behind his back about Luella wearing the pants in that marriage. But the truth was, Oscar loved his young and pretty wife so deeply that he would've done anything in the world for her...except join Wesley. He didn't join up there but now that the person he cared more for than anyone else in the world was an official member of the "proper" black church, he felt it was God's will for him to attend Wesley with his wife. When his son Clarence was born, Oscar had secretly wanted the boy to grow up attending Bethel where, the father felt, he would learn the real Negro religion. But, again, Lord, this was not meant to be, as Luella stuck the child under her wing and right away flew with him off to Wesley, where as a youngster he joined.

True, Oscar loved Luella madly but he certainly never understood her. To him, even after *she* almost asked *him* to marry her, she still seemed totally disinterested in anything he said or did, other than his fixing things and doing odd jobs around the house, which he was a master at and never appeared to tire of doing, nor she of telling him to do. Early on he saw that she was determined to raise Clarence *her* way, keeping him most of the time in the company of her and her select circle of friends and away from him and his much larger group of acquaintances. By the time the son was in his teens, the father, like towards the mother, found himself feeling self-conscious, totally uneasy, in the boy's presence. He never knew exactly what to say to Clarence, his own son, who by this time not only had a much better command of the English language than Oscar but could already talk even "whiter" than Luella. In their presence Oscar kept mostly shut up. Despite owning his mother's way of speaking, and manners, Clarence was built like his father—tall and big-boned. Even if Luella hadn't wanted the boy to go hunting with his father for fear of his getting shot, Oscar wished he'd been allowed to play football, a game he seemed so equipped to play. But again, here was drawn Luella's line. Oscar never really learned how to explain to his folks and friends why his big, athletic-looking son while in high school rather than play football read all the time.

All through his marriage, Oscar had kept, and still loved, his job at

Singleton, where he eventually became the first black supervisor in the history of the company. And for the first time ever, Luella, upon learning of this promotion, showed some interest in his job...for a while. Meanwhile, his Hemphill folks were extremely proud of his accomplishments at Singleton...but retained their strong doubts about his marriage.

When Luella switched her and Oscar's religious allegiances from Bethel to Wesley (where it was said that at baptizing time they washed folks' feet rather than dunk their souls) the couple's Sunday-after-church Hemphill visits came to a blasphemous halt. The families now saw each other in their homes only during special and rare occasions, such as on holidays or during the times of weddings, sickness, and funerals.

Luella, with the help of Oscar, kept an immaculate house, garden, and yard—oftentimes too much so for the husband, who, although he didn't mind, in fact loved, doing the handiwork around the place yet never felt really comfortable in the house itself, which he thought was kept a mite too clean and orderly for a man to kick off his shoes and spread himself out in. He and Luella had no mutual friends. His friends he felt she made no effort whatsoever to like and her friends he often tried to but just couldn't like, mainly because he felt they looked down at him. At the beginning of their marriage, on every Friday, payday, night he would bring home a friend or two and a few bottles of beer. This, except for on those special occasions of holidays, etc., was the only time Oscar drank, but even so just the smell of alcohol made Luella sick to the stomach. So, eventually, Oscar stopped bringing home a buddy or two and bottles of beer. Luella didn't complain. Now on Friday night after work he would visit a buddy or two, and his drinking over the years remained constant, an average of three beers per week. But three beers too many for the nondrinking Luella.

Oscar never truly thought Luella meant his family or his friends any harm by her actions. He just felt this was her lady way of doing things. But once in the bedroom he felt being married to her made everything else worthwhile. In there he would go out of his mind nearly over her petite, soft body, grabbing onto her beautiful butt, his favorite part of her to hold, and never getting enough of her, no matter how many times he had her. But, secretly, he sometimes wished she would be a bit more snappy in the bedroom like she was outside of it. He supposed, though, that being a lady meant a woman wasn't supposed to enjoy fucking like a man did. But more than her enjoying doing it with him, which he wished she could, Oscar wanted his wife's, *and* his son's, love, neither of which he had ever felt he truly had.

Slow of speech, Oscar certainly wasn't slow of foot, continuously walking the warehouse floor from morning to night busily supervising the handling of the daily incoming and outgoing seed shipments. Even at home he kept on the move, fixing and mending. Unlike his son, who could do so by the hours, Oscar didn't care for reading anything except for the newspaper, and when he tried to watch anything other than the news on television he always fell asleep and snored, causing Luella to shake and snap at him until he would get up and leave the room to go fix something or go off to bed to await his wife, who by the time she got there had lost all her snap.

He didn't like sitting and watching her for too long because it always brought him near tears to see life being drained from her still-young face that daily looked less and less like his pretty and petite Luella.

"You went to Bethel?" Her eyes were still closed.

"Uh...uh...yeah."

"When are you going back up to Wesley?" Her eyes now opened.

"I...I don' know. Maybe nex' Sunday."

"You've been saying that for a long time now. I'd like to know how some of the folks up there are doing. They are probably wondering what happened to me...to us."

"I'll git back up theah soon." He couldn't bring himself to tell her that that was why he had stopped going up to Wesley in the first place—not because she didn't take him like everybody claimed she'd always done but because on the Sundays he went up there alone following her illness not one single person, female nor male, had ever asked him about his wife, the die-for-Wesley-lover. That's why he had stopped going up the tracks to that stuckup church! Meanwhile, down the tracks at Bethel, the church his wife no longer liked and where now he'd started back going alone, practically everybody he saw wanted to know about Luella's health. Just that day, like every Sunday, some of his folks and a few others from Bethel were stopping in to see her, who, he sat thinking, was never too pleased at hearing this from him. But, he knew, that was his Luella. A lady to the last.

"It's funny that nobody from Wesley has been by to see me yet. Maybe they're thinking by you not coming up there to church anymore we don't want any of them coming down here to see me. That's why you ought to go back. Now be sure you go up there next Sunday. It would be nice to see some of the Wesley members again, rather than seeing Bethel folks all the time. You've got to *promise* me you'll go back up there this coming Sunday." Her eyes were still opened, aimed right on him.

"I...I promise."

"Good! You've never broken a promise to me yet, *that* I know. Now, honey, I want to doze for a few minutes before that Bethel crowd gets here, so go and find Sugarfoot and you two talk to one another, you hear?"

"I heah ya." He got up and left the room as she closed her eyes.

Built right after World War II, Luella's white frame house with the green trim and roof sat in the middle of one and one-half acres of lawn and garden in the nicest part of what was once known as "Dark Town" but had since officially changed to "Thompson Town." The new name came from the late Big Man, and his wife Little Bit, Thompson, called Dark Town's King and Queen from their marriage in 1918 to the husband's death in 1936 and the wife's in 1963. Luella's house stood directly across the street from the old Thompsons' throne, still standing in the form of a little two-room house since remodeled and now lived in by the couple's only child, Blue. A teacher at the local high school, Blue Thompson was better known, and loved or hated, for being the county's, and area's, most active civil, and human, rights activist. Luella's house had two bedrooms, a spacious parlor, a guest room, a huge kitchen large enough for the family to eat and entertain guests in, a laundry room, bathroom, long hallway, and screened-in front and back porches.

The house's interior was, no question at all, pure Luella. All bright, airish colors dominated by light blues and tans. Sitting in the living room on the seablue sofa watching the giant color television when Oscar walked in from his wife's bedside was Luella's "Sugarfoot," his son, Clarence.

"Hi you." The father came from the room adjoining and stopped alongside to peer down at the small figures on the big screen.

"All right."

"Who's play'n?"

"Braves and Cards."

"Who's winning?"

"Braves."

Figuring he had asked the right questions, Oscar moved on across the room to sit silently on the opposite end of the sofa from his son. Oscar, the doer, was an extremely poor spectator at anything outside the church. He definitely was not a TV man. The only things that interested him on the eyeball-box, sometimes, were the news, weather, and the spiritual singing which he'd once watched. But all of these things he much preferred listening to over the radio while he worked with his hands at something else. He considered everything on film as nothing

more than make believe, and therefore was unable to bring himself to take seriously either TV or the picture show. Even a church service on TV didn't move him; he felt folks ought to go out of the house for God rather than sit waiting for Him to come on "the tube" to them. Sports he felt the same way about. Games, to Oscar, were meant to be played, *and* watched, outdoors, not in the house. The house as far as he was concerned was meant mainly to eat, sleep, and stay out of the weather in—certainly not to be used to sit up and watch a ballgame in. But on this particular Sunday with his wife dying he felt it his duty for him and his son to spend some time together in the house to be near her...even if it meant sitting in front of an eyeball-box watching a children's game God intended to be played and watched outdoors. Oscar even suffered sitting at Wesley, where Luella had to constantly nudge him to keep him awake to listen to the, for him, dull sermon being delivered by the low-keyed minister.

Oscar came from that generation who enjoyed going to church because once inside the house of God they knew they would be kept awake by a preacher who knew how to entertain them. The preacher knew that in their hearts the congregation wanted to be told they'd sinned and had better get their souls right with God or else—while the preacher also flattered them by telling them their own sins were of enough importance to catch the attention of the busy Almighty Himself. The preacher put them each Sunday on center stage beneath the special spotlight beamed down from on high while God and Satan fought verbally 'twixt heaven and hell over their, immortal, souls. That was one reason why Oscar continued to drink his three beers every week—sin enough, he felt, to keep God fighting with the devil to win his soul. Also, being poor, the congregation just loved it whenever the preacher socked it to the souls of the rich by raving on about how *none* of them were going to enter God's kingdom. Only down here's poor would be up there in heaven, "po's paradise," where they'd strut their stuff beneath shiny gold halos in their long white silk robes and patent leather sandals while feasting on milk, honey, and grapes, loving everybody up there, praising God in song, and every so often sneaking a peek over the edge of the clouds down into hell where all the rich roasted. Amen.

Clarence, everybody said, took his body from his daddy and his momma gave him his mind. All through high school and college he kept busily answering no to all those wanting to know if he was an athlete, particularly a football player. Though he might've looked like a football player, Clarence didn't like the game of football at all. Too much planned violence, he told everyone. His game was baseball. He loved the game. There was just one drawback as far as he and baseball were concerned. He was no good at playing it. He couldn't hit the curve ball and couldn't throw the fast ball. He had a good arm from the outfield but baseball had no df, designated fielder. Yet he never stopped trying to play, or loving, the game. But with his physique everyone, including the local high school coaches, kept telling him he should go out for football, where he would stand a much better chance of earning a college scholarship than by playing baseball. All to no avail as Clarence, with assistance from Luella, insisted upon sticking with the non-contact sport of baseball, where he never made the high school team.

During his school days in Appalachee his peers were well aware of Clarence being a "momma's boy" but, and despite his mild manner, no one of them ever dared say this to his face because of his size. Big. Not baby fat big but muscular big. While growing up Clarence's father was always wanting him to do those things the son never particularly liked doing. Things like fixing, building, mending, growing, cutting, and countless other chores around the house. His father loved doing things with his hands. But Clarence loved doing things with his mind. His mind could hold many more things at one time than could his hands. The more his mind grew the more things Clarence wanted to do and be: baseball player, actor, pilot, adventurer, playboy, filmmaker, philanthropist, private detective, ad nauseum. While his father never seemed interested in anything he was, and vice versa, Clarence's mother appeared caught up in every single one of her son's dreams—all the while telling her husband not to interfere with the boy's dreams because someday he was going to be somebody famous. Yet she didn't quite want it to be in baseball.

So crowded was the boy's mind with daydreams that he rarely had room in there for anything else. Like school studies. But by being a bright student when need be, Clarence, accused by his teachers of always overcrowding the path to least resistance, managed good enough high school grades to be, barely, accepted into Morehouse College in Atlanta. Cousin Clarence's alma mater.

To be whom he wanted to be, someone famous or at least extraordinarily interesting, Clarence didn't know what to major in at college. But for sure he wanted *nothing* involving numbers. Suddenly, from the sky one day struck inspiration. He would become a writer! He'd always been an avid reader and a lover of the printed word, so he became an English major. But before reaching for pen and pad he went out and bought himself a pipe, a tan tweed sport jacket with dark brown leather elbow patches, and a best-selling novel to carry about the college campus with him at all times. Now Clarence was ready to be a writer, if not quite ready to write. He became obsessed with writers, spending most of his college freshman year in the library reading more *about* writers than reading their works. Eventually, he began seeking out on campus others interested in writing in order to talk to them about other writers, usually over a cup of java, or a cold one, all the while puffing on his pipe, wearing his tweed even during the warm months, and clutching a novel. Clarence read about and discussed writers from Homer to Baraka, spending so much time at it that his grades began suffering more than usual. He did little to no writing himself, figuring that once he was out of college inspiration would have a much better chance of striking through his then-less-crowded mind. Meanwhile, he continued to learn as much as possible about writers and their histories, believing that by doing so he'd somehow discover the real secret to writing. One thing he found out soon was that quite a number of history's famous writers never even went to college.

"Mother, I'm not going back to college," Clarence told Luella right following the end of his freshman year while the two sat in the living room on the seablue sofa watching television, she knitting in between peeks. From outside could be heard Oscar hammering.

"Why...why not, Sugarfoot?" Luella stopped everything to look straight at her son.

"I want to be a writer and college ruins writers."

"I thought in order to be a writer you had to finish college."

"Only if you write for a newspaper."

"Then why don't you write for a newspaper when you get out?"

"That's factual, not creative, writing."

"What's the difference between those two kinds of writing?"

"Night and day. Fact dictates what a writer writes. While the fiction, or creative, writer *is* the dictator."

"Oh."

"And in order for me to learn to write I've got to live the real life, not the insulated life college offers, and the sooner I get started the better."

Luella, tears blurring her vision, turned back to her knitting. Outside, Oscar hammered on.

Clarence's dream was to go live in the one place in America where he'd often read and heard that many great writers, and other artists, lived and worked: a village in the city of New York called "Greenwich." Thus, Lord, in the year of our Lord 1976, nineteen-year-old Clarence Henry Hemphill departed Appalachee, Georgia, for New York City, New York, to live the consecrated life of the writer. When he left on that early summer morning, Luella, after packing him a lunch large enough to last most writers a week and stuffing his wallet with money enough to last most writers a book, hugged and kissed her only-born goodbye before beginning a summer-long cry. Oscar, following a father-and-son hand-shake, went right back to hammering.

Clarence the writer didn't write letters. Instead, he telephoned home, collect, from New York weekly while Luella, unable to return calls to his phoneless apartment, answered him each time with a manuscript of a letter to which the writer would reply with another collect call. Then, Clarence suddenly stopped calling, causing Luella to write even longer manuscripts more often. After going nearly a month without hearing from her only child, the mother, fearing he had been the victim of a New York City terrorist, seriously considered calling the police department up there to check on her son. Instead she decided to pack and go North herself to find her Sugarfooot. But, Lord, before Luella could finish packing for the trip North, Clarence was back South.

Clarence returned just in time to enroll at Morehouse. He'd sud-denly decided that in order to live the way he wanted to as a writer he would upon graduation become a teacher and write on the side. He didn't volunteer any information about his summer in New York. When pressed he only talked about "the Village" and his favorite haunt there, a cafe he just called "Le Figaro's." But he never talked about why he suddenly left there and returned home.

Graduating from college, Clarence came back to Appalachee where he immediately landed a position teaching at Muskhogean County's middle school. Luella was ecstatic at having her Sugarfoot back home and insisted he keep his old room in her house, rent free. He accepted. Oscar, too, was glad to see his son returning and didn't mind him staying back home but did think it strange, and being one of few words found it even more difficult to explain to his male friends why a son of his built like a football player wanted to be a schoolteacher—a woman's job. Sometimes during brief pauses between hammering, although Oscar didn't want to, on occasion his mind would ask, was his son a sissy?

Clarence chose to teach middle school, fourth through eighth grades, because he knew children during these years were much more curious and eager to learn, especially the boys, and therefore easier to teach than high schoolers, who by their ages knew everything except what was in their textbooks. Clarence's students immediately took to him, the dreamer, with his limitless imagination, which kept them constantly entertained and, most important, interested. But it wasn't too long before he began running into disfavor with the school authorities. Clarence knew that in order to be true to the brotherhood of writers, it was his duty not to act normal. That is, he had to stray from the mainstream, the bourgeois, by finding, or creating, within Appalachee, his own "village." This, Lord, meant Luella's Sugarfoot hanging out among Appalachee's unpretentious. The no-putting-on-airs folks. The "po'."

Years earlier there'd been several hangouts for the black po' over in, then, Dark Town but now that the section was Thompson Town it, despite the housing project being over there, was busily striving for middle-class respectability. Even Appalachee's old back, black street, for more than a century known as the Alley, had been taken over by a ring of realtors, fathers of the bulldozer, and renamed "the Avenue." The only place in the black community where parents, and wives, could warn their children, and husbands, against going to now was way out on the outskirts, on the south end, of town. The Trailer Park. Lord! Capitol, or headquarters, of the Trailer Park was the only decent "knock down drag out" po' black juke joint yet alive in Appalachee, the Salad Patch. Lord! Out here on the south end of town at the Salad Patch, where the beer was cold and the music hot and one could always count on a good Saturday night argument, or even catch a fight or, if one got lucky, a shooting (among the young blacks the bullet had replaced the blade), came a pencil-and-pad-armed Clarence.

The Salad Patch crowd didn't right away take to drinking beer with a schoolteacher. Not that any of this crowd feared catching the "proper talk" disease, but they were puzzled as to why a schoolteacher, of all people, wanted to hang out with them? True, the schoolteacher talked all of that proper talk but, man, they all thought, he looked like a football player! Thus nobody out there gave the big man who taught the little children at school any lip for fear of getting it fattened.

The Salad Patch was mostly one huge square room of bare wood floor and tables with chairs. Sitting in one corner of the room was a big, old-fashioned juke box filled with soul sounds. From a small semiclosed kitchen nothing was served but beer and barbeque. The door to the much smaller back room, where there were only chairs, was always kept closed. Going back behind this door went only the elite, Appalachee's old-time juke joint crowd and their friends, the old-timers who remembered and talked about the days of yore of Dark Town: the, or Red, Alley, Earnest Moore's poolroom, Sam's Cafe, Red's, and the short-lived Baby Sweet's whorehouse. Sitting in the one rocker back there in the middle of the group reliving these long-ago days and nights day after night after day while recalling the deeds of Muskhogean County's legendary figures of those times—Boots, Big Man Thompson, Baby Sweet, and Appalachee Red—was an old-timer who upon hearing there was someone in the outer room who had been to New York City, immediately sent for him. Thus Clarence was led back into the sacred backroom where he met the man in the rocker, Big Apple. From this little, aged, prune-faced man, Clarence was to learn a side of Appalachee's history mothers didn't talk about and schoolbooks didn't print. Practically every weekend night soon found him in the backroom of the Salad Patch, listening.

The thing that had worried Clarence most about whether or not he would ever become a writer was his drinking. He felt he didn't drink enough. But, secretly, he hated the taste of the stuff, especially beer. Besides, it always made him sick. Whenever he got the opportunity he drank a little wine—white wine, as unlike the red it didn't purple his teeth, though being a proper-talking schoolteacher who talked about "preferring" wine over beer surely weren't virtues to endear one to the hearts of the Salad Patch crowd. Yet this group gradually came to accept this big football-looking weirdo who seemed to actually enjoy being around them and whom they came to call "Teach." Meanwhile, Teach had to stomach beer as the Salad Patch didn't sell wine of any tint.

Big Apple didn't sit in the rocker every night. On occasion the backroom throne would be occupied by a tall, lean, and real dark man a generation or so younger than Big Apple. Whenever this man appeared, about once or twice a month, Big Apple didn't. Talk was blood ran bad between these two. This younger man was called "Bird," said to've been an Alley badass at one time. But most important to Clarence was this man's claim of having pitched baseball in the old Negro Major Leagues. All Bird sat on the backroom throne talking about was baseball—except on occasion, when he got real drunk, and then his talk always ended near tears over the woman of local legend, Baby Sweet. (The same old Miss Baby Sweet who now lived alone on the top floor of the town's back street, the Avenue's, realtor building—the building folks talked about having once been a cafe...and then a house of prostitution—and who came downstairs every morning after the postman had gone to ask the receptionist at the desk right inside the door if there had been any mail for her. There never was. Talk was she for years had been awaiting a letter from an "Appalachee Red.") But it was after listening to Bird that Clarence finally hit on what his first book was going to be about. Baseball! Believing "real" writers only wrote about two sports, baseball and boxing, Clarence thus decided to concentrate solely on writing the Great American Baseball Novel.

Clarence, like most lovers of the game, especially writers, had always thought of baseball as being purely a battle of pitcher versus batter until one day he happened to mention this in the presence of his neighbor, Blue, who disagreed with this purist concept by saying,

"Baseball is *not* batter versus pitcher, it's batter versus *nine* men, the entire other team, and sometimes even the umpire. If you think not then tell the pitcher to send his eight defensive men off the field and face the batter one on one without their help. Unlike in basketball, where in a man-to-man defense one-versus-one takes place all the time and a teammate can come to the aid of the man with the ball by receiving a pass, the baseball batter is up there at the plate all alone and the only thing besides himself that can help him get on base is a misplay by the other team." Clarence listened to this with interest but he still liked the old time-honored pitcher-solely-against-hitter theory, which to him sounded more romantic.

Bird took to Teach. Because to him Teach listened. Teach liked Bird also because he now had a main character for his Great American Baseball Novel.

Clarence was very attractive, and attracted, to the opposite sex. He respected them. Whenever he had had the opportunity to place the female into the heat of passion and she gasped out to him "don't!" he didn't. Thus, as a teenager he never did. The biggest "don'ter" of his young life had been Inez Blackshear, his long-time childhood sweetheart. But along came his adult life and the year of the Salad Patch (Inez absolutely refused to ever go there with him) when he met Lizzie Lee Lester, who didn't "don't!" him and they did. So much so that:

"Mother."

"Yes, Sugarfoot." Luella put aside what she was preparing for Oscar to finish.

"I'm getting married."

"Oooh, Sugarfoot! I'm soooooo happy for you and Inez!" Luella cried and grinned from lobe to lobe while reaching up to throw her hands around her son's neck. Luella simply adored the beautiful Inez of the family Blackshear, considered Muskhogean's wealthiest blacks.

"But I'm not marrying Inez."

"Oh?" The grin quickly zipped up.

"No. I'm marrying Lizzie Lee Lester."

"Who?" Her hands slid down from around his neck.

"Lizzie Lee Lester. You'll like her."

"No I won't. Who's her family?"

"She's the daughter of Miz Annie Bea Lester."

"Who's her father?"

"I haven't met him yet."

"Has *she* met him yet?"

"I don't know. I never asked."

"Where does she live?"

"In the Trailer Park."

Luella fainted.

Clarence well knew Lizzie Lee wasn't the refined lady Inez was, and he also knew his mother adored Inez to death and had always wanted him to marry into the Blackshear family, those eminent members of Wesley. But he found Lizzie Lee much sweeter and less complicated than Inez and so, to the relief of (not Inez herself who despite all of her don'ts did dig Clarence) her family, whom he knew didn't want their daughter marrying a down-the-track Thompson Towner, Clarence married his Trailer Park pet. Not long following the wedding, Luella seemed to lose interest in everything and everybody around her, excluding Sugarfoot.

"Momma 'n some folks from Bethel will be heah soon to holla at Luella," Oscar cut in on his son's game.

"Did you tell Mother?" Clarence's eyes still followed the pitch.

"Yeah, I tol'er."

"What did she say?"

"She wanted to go back to sleep." The sudden crowd noise exploding from the box caught the father's attention for a few brief seconds before he continued, "You been up to Wesley lately?"

"No." Not being addressed as "sir" by his son also worked on Oscar.

"I ax 'cause yo' momma wondahs why nobody from up theah ain' been down heah to see her since she been sick. The two times I was up theah since she come home from the hospital not one soul at Wesley ax' me how she was. I ain' been back up theah since."

"Maybe they didn't know she was sick."

"They knowed. They up theah jes don' care. Nevah did care 'bout us. But I nevah could tell yo' momma that 'n I sho can' tell her that nobody up theah wanna come down heah to see her now." Oscar's voice almost broke. Clarence's eyes just kept following the pitch.

Unable to sit watching the box a minute longer and knowing sadly that he wasn't in any way going to get his son's undivided attention in discussing Luella, Oscar got up and quietly left the room. Moving on down the hallway he stopped outside the open door of the kitchen. In here his daughter-in-law was busy cooking Sunday's dinner in between watching the picture on the small color television talking from a corner of the kitchen. On her set, Oscar knew, one never saw a ballgame. Only picture shows. "Some folks from church will be com'n ovah soon to holla at Luella!" he hollered over the sound of the TV at her while walking straight through the kitchen's thick aromas on out the back door to his tool shed to something "real."

~ Chapter 9 ~

Everybody said Lizzie Lee Lester had been the prettiest child you'd ever laid eyeball to. So pretty had the little girl been that her mother, who still had the pictures to prove this prettiness, often told her during these young years that she was going to grow up to someday become a famous movie star and make her mother a lot of money. Then, Lord, innocently she'd entered adolescence and somewhere in the jungle of that awkward, sensitive, teenage nightmare the real Lizzie Lee had gotten lost, or became too embarrassed or frightened to emerge. Emerging with her name only was a tall, gangly, and no-longer-pretty imposter. Seeing this new creature everybody said that a girl couldn't do anything with such a tall, titless body except use it to play basketball. But Lizzie Lee had never liked basketball, even came to hate it when everyone kept insisting she go out for the girl's high school team. Lord, Lizzie Lee still wanted to be the movie star her mother had promised her as a little girl she would someday grow up to be.

The no-longer-pretty Lizzie Lee, the oldest of three children, saw her mother turn her back on her to concentrate on the youngest child, whom the parent promised was going to grow up someday to be a famous singer and make a lot of money for the mother. About Lizzie Lee, the mother regretted she wasn't a boy who with all of that tallness could someday become a famous basketball player and make a lot of money for his mother. Well, Lizzie Lee wasn't interested in making a whole lot of money for anyone; she, especially after seeing the old film *A Raisin in the Sun,* just wanted to be a movie star. Ruby Dee.

After graduating from high school in 1978 and in order to save enough money to take the Greyhound bus to Hollywood, or wherever Ruby Dee lived, Lizzie Lee got a job at the Salad Patch. Because it was there that while starring in a film on location in the area the actor Richard Pryor was rumored one Saturday night to be on his way to the Salad Patch. That was two years earlier and he hadn't shown yet, but simply on the chance he just might still show up, Lord, Lizzie Lee Lester would be there ready and willing to be discovered by Richard, whom she also figured must've known where Ruby Dee lived. Movie stars, she'd read, or heard, were more likely to be discovered in restaurants than in factories, where she hadn't bothered looking for a job. She didn't particularly like her job, as most of the customers weren't nice to her at all, so in order to get through the, especially weekend, nights, while she worked she pretended the whole Salad Patch scene was a movie being filmed with her playing the lead star, Ruby Dee.

It was here at the Salad Patch where she began taking notice of the big, good-looking, looking-out-of-place, quiet gentleman who always wore the same tweed sport jacket with the leather patches on the elbows and was never without his pen and notepad. And he was always smoking—mostly lighting—a pipe and nursing the same beer all night. He was usually in the back room puffing, lighting, and nursing while sitting listening to the old Black Jew, Big Apple, and the Bird talk on and on about way back yonder when. Sometimes he stopped lighting his pipe long enough to jot something down in his notebook. Lizzie Lee took an immediate liking to this big man because unlike most males she'd ever known, whenever he addressed her he always spoke softly and kindly— like when he ordered beer, which he always bought for those he sat listening to. In playing out her nightly role there at the Salad Patch she began pretending this big quiet man was Ossie Davis.

"What are you always writing?" Lizzie Lee stood at the table of the big nice gentleman sitting alone on this slow Salad Patch night.

"A book." Putting down his pen to light his pipe.

"You are a *writer?!*"

"Yes." Striking a second match to the pipe.

"Do you write for the movies?"

"Not yet." Striking a third.

"It's all right if you use me in your book because just as soon as I make enough money working here I'm leaving for Hollywood to become a movie star. Did you ever see the movie *A Raisin in the Sun* with Ruby Dee? She's my favorite."

"I saw *Raisin* but I enjoyed Ruby much better in person." Puffing, hard.

"In person?"

"On the stage." Striking another match.

"YOU SAW RUBY DEE ON THE STAGE?!"

"Yes." Another.

"Where?!"

"In New York." A third.

"New York City?! *You* been there?!"

"Yes. During my formative writing days." Puffing, hard.

"Why did you come back here?"

"I...I can write better here. The city, especially the Village where I hung out, offered too many distractions for a serious writer." Laying the pipe, unlit, on the table.

"Parties all the time?"

"All the time."

"Lord, God, you actually *saw* Ruby Dee! Did she do some good acting?"

"Exceptional."

"Someday I hope to be as good as she is. Did you get her autograph?"

"No. At the time I was with a group of people so I didn't go backstage. We were on our way to Le Figaro's in the Village."

"Did you meet many famous people in New York?"

"A few."

"Who?"

"One I met was Moses Gunn."

"You met *Moses Gunn?!*"

"Yes."

"Where?"

"At a party."

"Another one of those parties, huh? Was his bodyguard with him?"

"Bodyguard?"

"Don't all movie stars have bodyguards?"

"There were so many people at this party that I couldn't tell if Moses had one or not."

"Ruby Dee got Ossie Davis so she doesn't need a bodyguard. Hey, you wanna 'nother beer?

"This one is on me," she whispered upon returning and placing the cold can in front of him.

"I appreciate it."

"I'm Lizzie Lee. What's your name, besides 'Teach'?" She felt better around this man than any other male she'd ever been around before in her life.

"Clarence."

"Clarence who?"

"Hemphill."

"Oh! You Missis Luella Hemphill's son?"

"That's me."

"I know about you. Your momma is a real pretty lady. She sure keeps her house and yard looking real pretty too. I saw y'all house once."

"Thank you. Mother and Father work hard around the house. Are you at the high school?"

"No more. I finished last year. Is Ruby Dee your kind of woman?"

"Yes, I like Ruby." Picking up his pipe and striking a match.

After that night, Lizzie Lee sneaked Clarence at least one free beer every time he came in the restaurant when she was there, and the writer and the movie star nonathletes soon got to enjoy each other's company so much that he took to waiting for her after work and driving her home. Then came the night she snuck him an extra beer and before letting her out of the car at her door he, feeling his drinks, suddenly grabbed and, removing his, unlit, pipe, kissed her and she didn't "don't" him and it was done. Nicely.

Following their engagement, Lizzie Lee, strongly sensing from their very first meeting, or confrontation, that Missis Luella didn't cotton to her at all, suggested to Clarence they buy a trailer and move to Hollywood, or the Village, where they could get married and live. But Clarence, recalling seeing no trailer parks in the Village, insisted upon their staying in Appalachee until he finished, and sold, his book. He promised her that once the book was sold they, if the work was bought for a Broadway play, would immediately move to the Village or, if it was bought up for a movie, to Hollywood. Thus Lizzie Lee, until all this came to pass, agreed to put on hold, temporarily they both felt, her dream of becoming the next Ruby Dee.

Upon Luella's insistence the wedding, the reception, the honeymoon, and the couple all were held under her roof. Amen.

The Bethel folks came, hollered at and sad-faced Luella, and left. Then the family Hemphill ate their Sunday dinner. Finishing up the after-dinner cleaning, Lizzie Lee, apron over blue jeans, left the kitchen to look in on Luella, who had recovered from being "hollered" at and was now trying to recuperate from another bout with her daughter-in-law's cooking.

"Anything else I can gitcha?"

"No. But next time let your chicken cook a little longer. It shouldn't be bleeding."

"The piece I had won't bleeding."

"Where's Sugarfoot?"

"He's in the room writing his book. You want him?"

"If he's writing don't disturb him."

"If it's important...."

"*Nothing* a mother ever does is very important. You'll learn that someday, I hope. Where's my husband?"

"Out back in the tool shed. Want me to call him?"

"No. You finished up in the kitchen?"

"Yes, ma'am."

"What you got to do now?"

"There's a good picture coming up on channel 36."

"Don't you ever get tired of watching soap operas all the time?"

"This ain't a soap opera. It's an old movie filmed in Hollywood. I only watch soaps when there's no movie on or one I've seen to death."

"If you ask me they are all a big waste of good time. If you've got to watch why don't you watch channel 8 where the educational programs are?"

"That channel hardly ever have a movie. Most of what you see on there is something true."

"That's good for you. You can learn from it. That's the channel I started Sugarfoot out watching. I just hope he still watches it."

"That and baseball channels are *all* he ever watches. I just get sick of so many shows about animals. I like people shows, movies. Besides, on that channel you can never go to the bathroom without missing something."

"Too much unreal stuff is no good for you. It doesn't properly prepare you for life."

"You mean like watching the news do?"

"That can help. You watch the news now?"

"Not if there's a movie on somewhere. The news when it's all over just make you feel bad about everything and everybody. Movies don't make me feel that way."

"Lizzie Lee, I don't have the time nor the strength to argue with you about television. It would probably be for the best if this house didn't have one."

"Didn't have a *TV?* Then what would we do?"

"Then...maybe...by now Oscar and I would have a little grandbaby. All we've gotten since you've been here is another television set. And for the kitchen, of all places!"

"But...but didn't Clarence tell you?"

"Tell me what?"

"That we don't plan on having any children."

"No children?! No, Sugarfoot *never* told me any such thing! What, you can't have children?"

"I can have 'em, I guess. We just don't want any."

"Don't *want* any? Maybe *you* don't but I'm sure my Sugarfoot *wants his mother* to have a grandchild!"

"No, he doesn't want children. After he finish writing and selling his book we're going to either Hollywood or the Village, all depending on who comes up with the best offer for the book, the movies or Broadway. Anyway, with him concentrating on his writing and me working hard to become a movie star, children would just mess up our future. I thought for sure Clarence had told you all of this."

"No, he didn't."

"You want me to go get him to come tell you now?"

"No! Just please leave me alone and go watch your...your movie."

~ Chapter 10 ~

It was later on that Sunday afternoon with Oscar out in the tool shed tooling, Clarence in his room typing, Lizzie Lee in the living room TV-watching, and Luella abed shedding soft, self-pitying mother tears that, Lord, the front doorbell rang.

The doorbell rang a second time. Lizzie Lee waited for a commercial break before dashing out into the hallway to answer. Even more than her and Clarence's love-making, she hated her movie-watching to be interrupted. Miffed, she swung open the front door with a loud "YEAH?!" Standing out on the porch was a young woman near her own age. Lizzie Lee's in-a-big-hurry-to-get-back-to-TV eyes shot over the woman quickly. Petite and shapely, she was wearing heels and a beige dress whose color matched her skin. Besides her purse she was carrying a suitcase. But what caught Lizzie Lee's eyes and just stuck onto the balls for a good commercial three seconds was the woman's smile—teeth sparkling sweetly from a smooth, soft, oval face so full of warmth and so pretty that while staring into it Lizzie Lee for a moment forgot her miffiness, almost.

"Is this the residence of Missis Luella Hemphill?" The sweet smile briefly relinquished the mouth to words but right on the tail of the last syllable quickly recaptured the full, wet lips.

"It is. You wanna see her?"

"Yes...."

"Come on in then. Here, let me take your suitcase." That's when Lizzie Lee first noticed the woman was wearing white gloves. Pulling the door closed behind the sweet-smiling one and swiftly leading the way down the hall, Lizzie Lee hollered out, "Momma Luella, somebody here to see you! Go on in and sit down!" Lizzie Lee ushered the woman into her mother-in-law's room. "You kinfolk? She sick, you know, but she can talk when she awake. Sit down. I'll be right next door here if you need me." Dropping the woman's suitcase just inside Luella's door, then making a hurried pit stop in the bathroom and, without breaking stride, dashing to the refrigerator, she filled both hands and mouth with TV-watching fuel before scurrying back to the living room just as the movie was returning.

"Lizzie Lee, who was that at the front door?!" Clarence's voice thundered down the hall from the open door of his room.

"Just somebody to see Momma Luella! Now don't *bother* me, my movie is on!" Lizzie Lee from the living room shot back up the hall.

"Hello, Cousin Luella." The young woman stood over the bed talking down to the staring-up-at-her, now-dry-eyed, curious, sick woman. "I'm your cousin Clarence's daughter...your cousin Claire." Then came that sweet smile. Lord, Cousin Claire was there.

~ **Chapter 11** ~

"Oh, Cousin Clarence was the best-mannered, handsomest, most intelligent of all the young boys of Appalachee back then." Propped up in bed with pillows at her back, a beaming Luella held forth. The family had just finished their Sunday night supper of Sunday afternoon dinner leftovers and all were now in Luella's room. Oscar, Clarence, and Lizzie Lee all sat staring in amazement at the sudden glow now lighting up the sick woman's countenance. The reason for this abrupt burst of joyful noise exulting from the sick woman sat right next to the bed in the form of Cousin Claire, holding one of Luella's hands in both of hers while smiling at the talking woman ever so sweetly. "When Cousin Clarence left Appalachee," Luella carried on, "my whole world crumbled. I was never again to have such a wonderful playmate...and friend." Dew dropped.

"Daddy often told Mother and me about his growing up in Appalachee, especially about that sad day in his life when he had to move and leave behind his best, and dearest, friend, Cousin Luella. Then when he passed...."

"Oh, no!"

"...Mother was so heartbroken that, that she soon followed." Here Cousin Claire broke into polite tears.

"I, I hadn't heard about Cousin Clarence. When did he pass?"

"It happened while I was in high school," Cousin Claire sobbed softly.

"Are there any sisters or brothers?"

"There's only me."

"You poor, poor child."

Here the sprinklers went off in both women's heads.

Oscar, not wanting Luella to become too upset, yet never having seen her so concerned about anyone before, felt a bit confused, uneasy, somehow afraid for her. The only thing he'd ever known about her Cousin Clarence was what he'd heard from others. In listening to everyone but Luella this Cousin Clarence had sounded to Oscar like nothing but a real little stuckup snot. But, he also sat there thinking, Clarence certainly did have a pretty daughter and one whom Luella, who didn't take to people easily, had taken to instantly. He just hoped his wife hadn't taken to her too quickly and wasn't now sitting up there in bed "talking out of her head."

"Honey, ought'n you to be git'n some rest by now," said an apprehensive Oscar.

"Rest?" Luella dabbed away tears. "That's all I *ever* get! What am I tired from? Getting rest. Now I want to talk to and enjoy my kinfolk, Cousin Claire here. Y'all don't have to stay in here with us...."

"The Sunday Night Movie is coming up in a few minutes." With that Lizzie Lee shot out the door headed for all the necessary stops between her and the TV.

"...Lord, we got sooo much to talk about. Are you married, Cousin Claire?"

"No ma'am. I guess I've been too busy working lately to think much about it."

"A pretty girl like you wouldn't have one bit of trouble getting herself a husband once she put her mind to it. Don't we have a pretty cousin, Sugarfoot?" Luella looked straight at her taken-by-surprise-at-the-question son, who managed to stammer out,

"Er...er...yes, we do."

"Looks just like her daddy did and has that same beautiful smile. What kind of work do you do, Cousin Claire?"

"I'm a registered nurse."

"Really? Now that's real nice. You know, when I was a young girl I wanted to be a nurse sooo bad.... But then I got married."

"I'm sure you would've made a very good nurse, Cousin Luella."

"I think I would have. How did you get here, Cousin Claire?"

"I came on the bus from Atlanta and got a taxi from the bus station to the house here. But like Cousin Oscar said, you need your rest, so if I could use your phone I'll call a taxi...."

"Call a taxi, for what?"

"On the way here from the station I noticed a Holiday Inn sign...."

"A Holiday Inn? You'll stay there my foot! Now that Cousin Clarence and his folks have passed away my Sugarfoot here and you, Cousin Claire, are the only *blood* kin I have left on this earth. And you, poor dear, are all alone in the world. You're gonna stay right here in this house with your *kinfolks!* Sugarfoot, go tell your wife to go and take Oscar's bedding and things out of the guest room to the living room where he'll sleep on the couch. Tell her to then fix up the guest room for Cousin Claire to sleep."

"No, please, Cousin Luella, I can sleep on the couch. Don't make Cousin Oscar...."

"Oscar doesn't mind sleeping on the couch, do you honey?"

"Er...it's all right wit' me."

"Cousin Oscar, sir, you sure you don't mind because I...."

"Cousin Claire, you are going to sleep in the guest room tonight and every night for as long as you want to stay here. This is your home now. Even when I'm gone it will still be your home. Now as long as you live you will always have a place to stay under this here roof of my house. Sugarfoot, you and Oscar hear that?"

Lord, they heard.

And, Lord, Cousin Claire smiled sweetly.

When Lizzie Lee dragged out of bed and did her sleepwalk shuffle to the kitchen early that Monday morning to cook breakfast she found to her surprise that Cousin Claire had already been there and cooked and prepared her and Luella's breakfast and was now sitting in the sick woman's room, the two of them chatting and eating.

"It would've been all right with me if you hadda cooked breakfast for everybody," said a sleepy-eyed-and-voiced Lizzie Lee, leaning against the doorjamb of Luella's room, letting Cousin Claire know her true feelings about early morning cooking.

"I didn't know what everybody else ate but last night Cousin Luella told me what she could eat." Her remark, perioded by a smile, sent Lizzie Lee, feet dragging, on down the hall to the kitchen from where the next sound heard was the clicking on of the TV set.

This was to be the daily pattern. Before Lizzie Lee entered the kitchen to begin her meals, Cousin Claire would already have cooked her and Luella's food and cleaned up afterwards. She ate all of her meals sitting in with and assisting Luella with hers. Luella was showing signs of enjoying eating, living, again. Before her first week at the Hemphills' was up, Cousin Claire had paid a visit to the office of Luella's doctor and conferred with him about his, their, patient's condition, along with having Oscar drive her the twenty or so miles to Athens where she bought the white uniform of a nurse, plus the blue cape, which was all she wore now. She had taken over complete charge of the care and feeding of her Cousin Luella, who was acting very pleased about this new, sudden, arrangement. From Luella's garden each morning the neat and trim nurse would cut flowers and have a fresh bouquet in the vase on the table beside the sick woman's bed. Besides cooking for and feeding her, Cousin Claire spent her entire day reading, talking, and listening to and laughing with her Cousin Luella. In addition, the younger woman eventually coaxed the older woman to get out of bed and sit up in a chair for a short period of each day. Then, with the help of her personal nurse, Luella began slowly walking around the room, then outdoors on the porch and, finally, taking short strolls around, and longer sittings in the sun of, the yard. Everybody coming to visit the sick woman now left commenting upon what a vast improvement, especially in attitude, Luella had shown since the arrival of her Cousin Claire. More husbands even took to coming with their wives to visit the sick woman...and while there took note of the hip-hugging white uniform of the pretty young nurse.

Meanwhile, Oscar didn't know exactly what to think about this sudden, surprisingly optimistic change in his wife. She was more like her old self when they first got married, revealing interest around the house again by reminding him of the jobs she wanted done. Most of all, he was happy to see her out of her depressive, bordering-on-cynical mood, when every time anyone, except their son, said anything to her she seemed to snicker an answer back to them. Also, and most important, Cousin Claire appeared able to keep his wife's mind off her sickness pretty much. He remembered the time before the young woman's arrival when he had walked into Luella's room and she was crying.

"Wha's the mattah, baby?" He sat at her bedside taking her hand.

"I'm no use to anybody anymore. Just somebody to be looked after. A *burden!*" Her shoulders were now shaking.

"No, baby, that ain' true."

"It *is* true! I'm no more good to my family. No...no more good to you, my husband. I don't *feel* like a woman anymore. I'm *not* a woman anymore!" Here she let loose like he'd never heard anyone cry before.

"Baby," he soothed, trying his best to reassure her, "it ain' lak you was young...'n wan'ed some mo' babies.... They...they don't mattah, none...."

"They matter, *mattered,* to *me!* Maybe not to *you!*" At this she stopped crying abruptly and stared at him so hard and cold that he, not knowing why, turned scared. They hadn't talked about her sickness since. Nor had he ever caught her crying since that day.

Now he was happy to see her in good spirits again. Still...he didn't quite know what to think of Cousin Claire, who was so pretty, sweet, and nice to Luella, who just simply loved this young relative of hers. At times there he did feel a tinge of jealousy running through his soul whenever his wife got off on the subject of her Cousin Clarence who, having been made into a saint by the two women, she raved on more and more about each day. But more than being bothered by the never-ending subject of Cousin Clarence's nice manners, dare devilry, handsomeness, and intelligence, Oscar hoped with all of his heart that Cousin Claire in all of her sweetness wasn't in his wife's last few days taking Luella's heart farther away from him.

Clarence saw Cousin Claire's coming as a blessing. This way his mother had someone else to carry on over all the time besides him, giving him more time to concentrate on his writing and thinking. Not that he didn't love his mother and want her to live, which he truly did, but he'd never learned how to return all of the love she unabashedly lavished upon him daily. He was slowly beginning to suspect that all of this love

162

Benny Andrews
June 16, 1991

poured upon his head by his mother affected his father's attitude toward him. But now, with Cousin Claire here, his mother had someone else to pour her love over. This Cousin Clarence of theirs, he was beginning to wonder, must've been quite something for his mother to keep carrying on about all day, and on into the night, every day! He wondered, had this cousin been his mother's first lover? Whatever he was, he most certainly had left a deep impression on her. Also, he had sired a pretty daughter whose sweet smile always caused a meltdown in Clarence's system, which would be saved from total liquidation by a sudden rise out of him created by the hind end of the sweet-smiling one's white nurse uniform in motion.

Lizzie Lee thought such prettiness, rather than go to waste in a nursing uniform, should've been put to much better use somewhere else, like on a movie screen. But she was glad Cousin Claire had decided to come there because now Momma Luella had someone taking care of her whom she liked, loved. This way, a grateful Lizzie Lee felt, she now had much more time for her movies on TV.

Chapter 13

A sweet, pretty thing, Cousin Claire looked so innocent and vulnerable, gently toting around a smile so warm and soft it brought tears to the eyes of its recipients, causing them on the spot to secretly give thanks to their God for letting them be born and live long enough to bask within the glow of such angelicness and benignity. Not only the men but many women as well had to fight off the overpowering desire to just grab up the "little sweetie" and squeeze her in a great big bear hug and protect her forever...and ever...from the cruelties and dirt of this cold, heartless world. Lord!

True, Cousin Claire, ever in her clean, starched, white uniform with cap and, whenever away from the house, blue cape, had a bright sweet smile for everyone. But few, if any, words. Her whole life appeared consumed with caring for her Cousin Luella, as if she had been sent to Appalachee to do so by God Himself. By selecting, buying, cooking, and preparing all of Luella's food herself, along with continually surprising her with little presents of perfumes, books, items of clothing, and such, Cousin Claire was not only nurse, and sometime doctor, to the sick woman but also close friend and confidante.

"Cousin Clarence and I would sometimes just sit out on the front porch in the swing and talk," Luella one afternoon recalled to a rapt, smiling Cousin Claire seated at her bedside. "He'd tell me about what he wanted to be someday. Unlike the other boys around, Cousin Clarence wanted to do something far away from Appalachee. Something important. At first and for the longest he wanted to be an airplane pilot in the war but the war ended too soon for him to be that. And thank God it did because I lost my daddy in the war. Then just before leaving for Atlanta he wanted to be a doctor and wanted me to be his nurse. Lord, Cousin Clarence had the nicest hands, real long fingers just like a surgeon's...." This always brought a blushing smile to Luella's face. "Like I said, your daddy was sooo different from the rest of the boys around here. He read a lot, made good grades in school, but wasn't anybody's sissy because he would put up his dukes with anybody wanting to and would beat them up. Yes, Lord, Cousin Clarence was something else! He's gone on now, God rest his soul, but while here he, and I thank the Lord for it, fathered this beautiful and lovely child. Yes, you, Cousin Claire." This

brought a blush and stretched smile to the young woman's face. "I've only known about you since the Sunday you first showed up here but in that short time you've been just like a daughter to me. The daughter I never had...but the one who was meant to be mine. Your daddy and I being cousins, we never could've gotten married, but after he left Appalachee I never cared for another boy, or man, ever again. Not one! Not even Oscar, whom I only married to please my mama on her deathbed. I've never even had a girl, or woman, friend I could sit down and talk to like I can with you, Cousin Claire. I know everybody around here has always thought and still thinks I'm nothing but a 'stuckup.' But that never bothered me as all I ever wanted to do was to take care of my family right. If more folks were concerned about taking care of their families and not spending all of their time talking and worrying about somebody else's, then we would have a much better neighborhood here. Rather than that project down the street filled with all of those welfare mothers without husbands. But even after trying as hard as I did to run my family right, somewhere along the line I must've done something wrong because look what my Sugarfoot went and did. God knows I thought I was bringing him up the right way. Outside of that one summer he went to live up in New York right after his first year of college he never gave me one single bit of trouble until, after finishing Morehouse and getting himself a good teaching job, he, out of God knows where, ups and marries that woman from the Trailer Park. She has *no* class while trying to fool everyone into thinking she's serious about wanting to become a movie star. She? My foot! She just wanted to get her behind in there on the sofa where she can sit all day, and most of the night, watching television. Sugarfoot had the chance to marry a very nice, pretty, and beautifully mannered girl, Inez Blackshear, from one of the most respected, and wealthiest, families in the county. But no, he drags into his mother's house a Trailer Park bastard who's done nothing since being here but watch television. Sugarfoot even had her quit her job to take care of his sick mother. Which meant until you came I got on or off the bedpan only during a TV commercial break. The *only* thing that saved me is that she never watched the Public Broadcasting Station. Actually, the less she's around me the better I feel. Sugarfoot told me he met her where she worked, some knock-down-drag-out greasy spoon. Now what *he* was doing there in the first place I'll never understand, even though he keeps telling me he goes there for his writing. You know he's writing a book. He does look like a writer, doesn't he? But I asked him why couldn't he write the book, which I'm sure is going to be a good one, here at home near someone who loved him or at least write it in a *nice* restaurant? But what I *really* don't understand is, Lord, just *what is it* he sees in *that* woman in there? God, if my Sugarfoot had only met himself a *good* woman...a *good* woman like...like his Cousin Claire here." Cousin Claire blushed and just sat smiling on.

Because of her surprising rejuvenation on life many folks suddenly began thinking optimistically about Luella, believing that maybe with the help of Cousin Claire, and God, she just might whip the Big C. But Luella was still a very sick woman and knew it. The pain was always there to remind her. Cousin Claire, following doctor's instructions, administered the sick woman her medicine daily and as the pain grew so did the size of each dosage, eventually causing the woman to act and feel dopy or high all the time, either making her sleep or talk her head off. Cousin Claire was always at, or not too far away from, her side.

Then, Lord, came that stormy night when from the pouring rain and out of the hot glare of a flash of lightning onto the Hemphills' front porch stepped the black-clad "Bertha the Buzzard."

Tall and lanky, Bertha's stock in trade was her long, sad, ageless face, which she carried around to every house of the sick in, and out of, the community where like a buzzard she sat, hovered, at the foot of the bed of the ill whom she'd come to console, watching and waiting. Yes, it was said throughout the region that when Bertha the Buzzard came, you were gone. Bertha the Buzzard left no survivors.

The folks had first been introduced to Bertha the Buzzard many years earlier—everybody had lost count as to exactly how many—when as a total stranger she appeared out of nowhere to attend a local funeral and, uninvited, sat herself right down amidst the mourning family on the front row of the church. Ever since that day a seat was automatically saved for Bertha the Buzzard on the front row of the church, and in the lead car following the hearse in every black funeral, practically, in Muskhogean County—and she hadn't missed a burial. In fact, it was said, Bertha the Buzzard subscribed to several newspapers in the area, thus keeping a constant check on the sick and the dead, and she was also said to be in attendance at one funeral every week, at least, somewhere in the state. She was never seen out of her black mourning outfit, complete with hat and veil, and at the funerals themselves nobody could cry, moan, wail, or sing as long, as loud, or as sad as Bertha the Buzzard over the loss of the deceased, whether she had known them in life or not. Lord, *nobody* could get, and keep, a funeral going like Bertha the Buzzard— nor end one like her, as she always saved her best for the last and many, often strangers to the family of the deceased, came from afar just to witness Bertha the Buzzard's final and special "up from the gut" crying song over the grave that oftentimes even choked up the praying-for-pay preacher. It made you want to die. Following this moving graveside performance, Bertha the Buzzard, always leaving them crying, would fly (via Greyhound bus) off in search of another funeral. Now, Lord, her never-ending journey through rain, shine, sleet, and slime had brought her to the footpost of Luella's bed, where she now hovered.

Once Bertha the Buzzard had roosted in one's house there was no shooing her out—not even the pleading sweet smile and soft kind words of Cousin Claire worked—until she saw fit herself to fly off. "Just left the Funeral Home, Sister Luella," came the ominous screech of Bertha the Buzzard from the thin lips of her long, sad-eyed, vulture face. "But they hadn't yet displayed the body of Brother Willie Youngblood who, God rest his soul, you know by now was called home by his Maker early yesterday morning while he lay sleeping. God is merciful! But, as we all so well know, the poor man was sick for a long, long time. It was just last year they had to take off one leg. He was a diabetic, you know. Runs in the family. Essie Mae, his momma, died from it. Lord, what a beautiful funeral she had. Her family spared *no* expense in having her put away. She left here decked out in such finery that I'm sure when God saw her approaching the Pearly Gates He went out to welcome her home Himself. They said Brother Youngblood was doing right nicely for awhile there and it seemed he might make it all the way back until he took a sudden setback and then the other leg had to come off. That's when I went to see him...."

Thus sat Bertha the Buzzard that lightning-streaking-across-the-sky, thunder-thumping, rain-pouring-down, stormy night, digging up from the grave, digesting, and reburying old bones until, finally: "Sister Luella, I hate running out and leaving you like this but I must be getting on before it's too late for me to stop in at the Home to see if Brother Youngblood has been put on display yet. Funeral services will be held on Sunday, you know. The Lord giveth and the Lord taketh away, honey." The black raincoated, rainhatted, and galoshed Bertha the Buzzard, beneath her big black umbrella, stepped back out into the dark night's storm. Gone.

A week later, Lord, Luella, too, was gone. Amen.

Chapter 15

Luella's instructions to her family—"Get me in the ground as soon as possible after I'm dead even if it means the same day"—had miffed many who thought the woman wanting to be buried so quickly meant that even in death she was still putting on airs and snubbing the masses, who wouldn't get a chance to attend her funeral on such short notice. Cousin Claire automatically and immediately took sole charge of all funeral arrangements, starting from Luella's last breath to the last grit of dirt falling atop her grave. Also, she saw to it that her cousin's wishes of not wanting to be put on display, "like in some store window while folks stood around telling lies about you and you can't talk back," were carried out.

Most people she knew had respected Luella, but few outside of her immediate family had gotten to know, or like, her very well. This, plus the fact that the funeral occurred on a weekday, didn't produce an overflow crowd as did most local black funerals, the majority of which had always taken place on Sunday. And most of those showing up for Luella's funeral knew Oscar much better than they had known his wife. There were also those who came solely to get a glimpse of Cousin Claire, on this sad occasion out of her nurse's white into mourner's black, but nonetheless pretty, and as sweet as a Georgia peach. The funeral's being held at Wesley, upon Luella's insistence, assured a smaller crowd even if it had been held on Sunday. And even so, practically everyone attending the funeral up there was from down at Bethel or lived in Thompson Town. Though the funeral was held at Wesley, the burial took place in the cemetery behind Bethel where Luella was laid to rest in a grave beside her mother.

Oh yes, Bertha the Buzzard woke up Wesley. She more than made up for the crowd's lack in size, and sound, by crying, moaning, and singing a little louder than her usual loud over the deceased, whom she had only once ever spoken to, or even seen.

Oscar's family had wanted to fix an after-funeral feast at his mother's house but Cousin Claire insisted upon her and Lizzie Lee (who throughout the long day suffered severe withdrawals due to not having the time for even a quick TV fix, for which she substituted by chewing on a sweet onion, her favorite vegetable) preparing only a small luncheon and having it where Luella would have wanted them to have it, her home—and there it was held. Afterwards, everyone commented time and again upon how beautifully Cousin Claire had arranged and handled everything from A to Z surrounding Luella's funeral. To which Cousin Claire only smiled.

Funeral folks gone, Cousin Claire shooed all out of the kitchen and started cleaning up after the guests. Oscar, still in his funeral wear, drifted out back to the tool shed. Clarence and Lizzie Lee, also yet funereally dressed, went to the living room.

"It won't be as long as it was," said Lizzie Lee, once seated on the sofa beside her husband, speaking while biting on an onion. Atop practically everything she ate, Lizzie Lee added a slice of onion. She was even known to slap a slice on a piece of cake and gulp down the combination without shedding a tear. When the sweet Vidalia onion was in season she ate it like a piece of fruit, like she was doing now.

"What won't be as long as it was?"

"Before *The Jackie Robinson Story* comes on," she chewed, staring ahead wistfully at the blank screen of the turned-off television.

"Oh, no. Out of respect for Mother I'm not writing atall today and you agreed not to watch TV."

"It won't come on until after midnight and that's *tomorrow.*"

"No TV, or writing, until tomorrow morning *after* we've gotten up out of bed," said a never-more-serious Clarence.

"But Momma Luella is already buried now and this is Ruby Dee's second big movie, right after *No Way Out.*"

"I don't care."

"I've never seen this one before. You'll love it too because it's all about *baseball.*"

"If I can hold off from writing you can surely go a day without watching TV. Why don't you read something? You should read more. How far have you gotten on the Richard Wright novel, *Native Son,* I gave you to read?"

"I can't finish it. Those old-time books make me so sad and then mad. More mad at the black folks for sitting back and taking all of that stuff back then. If tonight you was to write after midnight I wouldn't consider it you breaking your promise."

"We must always carry out our promises to each other."

"How much longer you think you got to go on your book?"

"It's hard to say."

"How come? You said you know what you want to write so why don't you just go ahead and write it and get it over with?"

"Unfortunately, writing a book is not quite that simple."

"How long have you been writing on it now?"

"All of my life, really."

173

"I don't mean in your head, I mean with your hands."

"You know I don't like to go into details about my book."

"I know, I know, but if I am going to be in the movie or the play like you promised then I'll need some acting training to play a ballgirl. Why can't I play the ball player's wife?"

"He's not going to be married."

"Then why can't I be his girlfriend?"

"He's not going to have a girlfriend."

"He's not going to like girls?"

"He will. But no special girl."

"Why not?"

"When you bring in a female in a sports story it changes everything. Like when a girl enters a cowboy movie."

"What, would all the ball players go into heat and start killing one another?"

"No! It takes away from the game and there's nothing more important in a baseball novel than the game."

"Jackie Robinson had a wife. Ruby Dee!"

"Well, my ball player doesn't have one and that's all I want to say about the book."

"Well, if you don't finish writing it soon I might be too old to play a ballgirl and you might have to make me a ballgrandma. If we can't watch TV then what are we going to do now?"

"Talk, just like we are doing."

"That's silly when we could be watching something. Is there a game on?"

"No."

"There's one on after midnight. Don't you believe in Jackie Robinson?"

"Not tonight."

"When are we going to get a cable TV? Everybody else around here is getting one. They have *great* movies."

"You have to pay for cable TV."

"Now that Momma Luella is...gone, I can go back to work...."

"No, I want you to stay home and take care of the house."

"For that I oughta get a cable TV."

"Then you wouldn't get *any* work done."

"I *do* my work! If I stay home then what's she gonna do?"

"Who?"

"Cousin Claire?"

"Oh...I don't know. Now that Mother is no longer here for her to take care of she'll probably be leaving soon."

"She's a nurse and a good one. She could easily find a job here in town, I bet."

"But that doesn't mean she'll be staying here. She'll probably want her own place."

"Didn't you tell me that you and Daddy Oscar promised Momma Luella that Cousin Claire had a home here in this house for as long as she wanted to stay?"

"Yes, Mother did make us promise her. But it still doesn't mean Cousin Claire will want to stay here with us."

"I sure would. If *us* had a cable TV."

Lizzie Lee figured if she couldn't watch TV then she might as well do the next best thing in the world to watching TV. Using a persistent hand in the right spot she finally persuaded a still-somewhat-reluctant-at-first Clarence to retire early, and when she at long last got him into their room atop the kingsizer she, pretending she couldn't get enough of him, proceeded to wear him out. Now here it was after midnight, *tomorrow,* and he was sleeping like a baby while she sat munching and watching Ruby Dee on TV. At first she had prepared to watch the movie on the kitchen set, closer to the refridge and the bathroom, but after checking the living room and discovering Oscar wasn't sleeping out there on the sofa (he, she assumed, having gone back to sleep in the master bedroom, which, with Luella gone, he now had all to himself) she, quietly closing the door to the hall, switched on the set and, loaded down with TV-watching staples, happily plopped atop the couch.

So caught up did Lizzie Lee become in the aura and acting of Ruby Dee that even if she heard she paid no attention whatsoever to the hallway sounds of a door softly opening and closing, followed moments later by another door being quietly opened and closed. All the while, Lord, Lizzie Lee just looked on.

Chapter 16

When a foggy-eyed, fading-brown-bathrobed Lizzie Lee dragged her mules-shod feet behind her down the hall and on into the kitchen the next morning to start breakfast, she was startled to see a fully-dressed-for-work Oscar already sitting at the dining table eating. Shuffling on over to the TV in the corner to turn on the set (she couldn't think clearly in the morning without it being on), she asked, "What time is it?"

"Five after six." Oscar looked at his watch before sipping his coffee.

"For a minute there I thought my clock was wrong. I thought I was dreaming when I lay in there smelling breakfast cooking. You oughta told me last night you had to be at work early this morning and I would've set the alarm to go off sooner. You didn't have to get up and fix your own breakfast. That's my job." TV's sound and sight were beginning to awaken Lizzie Lee, standing in the middle of the kitchen with ears on Oscar and eyes on the set.

"I didn't fix it." Oscar continued eating.

"Who fixed it then?"

"I did." In walked a radiant-faced Cousin Claire wearing a soft blue bathrobe, Luella's. "From now on, Lizzie Lee, I'll be cooking all of Cousin Oscar's meals along with doing the rest of his housekeeping. This way all you will have to do is take care of Clarence's needs...and watch TV." Then she smiled. Lord, Lizzie Lee now had both ears and eyes off the set onto the smiling Cousin Claire standing right next to the seated Oscar hungrily eating his extra-early morning breakfast. Then for the first time her eyes saw sitting in the middle of the table the vase of freshly-cut-from-Luella's-garden flowers.

Lord, all of Thompson Town and all of those knowing, and knowing of, the family Hemphill were nearly shocked all the way out of their senses! The hereunto sober, practical, down-to-earth, two-feet-flat-out-on-the-ground, reliable, dependable, common, unimaginative, unpretentious, predictable, dull, and boring Oscar Hemphill was no more! Lord, no! Even before Luella could get her grave good and cold, everybody was quick to say, Oscar, acting in total disrespect of his late wife and his entire family, had shocked all by taking up with her kin, Cousin Claire, more than twenty years his junior! Even Luella's many old enemies were now coming to the dead woman's defense. Always the conservative dresser, Oscar had suddenly gone out and bought himself a brand new wardrobe of colors. You name the color, honey, Oscar had it *and* wore it! The former man of dark suits only was now seen wearing bright, out-of-this-world wild sport jackets, slacks, shirts, shoes, hats, and, seemingly, the loudest of whatever else he could find to fit. But everybody just *knew* this wasn't really *their* Oscar's fault. The poor, bereaved man had been "led," yes, "LED!" Lord, You know, because it was *You* who made men weak!

What totally convinced everybody of this Biblical fact of man's main weakness, woman, came that day when over into and down the main street of Thompson Town rode a shiny black, brand new T-Bird behind whose wheel sat a grinning Oscar right next to a smiling Cousin Claire! Lord! She and Oscar were now seen driving together all around town and throughout the area, sitting up there on the front seat with the radio blasting out soul sounds. No, Lord, they didn't hide at all. They were always somewhere in the public's eye, or talk—even seen together in church, in their sin! Many a time they were publicly caught holding hands or winking at one another, or were heard giggling together. Talk soon started going around that they were occasionally driving up to Atlanta where, supposedly, Oscar had even gone with Cousin Claire to a picture show! No longer was Cousin Claire seen in her starchy white nurse's uniform; instead she was now seen strutting her stuff all over town dressed in beautiful and expensive-looking dressy clothing, new! Yet she retained her same sweet smile for everyone. But the womenfolk were no longer taken in by it as they now wanted absolutely nothing whatsoever to do with her for stealing away the husband of their enemy in the grave. But, Lord, most of the town's males envied Oscar while still loving to watch Cousin Claire walk her walk.

As far as Oscar was concerned there was nothing too good for Cousin Claire—from being driven around in a brand new T-Bird to being daily supplied with dairy-fresh, not supermarket, products for her kitchen. Early on seven mornings a week Sid Mitchell's Dairy delivery truck from down county would pull up in front of the Hemphill house and leave each day a supply of milk and, whenever needed, cream and butter. After the dairy owner fell into poor health, the truck was driven by the young, teenaged hired hand, Le Bonbon. On occasion riding in the truck with him would be ol' Sid's young granddaughter, Lisa...and always with him, as if riding shotgun, was a woman named Reenie.

"You or somebody had better talk to Daddy Oscar soon before he spends all of his money on your Cousin Claire," Lizzie Lee told Clarence as they lay abed late one night talking in the dark.

"It's his money and life. He can do with them what he wants to."

"I know, but she's gonna run him both broke and crazy. I've never seen a grown man all of a sudden starting to cut the fool like this before.

And Daddy Oscar, a Christian man. Honey, who would've believed it? Just listen...." From behind the door of the father's room and echoing on down the hall to vibrate against their closed door came muffled laughter and song. "...She's in there teaching him how to dance. And, Lord, whatever happened to sweet lil' Cousin Claire, Cousin Clarence's 'darling daughter' that Momma Luella just loved to death? Your Momma only been outta that room for a month and just listen to what's going on in there now." Loud soul sounds sounded on.

"That's the only thing that really bothers me."

"What, the noise?"

"No. Mother. Out of respect for her they could've at least waited a little longer."

"When you are hot, honey, you are hot!"

"I guess I will have to have a talk with Father."

"When? They are boogying in there now."

"Tomorrow."

"What are you going to say to him? Tell him to stop what he's doing and go take a cold shower? Or are you going to stuff ice cubes up Cousin Claire?"

"No, I'll tell him to start watching TV. That'll cool him down."

"TV don't stop us."

"Thanks to the commercials. Father and I have never really talked to one another."

"Then tell him to watch the movie...."

"That you hear out there, Lizzie Lee, is *no* movie."

"I know, but you oughta see the movie too. It's about this son having to cool his papa down. In fact, I just saw in *TV Guide* today where that movie is on sometime this week. I can't think of the name of the picture but I know Ruby Dee ain't in it. If you'd let me bring the kitchen TV in here we could see if it's on now. You never say anything but I know you don't like to leave the room when you don't have to because you don't wanna know what's going on out there with them."

"Like I said, I'm only concerned about Mother's memory here in this, her, house. If he was to leave I wouldn't care what he did."

"Still, if I could just go get the set...."

"Lizzie Lee, there will be *no* TV set in this bedroom as long as I'm alive and that's final! If you want to watch...."

"Okay!" Lizzie Lee, popping up out of bed to go watch, shot through the bedroom door, letting in a loud female giggle riding down the hall atop the sound of soul before pulling it closed behind her.

Clarence had wanted to get his father out back in the tool shed where he knew they would have privacy to talk but Oscar hadn't been inside the building since the day Luella was buried. So the very next day following his and Lizzie Lee's talk and right after his father finished eating supper and went to his room, Clarence, knowing Cousin Claire was still in the kitchen cleaning up and Lizzie Lee in the living room watching TV, knocked on Oscar's door.

"Come on in."

"Father, you got a minute?"

"Why sho'. Some'n on yo' mind, son?" Oscar sat back in the large easy chair smoking a big after-supper cigar in a room that still had his mother's color but was at this moment decorated with several items of a younger woman's lingerie scattered about. "Let me put on a Billy Wright here." Putting a tape in a cassette player Clarence had never before seen, which sat on the small stand beside the easy chair, Oscar explained, "Billy is the man Little Richard and James Brown learned soul from."

> Oh baby please don't go
> Oh baby please don't go

Clarence stood trying to keep his eyes off the intimate female apparel lying on the bed and on this man sitting there in the chair who looked like his father but whose strange, exuberant, *sure* voice didn't sound like him at all. He was hit with the sudden feeling, fear, that he had now lost both his mother and father.

"I...I wanted to talk to you...."

"'Bout Cousin Claire?"

"Well...er...more about Mother...."

"Motha is dead."

"I know...but her memory...."

> Turn your lamps down low
> Oh, turn your lamps down low

"I keep her mem'ry, son. But since you the one brin'n it up let me tell you some'n. My mem'ry of 'Motha' is diff'nt than yo's. My mem'ry of 'Motha' is her not let'n me name my son aftah me lak my momma let my daddy name me aftah him. My mem'ry of 'Motha' is her not let'n me take my son hunt'n or anywheah else she didn' think he oughta go wit' his daddy. Son, I loved yo' 'Motha' but yo' 'Motha' sho didn' love me back. She loved her Cousin Clarence who she named you aftah. But what made it even mo badder was she was always mak'n me 'n my family feel we won' as good as she 'n you, my son who got my blood. Not even when ly'n in heah on her deathbed did she one time let me think I was as good as her. She went to the grave think'n she was bettah than me 'n my family. I nevah did lak her ways but the Lord in heaven knows I loved yo' 'Motha' 'n will always have a 'mem'ry' of her no mattah what she thought 'bout me, yo' 'Fatha.' Now fuh the fust time in my life I met a woman who makes me feel lak a *real* man. 'N, son, she's mak'n me feel lak I nevah knowed I could. Lak 'Motha' 'n me oughta did. 'N I don' care what folks is now say'n. Even my folks. Even you, my son!"

Oh, turn your lamps down low
Cause I'll never never let you go

"But...but what about all the money you are spending on...."

"It's *my* money. I couldn' spen' a penny befo' widout tell'n Luella, who put evah cent I made she could git in the bank in *her* name. Now jes as long as I pay my part in run'n this heah house I don' hafta tell *nobody* how I spen' *my* money. Not even you, my son, my flesh 'n blood. But if you think I'm spen'n too much of my own money now don' worry none 'cause lak I tole Cousin Claire theah's plen'y mo' of *my* money lef' in Luella's will." That seemed to open the door at Clarence's back, admitting Cousin Claire, smiling.

Oh baby please don't go
Oh baby please don't go

~ Chapter 17 ~

That following week Luella's will was read. In it Clarence was left the house and thirty-six thousand dollars in cash and U.S. government bonds. Lizzie Lee got *both* television sets. Oscar was left the tool shed and all its contents...and a home in Sugarfoot's house for as long as he lived. Amen.

You got me way down here
Oh, you got me way down here
Where I'm all alone

~ Chapter 18 ~

That night following the reading of Luella's will there sounded no soul in the house of Sugarfoot Hemphill. In fact, the heavy sound of silence blitzed the entire house. Except for Lizzie Lee. "With all of that money, honey, we can now get cable TV!" Which Clarence did and after that day, unless he had business in the living room, he rarely saw his TV-watching wife.

Feeling pounds of guilt over all his mother had left him in her will while all but ignoring his father, Clarence on the day following the reading had gone to Oscar's room where the older man was sitting alone in his easy chair. In one hand he held a just-opened can of beer from the twelve-pack on the floor at his feet. Oscar was a three-bottle-every-Friday-night man. This was Tuesday night. On the tape deck Billy Wright was bluesing.

"Father, you can have the cash and bonds Mother left me. I'm a writer, I won't ever need that much money."

"No, son, yo' momma wanted you to have it so it's all yo's."

"But it's money she saved from your paychecks. It's *your* money."

"No it ain't. That's the rent I paid to stay heah in her house. But if you really wanna givya daddy some'n then go in theah 'n drag yo' wife 'way from that TV long enough to gimme a lil' gran'chil' who you could one day give that money to fuh me. But right now it's all yo' money 'n all yo' house, 'cord'n to the law 'n Luella. Even when she's in her grave I ain' good enough fuh her." Standing there listening to all of this, Clarence had wanted to run over and hug his father and tell him that his mother had loved them both equally as much. But he knew this wasn't true. His father was right. He'd never thought about it before, whether or not he loved his father, but right at that moment he did love him—yet not enough for his feet to take him that short distance to where his father sat with chin on chest to hug, or just touch, the older man. Instead, without a single word of solace, the son turned and left the room, now not sure whether he loved his father or pitied him.

Long past midnight that next morning, Clarence, the deep sleeper, was awakened by a loud noise. His body jerked straight up in bed awaiting his mind to catch up and figure out exactly what was going on.

Lizzie Lee awakened too after dreaming she had left on the TV, which she had stopped watching an hour earlier to come to bed. Then, Lord, came the scream that tore up Thompson Town. When Clarence, followed by Lizzie Lee, reached the master bedroom where Cousin Claire's scream had come from, she was standing in the open doorway in her bathrobe crying hysterically and pointing to Oscar lying back in his easy chair, blood spurting from the bullet hole in his temple. Down beside his chair among the several empty beer cans at his feet lay a .38 bulldog special. From the tape deck on the stand on the other side of the chair Billy Wright kept right on bluesing.

> I believe your man done come
> Don't leave me here all alone

Oscar was dead—killed instantly, the law later surmised, by a self-inflicted bullet to the head from a pistol he had just bought the day before. Thompson Town went into shock. First, everyone naturally blamed his death on Cousin Claire, who on that fatal night reportedly had been awakened by the shot and jumped out of bed and ran from her room down the hall to investigate. But once discovering the body, she herself went into shock and had to be put under sedation by the doctor, causing everyone to look around for someone else to blame, temporarily, until Cousin Claire recovered enough to shoulder the role of "devil." Luckily, though, for those knighted with the responsibility for the placing of blame, word, somehow and immediately, leaked out about Luella's will. In being fair to the dead, and the in-shock, yet in desperate need of a blamee, the blamers blamed the inheritor of Luella's house, Clarence—though out of respect for the grieving, Clarence's blame was suspended by the blamers until following Oscar's funeral, during which time the blamee's wife, Lizzie Lee, with her TV-watching habit, was blamed for the whole thing. Amen.

Despite his father's wish, Clarence didn't run into the living room, grab Lizzie Lee away from in front of the TV by the hair, and drag her hollering back to their bedroom and squirt a baby up her. It had been his idea, not Lizzie Lee's, to wait until he'd published his first book before they had any children. He wanted to be a famed father—though Lizzie Lee kept reminding him that if he didn't read so many other books all the time then maybe he would finish his own quicker. But he read mainly to find out how other writers did it. God, a writer *had* to get the outline right! Burying both of his parents in less than two months' time had caused Clarence to bury himself deeper and deeper into his novel's outline...outlining in more detail parts and chapters of the book while writing more and lengthier character sketches.

Cousin Claire, on doctor's orders, didn't attend Oscar's funeral, but not very long following the burial she was on her way back to normalcy, though her smile now reflected a respectful touch of sadness. During the few days she spent confined to her room she was waited on by Lizzie Lee, during TV commercials and the news. Clarence visited her room only once to find out how she was feeling. It was the first time he'd been in the guest room since she moved in. All of his mother's bright, airy colors in there had either been removed or covered over. The room was yet spic and span but colorless...and, Clarence felt, like a hospital, sterile.

On the opening day of school for the fall term and less than a week following Oscar's funeral, Clarence found himself extremely happy to be back teaching his youngsters. So happy was he that he hated to leave the school building that first day, finally reaching home late in the afternoon. To his surprise, and delight, awaiting him was not a heated TV dinner, which he'd grown accustomed to, and tired of, eating, but a hot, cooked meal. Cooked by Cousin Claire, who stood right there in the middle of the kitchen to greet him wearing a white apron over her black, skin-tight mourning dress and a big, warm smile. Lizzie Lee had taken her Cousin-Claire-cooked supper to eat in the living room while watching TV. Cousin Claire immediately left the kitchen for her room but when Clarence had finished eating and sat drinking a cup of, noninstant, coffee she returned to sit down at the table across from him drinking a glass of ice water. The health-and-body-conscious Cousin Claire didn't drink coffee, tea, or any alcoholic beverages. Nor did she smoke. But now she was suddenly talking.

"Cousin Clarence," she began with a smile, "I would like to ask a big favor of you," she ended with a smile.

"Go ahead." Clarence, never having been this near to his pretty cousin before while they were alone, sat feeling the fact.

"I know you and everybody else feel I'm responsible for Cousin Oscar's death and I don't blame you for thinking so. But your father was a lonely, unloved man whom I cared very much about. But, God, I had no idea how unloved and hurt he was.... Anyway, that's not what I want to talk to you about. Tomorrow morning I have to go up to Atlanta to make final arrangements for me to begin work there this coming January as a private nurse. But until that time I'll be unemployed and right now wouldn't want to accept another job knowing beforehand I wouldn't be staying with it beyond January. What I want to know is, would it be all right with you, and Lizzie Lee, for me, upon returning from Atlanta day after tomorrow, to stay on here with y'all until the first of the year? While here, in order to earn my keep, I can help Lizzie Lee with all of the house, and outdoor, work. I'll gladly do *all* of the cooking if you two want me to. I *love* to cook." Smile. "I sure would appreciate it if you and Lizzie Lee talked it over and then let me know what you both think. Meanwhile, I'll take care of these dishes...."

"Cousin Claire, sit down, please," Clarence urged. "Sure, you can stay. Before Mother died she promised you on your very first day here you would *always* have a home under this roof. Well, nothing's changed. You *still* have a home here under this roof of, now, *my* house for as long as you want to stay. That's the way Mother wanted it and that's the way I want it. As far as you and Father...well, that was y'all's business. Neither one of us was responsible for his death." Cousin Claire's answer to these words of kindness and understanding, in addition to her two wet eyes and warm smile, was to reach across the table and grab her Cousin Clarence's free hand and tightly squeeze it. Sugarfoot blushed.

Lord, Lizzie Lee loved it! With Cousin Claire back from an overnight stay in Atlanta doing *all* of the cooking, Lizzie Lee suddenly found herself with even more available time to concentrate on being the next Ruby Dee by learning to act by watching more movies on the family's new cable TV. In addition to his getting cable, Lizzie Lee talked Clarence into buying her a portable TV, which she took with her on her cleaning tours of the house and yard. As a result, Cousin Claire had to follow behind and clean Lizzie Lee's cleaning. Eventually, she was to tell Lizzie Lee that along with the cooking she didn't mind at all doing the house and yard work, all of it. Lizzie Lee kicked up no dust over this arrangement. Soon she was living in the living room with Cousin Claire serving her three meals a day in there (Lizzie Lee managed to get her own snacks) while dutifully watching TV from the moment she arose to catch the first morning movie until seeing her last one long past midnight, while ever at her side was her trusty portable for whenever nature or snacks called or for any time she went outside, or left, the house—but never in her and Clarence's room, where the husband refused permission to the portable, which each night was left outside the bedroom door. Also, with Lizzie Lee all the time was her TV remote control, which she kept in her purse when away from home and each night took with her to bed, where while sleeping, she lay with her thumb, apparently, switching channels with her dreams.

Meanwhile, Cousin Claire, now with free reign, went about the place working like a whirlwind. Her vacuum cleaner, broom, wet and dust mops, and sponge missed nary a spot in her effort to keep the house of Hemphill dirt and dust free by continually washing, scrubbing, scouring, waxing, polishing, and shining. In addition to taking care of the yard, with its ever-neatly-trimmed grass and hedges, flower garden, and porch hanging plants, Cousin Claire began a winter vegetable garden. Some of the produce she canned. When she did the cooking for them before their deaths, Cousin Claire had filled Luella's and Oscar's diets with plenty of fresh vegetables and fruits, and now that she was doing all of the cooking at Sugarfoot's house she continued the practice. A good cook who loved cooking, yet ate very little herself, she right away began adding new dishes to Clarence's and Lizzie Lee's diets. When she had arrived the family ate mostly local soul food, plus Lizzie Lee's TV-heated meals, but now Cousin Claire added Cajun, French, Mexican, Italian, and other new foods to the Hemphills' menu, clipping recipes religiously from the food section of the Atlanta newspaper Clarence daily subscribed to. Clarence took a quick liking to Cousin Claire's cooking (even tastier than his mother's, he admitted to himself) and her many different foods. It was a beautiful reminder to him of his eating-out days in the Village. Cousin Claire even asked him to make suggestions for food for her to cook but he, not knowing nearly as much about menus as he did about novel outlining, gave her free reign to cook whatever she wanted to.

Even Lizzie Lee right away noticed the difference between Cousin Claire's cooking and TV dinners. Cousin Claire's food always arrived in the living room aboard china rather than aluminum.

Daily, Clarence was seeing less and less of his wife. Even for sex. In the old days this eventually-to-be-perfectly-timed act would be carried out by the well-trained couple during TV commercial and station breaks when a readied, and pantless, Lizzie Lee would zip back to their room and jump atop her waiting husband for a quickie and get back to the living room without missing a moment of her show. But with the new cable TV and no commercial breaks, Lizzie Lee couldn't chance leaving the living room for fear of missing a moment of show, and thus whenever sex signaled, Clarence followed his need to the Source where on the sofa's folded-out couch in there Lizzie Lee always got on top facing the TV screen in order not to miss any of the movie.

The living room now had the atmosphere of a real movie theater, with its drapes kept drawn at all times except the time it took every Saturday morning for Cousin Claire to go in, vacuum, and throw out all the empty popcorn boxes and soda cans.

Having lost his wife to TV and the living room, Clarence, when not watching baseball on, now, the kitchen set, was usually found in his room working on a new, or extending the old, outline for his book. Sometimes after supper, or Sunday dinner, he would linger awhile in the kitchen at the table talking to a busily-cleaning-up Cousin Claire who still volunteered little in return but a smile. This is when he first began thinking about how little he really knew about his cousin, who'd been living in the same house with him and his family for nearly six months.

Chapter 20

Each day after finishing his meals at home (Cousin Claire packed him a lunch for school), Clarence, except for breakfast on class days, sat at the dining table sipping coffee and talking while Cousin Claire cleaned up the kitchen around him. As hard as he, the talker, tried he could get very little to no talk out of his cousin. She only answered his questions, never volunteering any information, and other than asking something about the meal she never initiated a conversation on her own. But she always offered a smile when facing him and when turned away bounced back at him that beautiful butt. Gradually, he began to cut back on his own talk...and just watch...until one day,

"Are you feeling all right, Cousin Clarence?" Cousin Claire suddenly turned from the sink to catch him sitting at the table eyeballing her butt.

"Oh...er...yes. I feel fine, why you ask?"

"You've been very quiet the last few days. Has there been something wrong with the food?"

"Oh, no. The food's been just fine, as usual! I'm all right. It's just that I thought I would give you a break by not talking your ears off every day."

"Oh, no! Please don't feel that way, Cousin Clarence. You always have so many interesting things to say and topics to talk on. I learn a lot by just listening to you. *Please* don't stop talking because of my saying nothing. I just never know of anything interesting or have anything important to say. I just *love* listening to you!" This was followed by the most beautiful smile she'd ever given him.

Thus, Lord, the floodgates were opened for Clarence's tongue to let flow at will. Now he couldn't wait to leave school or his room to go to the kitchen where daily waited Cousin Claire to listen to him talk about his day, his expectations of the upcoming one, writers, baseball pitchers, and whatever other leftovers his brain could find to drop down upon his erupting tongue until long after the meal had been eaten and cleaned up afterwards. These moments, or hours, spent in the kitchen soon came to be the most important and enjoyable ones of Clarence's day. He sat talking away beneath the glow of Cousin Claire's smile...and within eyeball distance of her beautiful bouncing butt.

Meanwhile, out in the living room, lit only by the flickering TV screen, sat Lizzie Lee, chewing and watching.

One October Friday after school, Clarence, thanks to a faculty meeting, arrived home much later than usual. He daily walked to and from school (a ten-minutes-one-way trip for him), leaving the car home for Lizzie Lee, who never used it as all the shopping for the house had been taken over completely by Cousin Claire, who drove the T-Bird. Following his father's death, Clarence, not wanting the automobile for himself, told Cousin Claire the T-Bird was hers to do whatever she wanted with. She quietly, but quickly, accepted his offer by keeping the car, he automatically picking up the payments. On this day he walked home in a steady rain and was glad to get out of the weather into the comfort of his own house. Ridding himself of his wet umbrella and raincoat, he immediately made his customary first stop in the living room. "Hey, baby." His lips groped through the TV-screen-lit room in search of Lizzie Lee's to plant atop them a kiss.

"Don't! That's the ad for Ruby Dee's movie, *Edge of the City,* coming on at midnight!" she complained, pushing his face away from between hers and the screen. *"There she is!"* Not turning to see, a sharply disappointed Clarence, suddenly feeling the intruder, left the living room for the kitchen, where was awaiting him Cousin Claire's warm smile.

While sitting eating his food with the sound of rain beating against the outsides of the kitchen windows, Clarence felt tired and annoyed. Tired after a long week of work and annoyed at Lizzie Lee's indifferent greeting, making him feel a trespasser in *her* living room. He tried thinking how long it had been since he and his wife had sat at the same table and eaten a meal together. He couldn't remember the last time. The only times she came out of the living room now were to go to the bathroom and to get her snacks from the kitchen, times when he was usually at school or in his room doing his classwork or working on his novel's outline. It had reached the point now where she no longer came to bed with him, instead sleeping on the living room couch watching the night's last movie and being there ready for the morning's first ones. He decided right then and there that he and Lizzie Lee had to have a heart-to-heart, husband-and-wife talk. A TV talk.

Now he'd finished eating and sat sipping coffee, but before he could think anymore on the talk he wanted to have with Lizzie Lee, Cousin Claire suddenly popped through the kitchen door and swooped down atop the middle of the table in front of him a chocolate cake with one candle.

"Happy birthday, Cousin Clarence!" She smiled.

"Birthday? That's right, today's October tenth! How did you know today is my birthday?"

"A little bird told me."

"That little bird forgot to remind me."

"Because you've been so busy lately that even he didn't want to bother you."

"Did *you* bake the cake?"

"Yes. I don't believe in buying something so personal as a birthday cake."

"Cousin Claire, you didn't have to go to all this trouble."

"It was no trouble at all. It was the least I could do after how good you've been to me."

"My, what a beautiful cake and behind it an even more beautiful thought. I wonder did Lizzie Lee remember? Let me go get her so she can see this," he said, rising.

"She knows. I told her what I was doing. She said to say 'happy birthday' to you for her and for you to save her a slice for the Ruby Dee midnight movie." Clarence sat back down. "I didn't ask Lizzie Lee your age so I just put on one, symbolic candle." Cousin Claire's fingertips lightly caressed the huge black candle sticking straight up from the center of the chocolate cake. "Now make a wish," she smiled straight down into his eyes, "and blow it out. There. They say it'll come true if your wish was hard enough." She continued smiling into his eyes while her fingers fondled the candle. "Now let me cut you a real nice piece."

"You have a piece too."

"I don't like eating my own stuff that much but I'll enjoy you eating it." For this special occasion Cousin Claire was wearing a new, low-cut dress revealing more cleavage than Clarence ever suspected cousins of having. Trying hard to keep his eyes off all the upper-body area the dress didn't cover, along with the area it was straining to shield, he nearly missed her cutting the cake and putting before his face a piece.

A slab of a slice and two cups of coffee later, Clarence was feeling full but much better mentally. Then when Cousin Claire placed on the table another surprise, he took his eyes off the rest of her long enough to watch her hands corkscrew open a bottle of chilled white Rhine wine.

"I hope I'm not overstepping my boundaries here with this but I thought today being so special I would take my chances." She smiled as she, leaning her cleavage right over into Clarence's eyes, poured him a glass almost to the rim.

"I love wine. But I'll only drink it if you join me in a birthday toast."

"All right, but just a little. Wine makes me giddy." She poured a glass about a quarter full. "Now, Cousin Clarence, make another wish." Standing, she looked over her cleavage directly down into his eyes. "Happy birthday, Cousin Clarence, and may all your wishes come true, tonight." They clinked glasses.

With the rain coming down outside and the wine going down inside, Clarence from time to time would remind himself that later that evening he had to watch on the kitchen TV the American League baseball playoff third game between the Yankees and the Royals, as he wanted badly to see one of his favorite pitchers, Tommy John, pitch. But he never managed to stagger over to the turn-on button. Instead, sometime during the evening Cousin Claire produced a short-wave radio on which she picked up the sound of jazz music from Atlanta on the Clark College station, WCLK, that he had always listened to while in school at Morehouse. Once he managed to stand up from the table to go bring back Lizzie Lee to join in the fun, as he wasn't feeling quite right about her not being there, but Cousin Claire pushed him back down and went down the hall to the living room herself only to return with the news that his wife said 'happy birthday' again but sent her regrets that she couldn't leave her movie where it was at that moment to make it back to the kitchen, yet still would be in there at midnight to pick up her snack and see them both then. And be sure, she'd emphasized, to leave her some birthday cake to watch Ruby Dee on. Also, Lord, every time Cousin Claire got up from the table to move about, Clarence's eyes followed the mad reaction occurring each time with her behind, when at the precise instant of one of her fallen steps her seat's cheek atop the leg of the implanted foot would shoot heavenward in an all-out attempt to escape from the bottom of the body. But just an instant before grasping the spinal cord to make the long climb up the back to freedom, the cheek would be abruptly grabbed from beneath by the Man—the Law of Gravity—with this entire side of the butt given a spasmodic soul shaking, handcuffed, and quickly dragged back down the body to await its leg's next step...while watching helplessly its sister cheek atop the other leg make the same futile escape attempt. Lord, Lord!

He remembered Cousin Claire pouring him a second glass of wine (she was still sipping on her first) and every time he looked after that, his glass was always near full no matter how much he drank from it. Then, he saw why. Cousin Claire had produced another, bigger birthday bottle of Rhine wine. He'd never drunk so much at one sitting before in all his life, including his summer in the Village. But, as a constantly pouring Cousin Claire kept smiling out to him, it was his birthday and he didn't have to go to work the next day. Lord, he'd never felt so good, spiritually, before in all his life, not even at Le Figaro's. He sat there at the kitchen table, when not stretching his eyeballs out of joint watching her strut about the room, talking his guts up to an ever-smiling and, he felt on this particular and special night, understanding Cousin Claire.... "Yes, Lord knows, I love Lizzie Lee and you can see for yourself where we both get along wonderfully together but lately I haven't been able to talk to her like...like...like I've been able to talk to you, Cousin Claire." Who just smiled and smiled, poured and poured, and strutted and strutted.

Such a good time was he having with Cousin Claire that he eventually forgot all about his early feelings of guilt suffered because of Lizzie Lee not being back there with them in the kitchen to enjoy his birthday like they sure as hell were doing. The wine drowned all guilt, along with the thought of watching Tommy John pitch some baseball game. He talked on and on, soon forgetting what about, but still blabbing away all the same at that sweet-smiling, pretty face in front of him—though he did remember it saying something in reply to a question he must've asked about his father, "He was a good, decent man but a very lonely one who felt unloved, unwanted, by the one he loved the most...." Then he heard his voice again.... "Lizzie Lee and I are not, as you can easily see, that way and are *not* going to be the way my parents were...ever! Lizzie Lee's going to play a part in the movie that I plan on having made from my book I'm writing just as soon as I finish this last outline. Would you like to be in the movie too?" The kitchen was hot with cool jazz and Cousin Claire's sweet smile welded onto his every word.... "If a writer doesn't have the right characters properly arranged in his mind as they are to appear on paper, then, believe me, Cousin Claire, his, or her, book is in d-e-e-p trouble. That's why a good outline plus lots of good notes are the keys to good writing. I read that...." He bottom-upped his glass only to look down and see it nearly full again. The rain beat against the kitchen windows and the cool jazz cooed. Lovely, Lord, lovely!

Moments before midnight, out of the living room, down the hall into the bathroom and, following a quick flush, on into a now-quiet, deserted, kitchen to pick up from the table the plastic-covered saucer holding her slice of birthday cake, along with the jar sitting alongside, shot Lizzie Lee—to shoot back down the hall into the living room and land atop the couch without missing a moment of the just-starting *Edge of the City* movie. Hallelujah!

And, Lord, the rain just kept right on beating against the window of Clarence's bedroom. Amen.

Chapter 21

She had never felt so good since the moment she was handed her diploma for graduating from nursing school. Now she just *knew* things were, finally, going to work out for her...and her mommy. God knows she had worked hard enough to get them going her way. Lying there snugly listening to the rain beating against the window, Cousin Claire's mind began slowly floating back, back...back....

When she was little it seemed that every Saturday night her daddy, dressed so beautifully with that flower in his lapel, would leave the house, leaving her mommy behind to cry all night. Early on Sunday morning she would be awakened by her parents arguing, her mommy crying and accusing her daddy of being out all night with "that woman." She always lay wondering, why would her daddy want to spend every Saturday night out with "that woman" rather than staying home with her and her mommy? As the Saturday nights out continued, her mommy cried and argued with her daddy more and more these Sunday mornings—to the point where he often ended up saying, "One of these days, baby, I'm gonna go back from where I came. Back down to Appalachee where I *know* I would be appreciated by Luella, who owns her own home and would be only too happy to take me in and away from this dump and all your never-ending accusations and crying. Besides, I got the letters from her *proving* she wants me to come back home to her!" With that he would stalk out of their apartment, banging the door shut behind him. This was the cue for little Claire to leap out of bed and run into the kitchen to try and console her now-crying-out-of-control mommy. Then came that time following one of these early-Sunday-morning quarrels when she'd awakened to hear her mommy cry out, "But Luella is your *cousin!*"

To which her daddy had replied, "Kings marry cousins!" before stalking out and this time never coming back.

She had never understood why her daddy and mommy argued all the time because to her they were the two most beautiful people in the whole world. Their wedding picture showed everybody that. And, Lord, her mommy loved her daddy so, but now was so unhappy, and starting to drink liquor, all the time. One night after her daddy had gone for good, her mommy, between sobs and swallows of liquor, told her only child,

"Your daddy and I were the most beautiful and popular couple on the campus of Booker T. Washington High School. He played football, basketball, and baseball and ran track, and I was a majorette. I could twirl two batons at once. Right after high school we got married and I went to work to help send him to college. But in his very first year of college he got hurt playing football and soon after gave up the sport, all sports. He stopped playing the game to start 'playing the field.' And he hasn't stopped running after women since. Years later I learned that around the same time you were born that woman over on the west side of town gave birth to a daughter of your daddy's. I've never seen the child but I hear she could pass for your twin...like you, they say, she got that same pretty smile of Clarence's. But, God only knows why, I *still* love my Clarence! Lord, his sweet smile, I just *can't* do without it! Now he done took it and gone. And I just *know* he went back to his Cousin Luella down in Appalachee because all of those love letters she wrote him a long time ago, which he kept every one of in the dresser drawer, are now gone too. Along with the clothes on his back and those old love letters, he took away with him my heart. Oh, Luella, *please* send my sweet-smiling Clarence back to me because after all these years you *can't* need him as much as I do right now! Please, God, send my sweet-smiling man back to me and I *promise* You I'll *never* complain *ever* again!" Then she got too busy crying to talk.

Later, little Claire went to bed. Stunned! Too much so to even cry. She had believed her daddy had loved her like he'd always told her he did, only now to find out he had "another" daughter who looked just like him and whom he must've loved better than she because he'd gone off and left her and her mommy all alone. She went to sleep, still too stunned to cry, starting to slowly hate her daddy's "other" daughter *and* his Cousin Luella—at the same time starting to love even more than before her poor, dear, left-all-alone mommy. Early that next, Sunday, morning, now with the tears starting to pop up in her eyes, nine-year-old Claire went to her mommy's bed, awakened and hugged tightly the still-suffering soul, and said to her, "Please don't cry anymore, Mommy, someday God's going to make Daddy's mean ol' Cousin Luella down in Appalachee pay for taking him away from you and making you cry all the time. I *promise*. And don't you worry none, Mommy, because I'm going to take care of you *always*. When I grow up I'm going to get a job and buy just you and me a nice pretty house to live in. Mommy, I *promise*."

Claire grew up poor in Atlanta's Grady Homes Housing Project in a small, cramped apartment where the noise coming from outside sounded more inside than out there. What kept her nose above the neighborhood was daily seeing and idolizing the nurses in their spotless white uniforms working at the nearby Grady Memorial Hospital. Looking out from her grimy surroundings, little Claire swore to herself that one day she was going to be one of those *clean* females.

Her daddy never came back home, causing her mommy, who continued to cry and drink over him, to go out and get a job to support herself and her only child. So determined to someday buy her and her mommy a pretty house all their own, Claire, upon entering high school, lied about her age in order to get a part-time job waitressing after classes each day and on weekends. So busy was she working after school and during the summer months that she never did get around to making any close friends in school or within her neighborhood. For her peers Claire, in place of friendship, substituted that warm, sweet smile she got from her daddy. But nothing else she gave them.

Upon completing high school, Claire entered nursing school at Atlanta's Georgia State University. But by the time she graduated at the top of her class from this institution, her mommy's physical and mental health, thanks to years of too many tears and too much tippling, had deteriorated to the point where she had quit work and, in order to receive the care the daughter hadn't the time to give, been put into a nursing home. But Claire, now an RN, felt this would continue only until she worked and saved enough money to make a down payment on a pretty new house for her and her mommy.

Lord, for as long as she lived Claire would never forget her first visit to see her mommy in the home right following her graduation from nursing school. Her dream of someday becoming one of God's *clean* children, a nurse, having finally come true, she felt so happy and proud standing before her dear mommy, showing off her spotless, starchy, white uniform topped off by the beautiful blue cape. With tears of happiness in her eyes she leaned down and hugged her seated mommy and said, "Mommy dear, your daughter is now happily a registered nurse and it won't be long before I'll have you out of this ol' place and into a new pretty house that will belong to just us!" Then she flashed her mommy her biggest, warmest, and sweetest smile. Her mommy started to cry. "Now, now, Mommy, please don't cry. The worst is over. I'm out of school now and I'm coming to see you more often. Just try to think only about the new pretty house...."

"Every time I see your smile it makes me think of my sweet Clarence...." The dam behind her eyeballs burst. Claire, without a word, kept holding her shaking-with-sobs mommy tightly. But, God! She'd been suddenly stabbed with a sharp, cold, and unexpected pain of disappointment. Here she was, finally a registered nurse and eager to share this precious moment with the one person who meant the most in the world to her, her mommy. But all her mommy could think about at this, her only child's big moment was her "sweet Clarence's" Goddamn smile! God, she had worked *hard* for this particular moment—had worked most of her life for it. This moment with her mommy belonged to *them*—*not* her no-good daddy! A daddy who'd stolen *all* of her mommy's moments! A daddy who'd left them high and dry eleven years earlier and whom they hadn't seen nor heard word of since but who *still* lived strongly in her mommy's head and heart—lying there sneakingly stealing Claire's one, *happiest* moment. It just wasn't right! Claire was pissed! And that, Lord, was when she first started truly hating her long-gone daddy with the "other daughter." First, for stealing her mommy's life, heart and soul, and then, from his stationary stand in that heart, stealing his daughter's happiest moment. Still hugging her mommy while listening to her babbling between sobs about her "sweet Clarence," Claire right then and there decided to go daddy digging, to let hers know eyeball to eyeball how he'd ruined a good woman, her dear mommy. And, Lord, her first finding-father stop was way down yonder in Appalachee. Amen.

After discovering that Cousin Luella hadn't seen nor heard from her daddy since they were children, Claire's first reaction was to go back to Atlanta and to her mommy. However, she happened to fall immediately and helplessly in love with the Hemphill home—not the family, though she did take a strong liking to Cousin Luella, a much stronger woman than her mommy though not as sweet—but the house. Claire wanted it. Though not new, the Hemphill house was just the pretty type she'd always dreamt of someday owning for herself and her mommy. This was her first trip outside of Atlanta and after only a few days away, she found herself loving being out of Atlanta. This is when she knew she wasn't ever going back there to live. Here in Appalachee she had found her, and her mommy's, home. Thus, Lord, Claire became determined to get this house. At *any* cost.

Once the house was hers she would go get her mommy out of that nursing home in Atlanta and bring her back to the fresh air of Appalachee. Most people knowing of her mommy, including those at the nursing home, thought the woman was gradually losing her mind, but Claire felt differently. A pretty house in a small-town atmosphere away from the filth and noise of Atlanta would, Claire felt, be just the cure for what ailed her mommy, not yet fifty years old. A fresh start in a new surrounding—and Claire wanted the Hemphills' house to be that start.

She had been touched beyond words when Cousin Luella told her she had a place to stay there in the Hemphill house for as long as she wanted to stay. But as time passed and Cousin Luella crawled closer and closer to her grave, Claire's thoughts became more and more concentrated not on keeping a bed in the house following the older woman's death but on owning the house itself. But how? Then one day, Lord, it hit Claire right where she lived, died, cried, and couldn't hide. Cousin Oscar. Amen.

With a long-time-sick, dying wife, Cousin Oscar, Claire figured at the time, must've been starving for the need of a woman, in every way.

She pretended not to but couldn't help but notice that whenever he was near her his eyes moved on her every move. She just smiled and kept on moving...just a shake ahead of his eyes. Now she, a virgin, knew absolutely nothing about men except for suspecting them all of being interested in some other, or "that," woman. In fact, after living through what her daddy caused to happen to her mommy, and seeing his effects on Cousin Luella, Claire didn't *ever* want to fall in love with a man. She had had several opportunities to do so but had purposefully seen to it that her goal in life had always gotten in between her and the male. But getting this house, she knew, couldn't be gotten without first getting the man. She would get the house, she decided, then she would figure out what to do with the man.

Claire suffered no guilt feelings around Cousin Luella because of her secret thoughts regarding the dying woman's husband and house. A realist in this sense, Claire knew Cousin Luella had little use for Cousin Oscar in the first place and once in the grave she would have no use for the house. So, Lord, late that very first night following Cousin Luella's burial, the virgin Claire had gone straight to Cousin Oscar's bedroom and given herself unto him. WOW! Cousin Oscar, acting more the virgin than she, went berserk with passion, excitement, joy, and other exclamations over her. She couldn't understand a grown man totally losing his head over a little hairy hole. She let him do whatever he wanted to do with her in bed, or out, while quickly learning to help him on—all leading to the night when he asked her to marry him and she, blushingly *and* smilingly, accepted. Now her and her mommy's house was just one "I do" away. She thought. Then Cousin Luella's will was read. Shit! to herself she, unblushingly *and* unsmilingly, said.

The night following the reading of the will, she and Cousin Oscar lay abed for the longest time, not talking, until she said, "Tomorrow, darling, you've got to buy me a pistol."

"What fuh?"

"In the morning I'm going to the hospital here to apply for a nursing job and if I get it I'll no doubt be doing shift work. When working late nights I'll need a pistol in my purse for protection."

"Sweetheart, ain' nobody 'roun' heah gonna botha you. I kin pick you up...."

"You have to get your sleep. Honey, I'm from Atlanta and out there at night I don't trust a soul I don't know. Buy me the pistol tomorrow, but don't tell anyone who it's for, not even the storeowner, because I don't want anybody thinking I'm scared. I'll get the permit later."

"Look, sweetheart, you don' hafta go look'n fuh a job jes 'cause of Luella's will."

"Yes I do. I want to work no matter what. I'm a nurse. Just please get the pistol for me tomorrow and I'll cook you the best supper you've ever eaten. Just remember not to tell *anybody* who the pistol is for.

Please, darling." She turned to him with a smile and a hand to squeeze *his* pistol.

That next night she shot him. Lord, she hadn't really wanted to kill poor Cousin Oscar but he didn't get the house, and for her and her poor dear mommy she *had* to have the house. But, doing the least she felt she could do, she did prepare him a delicious last supper. The pork chops were just the way he liked them, breaded, plus the baked sweet potato and turnip greens were fresh from the garden. She also baked his favorite dessert, pecan pie—the pecans were right off the tree, too. She even bought him a whole twelve-pack of beer, which he had fallen asleep in the chair from drinking too much of when she stuck the pistol to his temple and pulled the trigger. Dropping the pistol down beside him and pulling off the gloves used to keep her fingerprints off the gun and powder burns off her hands and jamming them in the deep pockets of her robe, she exited his bedroom through the door leading into the living room. From there she stepped into the hall, across from the open door of her room. Seeing that the door of Cousin Clarence's and Lizzie Lee's room hadn't yet opened, she ran back down to and on through Cousin Oscar's bedroom door opening onto the hall. Back in there was when she began to scream loud enough to wake Thompson Town and was immediately joined in there by Cousin Clarence and Lizzie Lee. That's when she went into her fake state of shock, taking her off the scene for a few days, especially delivering her from having to attend another funeral so soon after poor Cousin Luella's.

True, she'd said yes to Cousin Oscar's marriage proposal but no one knew about this but the two of them, and she certainly hadn't loved him. In fact, she'd felt sorry for the poor man for how he'd loved a woman who hadn't loved him back. Sort of like her poor dear sweet mommy. Then, following the reading of the will, Cousin Oscar was in such misery that she didn't feel too terribly bad about putting him out of it. Sort of a "kindness killing." Besides, without his owning the house she never could've brought herself to marry him. And she couldn't have stayed on in the house without marrying him. So he had to go. Poor Cousin Oscar. But she did show him a good time his last month on earth. He just could never get enough of her body and her cooking. The moment he got to heaven, Claire bet, he probably looked Cousin Luella up right away to tell her about his last supper down here. But besides her cooking, she doubted if Cousin Oscar would mention much else about her to Cousin Luella.

She had been extremely thankful to the police for how nice and understanding they all had been, asking her very few questions and none she wasn't prepared for. She knew exactly when to cry, smile...and cross her legs. They only questioned her once...after she'd burned the gloves she wore to pull the trigger. Finding the pistol, which he'd bought just that day at the town's gunsmith, right near his body with only his fingerprints on it, along with several empty beer cans at his feet, then later learning about Cousin Luella's will had satisfied the law that Cousin Oscar's death had been a suicide. All the lawmen had been so sweet. And poor Cousin Oscar, she did miss him, especially his strong hugs! Lord, she loved tight hugs! But, again, a woman has to do what a woman has to do.

It was while lying abed following Cousin Oscar's bit of bad luck in, supposedly, shock that her mind got busy planning her next move to get her and her mommy the Hemphill house—but not before she lightly chastised herself for automatically assuming that Cousin Oscar would get the house instead of waiting until Cousin Luella's will had been read and officially declared the true owner, Cousin Clarence. She, trying not to arouse suspicions, had tried to find out about Cousin Luella's will before the woman's death but got nowhere as all the sick one ever wanted to talk about was any, and every, thing to do with her "sweet Cousin Clarence." So Claire had to assume the house would be going to Cousin Oscar...shot in vain.

Now, she realized, the married son was going to present more of a problem to get next to, or in bed with, than had the widowed father. But after Cousin Oscar, Claire felt she could eventually get to any man she wanted—even Cousin Clarence, though he didn't interest her very much as a man as he was too much talk and too little toil for her taste—though perhaps with his big broad shoulders he would be good for a hug. But to get this hug she knew she had to go around, or through, another woman. The toughest thing of all. Yes, Claire admitted to herself, Lizzie Lee was going to be the problem.

After making sure with Cousin Clarence that she would be able to remain in his house until at least the beginning of the following year, she, in her T-Bird and under the pretense of lining up a job, drove up to Atlanta for a day to see her mommy in the nursing home. Her mommy greeted her by commenting upon what a beautiful, familiar smile her daughter had before bursting into tears. Then she realized more than ever that as soon as possible she had to get her mommy out of that place, and Atlanta, into the much friendlier and healthier environs of Appalachee. She *had* to have the Hemphill house. (True, she had told the Hemphills both her parents were dead—and, as far as she was concerned, her daddy, whom she hadn't seen nor heard one single word from since she was a little girl, *was* dead. About her mommy? She had always been prepared to tell the Hemphills, if and when the time ever came, that she had said what she said about her mother being dead only because after seeing the Hemphills' beautiful home she became so ashamed of her mommy having to live in a nursing home that she just couldn't bring herself to reveal this sad fact. This confession would be followed by a few tears, and she was more than sure she would be forgiven by the family Hemphill for having told a fib.)

And, Lord, it was while in Atlanta that it came home to her how to get the house. She went out and bought a book on canning.

Upon returning to Appalachee she proceeded to use her new book by canning produce from her garden, plus fruit and vegetables she bought from the market. She canned everything by the book, including her nonacid vegetables...except for three jars of Vidalia onions (onions, her canning book stated, were one of the nonacid vegetables the Department of Agriculture did not recommend to can at home due to the strong possibility of the deadly germ *Clostridium botulinus* developing within the canned vegetable). These jars Claire put separate from the rest of her canned goods. Then just that very day, a month later, she opened one of these not-canned-according-to-her-canning-book jars and put on Lizzie Lee's "Cousin Clarence's birthday" supper plate, along with her pan-gravy-covered roast domestic duck, polenta, and English peas, a second Vidalia onion (not washed before canning nor, as the U.S. government warned in her canning book, boiled in an open pan for fifteen minutes before serving), having served Lizzie Lee the first one from the jar earlier with her lunch. Then, before leading from the kitchen that night a not-too-accustomed-to-drink, drunk Cousin Clarence to his room and without his seeing her do so, Claire placed on the dining table alongside the plastic-covered saucer holding a thick slice of birthday cake the opened jar of Vidalia onions for Lizzie Lee's midnight-Ruby-Dee-movie snack.

Cousin Clarence passed out the instant he hit the bed. It took her a good half-hour to undress him and put away his clothes her way. She didn't want any clothing covering him when he awoke the next morning naked next to her naked body.

Lying in bed next to Cousin Clarence's snoring body while listening to the rain beating against the window, Claire knew this time she *couldn't* lose. Even if that first jar of onions she opened hadn't developed botulinus, she had two more not-properly-canned ones to experiment with on Lizzie Lee during the upcoming days. While busily watching TV in the dark of the living room, Lizzie Lee, Claire knew from having observed several times, never looked at what she ate nor ever commented upon the taste of anything. If all three jars didn't work? Well, when Cousin Clarence awoke that next morning naked to find her naked body beside him, it wouldn't take much for her to convince him they'd had sex during his drunken, birthday-celebrating night. And if he denied it? It didn't matter, as she already had her ace in the hole. After missing her period next month, like she had done last month and was doing this month, *that* would get the attention of Cousin Clarence, a humane soul if she ever met one...who wouldn't want to see his baby sibling (or baby, if he wanted to claim the child) grow up outside the Hemphill house. Yes, Lord, Cousin Oscar's last two nights on earth had both ended with a bang.

Chapter 22

Late that following Saturday morning while Clarence lay abed hungover, shocked, ashamed, and trying desperately to go back to sleep in please-God-I-won't-do-it-ever-again hope of waking up later that morning to his twenty-four-hours-earlier world, Cousin Claire, in her bathrobe, left his bedroom and walked down the hall into the TV-lit living room. The television was on but Lizzie Lee wasn't watching. From the dark of the house came her voice saying, "Cousin Claire, I don't feel too good," weakly.

"It's no wonder, after eating a whole jar of onions." Cousin Claire picked up the empty Mason jar from the table beside the couch.

"I've been throwing them up all morning, too. And something's wrong with my eyes. I can't see the TV right, every time I look at it I get dizzy. Clarence always said if you do it too much you'll go blind."

"Let me take your temperature." Cousin Claire whipped from her pocket a thermometer she happened to have on her and stuck it in Lizzie Lee's mouth. After feeling her fiery forehead and taking her pulse, Cousin Claire spoke softly and warmly. "Just lie here, Lizzie Lee, honey, and I'll get you something to make you feel better."

"Thank you, Cousin Claire. It sure is a good thing we have you, a trained nurse, here in the house to look after and take care of us. I don't know what we would do without you. You must've been sent to the Hemphill house by God." A touched Cousin Claire smiled sweetly down at the extremely, ostensibly-food-poisoned, sick young woman. Then from the glare of the TV she couldn't help but notice Lizzie Lee's right thumb. It was abnormally huge, muscular, appearing to be the only alive part of her body. With the remote-control (yet clutched in Lizzie Lee's hand) button-pressing TV junkie, Cousin Claire believed, the thumb, at the body's death, was the last thing to die.

Cousin Claire left the living room a tad sad. Unlike Cousin Luella, she had never disliked Lizzie Lee, who had never caused her one ounce of trouble, personally, asking of life only a Ruby Dee movie and an onion sandwich. Cousin Claire hoped Lizzie Lee had finished the jar's, and her last, onion during Ruby Dee's last *Edge of the City* scene—making her, to the very last, a true trouper. Cousin Claire was going to miss fixing for and cleaning up after Lizzie Lee. But she, poor soul, had stood in the path leading to Cousin Claire's ownership of the Hemphill house. And, Lord knows, a woman has to do what a woman has to do. Now Cousin Claire had to get Lizzie Lee something for her tummy...then just wait. Eventually, she would call the doctor, but in the meantime would arrange her kitchen and canned goods, including the now-empty onion jar that got her the Hemphill house, in a proper manner to be later inspected by the authorities. She had already made sure there were no raw onions on the premises, thus making it easier for anyone to believe that Lizzie Lee, the onion addict, in search of a quick midnight movie snack fix, had grabbed, opened, and eaten one of Cousin Claire's canned jars of the contaminated vegetable. Too, the canning book, which no one besides herself knew she had, would be burned, with her, if asked, saying she learned all of her canning from her mommy. (This time she wanted to leave *nothing* to chance. The last time she had been extremely lucky when the police, no doubt taken in by her state-of-shock act, her smile...and legs...believed immediately and throughout that Cousin Oscar had committed suicide, not even bothering to check for gunpowder burns on his hands, where they would've found none. At least, she didn't believe the police checked.)

Lord, she was feeling pleased with herself. It wouldn't be long now before her dear mommy would be there safely with her. And, then, her baby. Every *real* home, not a home like Lizzie Lee ran one, needed a little baby. After the birth of her baby, whom her mommy would take care of while she worked, she would finally have all she ever wanted or felt she needed: her mommy, a baby, a nursing job, and a house. She would then begin figuring out how she was going to get Cousin Clarence out of her, her mommy's, and her baby's house....

That's when the front doorbell rang.

~ Chapter 23 ~

Opening the front door, Cousin Claire felt as though she suddenly left her own body to leap over into the body of the pretty young woman standing on the porch with suitcase in white-gloved hand.

"Is this the residence of Missis Luella Hemphill?"

"Yes...er...."

"I'm her Cousin Clarence's daughter from Atlanta. Her Cousin Claudia. And," motioning to the older, sad-eyed woman standing next to her, "this is *Mommy*." Then the pretty young woman who could've easily passed for Cousin Claire's twin, Lord, flashed a sweet smile.